SYMPHONY HALL SERIES

LAUREN E. RICO

This book is a work of fiction. Names, characters, places, and incidents are the product of the author's imagination or are used fictitiously. Any resemblance to actual events, locales, or persons, living or dead, is coincidental.

Copyright © 2017 by Lauren E. Rico. All rights reserved, including the right to reproduce, distribute, or transmit in any form or by any means. For information regarding subsidiary rights, please contact the Publisher.

Entangled Publishing, LLC
2614 South Timberline Road
Suite 109
Fort Collins, CO 80525
Visit our website at www.entangledpublishing.com.

Embrace is an imprint of Entangled Publishing, LLC.

Edited by Jenn Mishler
Cover design by Erin Dameron-Hill
Cover art from Shutterstock and Period Images

Manufactured in the United States of America

First Edition May 2017

embrace

For the dedicated music students who spend long hours locked away practicing.

Whose parents wish they would just outgrow this whole 'music thing' already and get a business degree instead.

Who spend way too many late nights roaming the music department preparing for lessons, juries, auditions, and recitals.

You can do this! Just remember to find a little time for friends, and fun…and love.

God bless you and good luck!

Chapter One

Kate

I don't know what I expect to see when I raise the hood of the car. It's not as if there'll be a neon sign flashing *Broken Hose* or *Blown Tranny*—whatever the hell a tranny is. But there's nothing like that. Just the greasy, metallic guts of my old Toyota. I recognize the plastic container that holds the blue washer fluid and the cap that I twist off to put antifreeze in. I see the dipstick I use to check the level on the oil that this bucket of bolts guzzles down and smokes out the tailpipe. But that's it.

"Hey, do you need some help?"

I'm so startled by the voice behind me that I jump and hit my head on the hood of the car. The pain comes in a single blinding flash.

"Shit!" I hiss, my fingers flying to the spot on my forehead. When I pull them away, they're smeared with blood. Great. Just great. This is exactly what I need this morning on top of car trouble. On top of being late. On top of freezing my ass off in this parking lot.

"Oh, hey. I didn't mean to startle you. Are you okay?"

The voice is right next to me now, and when I turn to face it—turn to face *him*, I'm met by some seriously broad shoulders. *Wow*. His concerned eyes are a blend of blue and green that are sexy as hell. His hair, just a little too long in the back, is a sandy blond and he's got a little matching stubble. Like Ryan Gosling. Make that a double *wow*.

"Here," he says, pulling a crumpled McDonald's napkin from his backpack. "It's clean. It's just a little squashed is all."

"I…uh…thanks," I mumble, accepting his offering and his apologetic smile. I use the napkin to apply pressure to my bleeding head.

He looks amused, the corners of his eyes crinkling into the slightest hint of crow's-feet. It makes him look a little older than I thought at first glance. He must be a grad student. No, actually his clothes are too nice. Grad students don't have money for nice clothes. He must be faculty or staff. Older, for sure. But that's okay. I can work with older.

"Something wrong with your car?" he asks, his gaze moving between me and my eighteen-year-old Corolla.

I swivel to look down at the vehicle that is the bane of my existence most days.

"It won't start," I say dejectedly.

"And…you know something about cars, do you?" The amusement in his tone tells me that he's wondering why I even bothered to raise the hood and have a look.

I shake my head and immediately regret the movement, wincing through another surge of pain.

"No, I just thought it might be something obvious. A broken hose or something. But it's not anything I can see."

"You know, you really should have that looked at."

"Yeah, I guess I'll have to get a tow truck," I mutter.

His cheeky grin grows into a broad smile and he throws

his head back, laughing loudly.

"What?" I demand, suddenly embarrassed over something I can't even identify.

"Not the car, your head!"

"Oh. *Oh*." I laugh with him now. "Are you suggesting I have my head examined?" I ask with faux indignation. God! Am I flirting with Hot Older Guy?

"I am, actually," he says, still smiling but not laughing anymore. "That looks like a pretty deep gash. And you know how those head wounds are. They bleed a lot. You might need stitches or something."

He's not wrong. I can feel the blood soaking through the napkin. But at the same time, I can also *hear* the *ka-ching!* of the cash register as I do the mental math on a car tow, car repair, *and* a trip to the ER. The blood will regenerate; the car won't.

"If it's still bleeding in a little while, I will." I lie through my reassuring smile. "But hey, thanks for checking on me."

"Yeah, well, maybe if I'd left you alone you wouldn't have a gash in your forehead," he says, looking remorseful. "Listen, the least I can do is give you a lift. Where're you headed?"

"Oh, the Music building. But it's not too far. I can walk from here," I say, pointing toward a cluster of brick buildings barely discernable across a small lake and through some trees.

"Yeah, not too far if you have forty-five minutes to kill." He snorts, closing the hood of my car. "That's all the way on the other side of campus. What are you doing over here? Do you live in the dorms?"

I shake my head. "No, I work in the North Dining Hall. But you know, I'll bet I can catch a shuttle."

"Nope. I just saw it go past. Won't be another one for twenty minutes. Why don't you let me give you a lift? I was headed to the Art department anyway and that's right next door. I mean, unless you have the time to wait."

I pull my phone from the pocket of my jeans for a time check. Seven forty-five. That's the thing. I don't have the time to wait. There's no way I'll make it to my eight a.m. Orchestration class if I try to walk it now. And by the time the university shuttle gets me there, I might as well just skip class all together.

I consider the hot guy. I don't know him. Not even a little. What if he's some handsome sociopath who picks up girls in parking lots? With my luck, I'd become a Lifetime Movie of the Week. Some C-list actress will play me as the stupid, unsuspecting girl who gets into the car of the tall, handsome stranger. Next thing you know, my picture is on a poster, they find me stuffed down some drainpipe in Encino, and *Dateline NBC* is interviewing the jurors in my murder trial.

When he extends a hand, I don't have to wonder if my reluctance is on my face. Everything shows on my face.

"By the way, I'm Kevin," he offers.

"Kate," I reply, giving him a quick shake with my free hand.

"Music department, you said?"

I nod. He squints thoughtfully, turning to walk away from my immobilized vehicle.

"Do you know Dr. Markham?" he asks.

"Ohhh, yeah. It's his class I've got at eight."

"Seriously?" he asks, eyebrows up, like I might be messing with him.

"Seriously," I say solemnly.

"Well, that's that, then," he declares as he puts a reassuring hand on my forearm and starts to steer me through the rows of parked cars. "I've heard what a dick he can be and I refuse to be the reason you're late for his class. It's the least I can do."

"How do you know him?" I ask, allowing myself to be pulled along. The question is part test, part curiosity.

"I'm a teaching assistant in the Art department.

Everybody over there knows him. Or, *about* him, anyway. His dickishness is kind of legendary." He grins at me over his shoulder.

I chuckle at the idea of that, but I still can't quite shake the niggling feeling that something's not right with this guy.

"So, what are you teaching?" I press, needing just a little more convincing to reset my *stranger danger* radar.

"Art Appreciation for non-majors," he says, edging sideways through two closely parked sedans. I follow him as we cut through to another row. "I get all the business majors who consider the Mona Lisa to be a financial investment rather than a work of art. They'll be lucky if I don't strangle one of them before the semester is over." He laughs and then stops himself with a look of faux alarm. "I'd better be careful or *I* might get a reputation as the next Markham."

"Not likely." I groan, rolling my eyes.

"Well, come on, there isn't much time to get you to class."

I stop and look at him.

"Really, be honest with me. Do you mind? Am I taking you out of your way? Because I can walk," I offer with some reservation in my voice.

I get the dazzling smile and the crinkly eyes again.

"Kate, please. I really am on my way over there. Same parking lot. You won't be taking me a single foot farther than I was going to go anyway. I swear to God."

I nod, satisfied at last, and follow him through the sedans and small SUVs until we're standing in front of a shiny white BMW X-something or other. Someone's got a little cash, I see. My reflection in the tinted window gives me my first glimpse of the gash on my forehead. "Ughhh," I mutter as I rearrange my long, dark hair to try and camouflage it. But it's no use. I return the saturated napkin to my head and get into the leather passenger's seat with a frustrated sigh.

"I hope you don't mind me saying so, but your ride's seen

better days. Might be time for some new wheels," he suggests as he slides into the driver's side and shuts the door. "Just saying."

"Yeah, well, not everyone can swing a bimmer," I counter.

"Oh, come on now," he coaxes. "What are you? A junior? Senior? You must have family to help you out."

"I'm finishing up my masters, actually," I respond, ignoring the family comment as he pulls out of the lot and onto the main road through campus.

"What? No way!" he says, giving me a surprised sideways glance. "Good for you! Got plans for after graduation?"

"I'm going to sleep. For about a month," I mutter.

"Oh yeah. I crashed at my parents' place for the entire summer after I finished my grad degree and I don't think I left my bed for the first week. What about you? Will you be headed back home to your folks, too?"

"Nope," I say, poking at the napkin over my wound.

"No?"

Oh, hell. I know this trick. He's hoping I'll feel compelled to elaborate. I won't. But it's got me wondering if maybe Hot Teacher Guy recognizes me as the daughter of "Senator Satan" and is fishing for a little info. It wouldn't be the first time a potential date has started out by way of morbid curiosity.

"I'm sorry," he says before I can comment. "I don't mean to be nosy. It's just a bad habit of mine. I meet an interesting, funny, pretty woman and I jump right into the personal details."

"Nah, it's okay," I say softly, his compliments making me feel suddenly bashful.

"Hey, you wanna have coffee sometime?" he asks, quickly looking over at me. He seems a bit taken aback by his boldness, with the lip biting and all.

"Really?" I laugh. "I'm bleeding all over your posh leather interior and you actually want to see me again?"

"Why not? I like being the white knight."

"What? Rescuing the damsel in distress from the parking lot, riding in on your white BMW?"

"Sure." He shrugs. "I'll rescue you from the big, bad Dr. Drew the Dragon, too, if you want. We could run off to the Pancake Cottage and live happily ever after. Well, for an hour or two, anyway."

"Oh, so tempting." I groan and grin at the same time. "You've just stumbled upon my Achilles' heel."

"Breakfast?"

I nod enthusiastically.

"Well, come on, then! You can get the notes from someone else, can't you?"

I sigh heavily, allowing my mind a nanosecond-long fantasy involving this Kevin guy and pancake syrup.

Stop it!

"No, I can't," I reluctantly decline. "I have an assignment due and Markham won't take it if I don't come to class."

He looks a little disappointed, but still determined.

"Okay, well, how about a cup of coffee later, then?" he presses.

Oh, what the hell? What else have I got to do except study scores in my apartment and work on my midterm project?

"Um, yeah, I think I'd like that," I agree at last.

"Great! What time are you free?" he asks just as we're pulling into the Arts Complex lot. I notice that it's already full. Even if I had been able to get my car running, no way I'd have found a parking spot. I glance at the dashboard clock: 7:58. If I fly into the building and right up the stairs, I should *just* make it.

"Uh, noon?" I ask as I reach for the visor so I can flip it down and take a quick peek in the mirror. I want to be sure my face is blood-free before I get out of the car. The car which now jerks to a sudden stop, propelling me forward against the seat belt.

"Oh, wait, don't..." Kevin says, reaching toward the visor and sounding suddenly alarmed.

But he's too late. I see it.

My heart sinks, breaks, and explodes all at the same time. This guy is obviously not who he says he is. And I am obviously a fool. I twist around to face Kevin, who looks considerably paler than he was the last time I checked.

"I—uh... That's just a..." he stammers.

"Microphone," I say coolly, examining the small black disc about the size of a button. There's a black wire running from it. When I follow the line, I see how it's carefully tacked around the headliner.

The epiphany or realization or frying pan to the head or *whatever* the hell this is, takes my breath away as everything snaps into crystal clear focus. I'm adding it all up in my head—something I *should* have done much sooner. Along with the slight crow's-feet, I now spot a few threads of silver hair camouflaged by the blond. Then there's the BMW. And the expensive clothes he's wearing. Why didn't I put it all together before? My eyes narrow on him as the last of the pieces falls into place. How could I have been so goddamned stupid? I *know* better.

So, so stupid, Kate!

"Who do you work for?" I ask quietly.

"I don't know what you mean."

"Who do you work for?" I demand louder this time, a little surprised by the edge in my tone. "The *Post*? The *Sun-Times*? The *Ledger*? Christ! You don't work for the *National Enquirer*, do you?"

Kevin—if that's even his name—takes a deep breath. His voice is calm and soft.

"Kate, it's not what you think."

"No? Then what the fuck *is* it?"

"I'm a reporter for the *D.C. Courier*," he explains slowly.

Of course he is. Because, why would a good-looking, smart, funny guy want to help me out? Or *ask* me out for that matter?

I take a deep breath and regroup. This is not the time for self-pity. *Anger*. That's what this situation calls for. Good, old-fashioned rage.

"What did you do to my car?"

Seeing that his cover is totally blown, Kevin tosses charming out the window, replacing it with smugness.

"Not that I'm admitting to anything," he begins coyly, "but you might want to have your battery cables tightened. And, just out of curiosity, why *is* the daughter of a senator—and a presidential hopeful at that—driving around in that piece of shit?"

"You son of a bitch!" I hiss, unable to restrain myself any longer.

"Oh, come on, Katie," he says, turning to me with a conspiratorial grin. My fingers twitch with the temptation to slap it right off his face. "Your father's the most detested politician on the Eastern Seaboard! And, I'm guessing, he's not exactly 'Father of the Year' material. I mean, aside from the clunker you're driving, you're working a crap job. I know you don't have any health insurance. I mean, Christ, Katie! You don't even have a winter coat! Does your father know you live like this?"

"What? A winter coat? What the hell are you talking about?"

I can't follow his line of thinking, so he fills me in.

"Yeah, well, look at you. It's thirty degrees out and you're wearing a hoodie. And, before you feed me some bullshit about leaving your coat at home, I haven't seen one on you in the last six months."

Wait, wait, wait…

"Y-you've been watching me for *six* months?" I ask, sounding a bit shakier now because I *am* a bit shakier now. I see, with growing dismay, that this guy isn't your garden-variety journalist out for a quick pic and a sound bite. He's one of a very specific, very tenacious breed known as a stalkerazzi. And that makes him more than a nuisance. It makes him dangerous.

He shrugs, as if reading my thoughts. "It hasn't been that hard, you know. I mean, all you do is go to class and work. No dates. No friends. Why is that, Katie? I'd have thought a pretty girl like you would have some hot trumpet player in your bed by now. And judging by the way you've been drooling over me for the last twenty minutes, I'm guessing it's been awhile since you've had *anyone* in your bed."

That's it. I reach for the handle of the door so I can get as far away from this guy and this car as fast as I can. But the handle doesn't budge. I poke at the button, but he must have some child safety feature so it can't be unlocked from this side.

"Open the door," I say flatly.

"Oh, now, Katie, don't be like that. You know your dad's bill is gaining momentum, right? He's in the spotlight now, and all signs point to a presidential run. I'm just wondering why you aren't a part of his campaign? Come to think of it, why aren't you a part of his *life*? I mean, his only daughter, and him being a widower and all. You're his only family. And yet, you're never anywhere to be seen. You refuse to give interviews. You're never quoted in the press. He doesn't mention you. Ever. Why is that, Katie?"

If he calls me Katie one more time, I'm going to wrap my hands around his neck until his eyes pop out onto the dashboard.

"Open. The. Door," I say in the most menacing tone I can muster. But he just prattles on, hoping, I'm sure, that I'll give him something that he can use against my father. Against me.

"Near as I can tell, you haven't been home to Virginia in years. You spend the holidays by yourself up in that dumpy little apartment of yours. I mean, I don't know how you do it. What is it, like two hundred square feet? You've got a nice view of the mountains, but still. Put a little color on the walls or something, it's depressing as hell in there."

I can only stare at him, my mouth hanging open. Oh. My. God. He's been inside my apartment!

"What are you going to do when he comes here in a few weeks?" he's asking even as I'm trying to sort through this mess in my head.

Whoa! Wait just a minute. Did he just say my father is coming *here*? Since when? Seeing my shock and confusion, the son of a bitch starts to chuckle.

"Surprised by that, are you? He's part of the panel at a bipartisan town hall that the Poli-Sci department is sponsoring. Word is, he might even announce his intention to run for president."

I close my eyes and take a deep breath. It's time to put on my big girl panties and take back the power in this situation. I pull the phone out of my pocket and snap a picture of him.

"Hey!" he objects. "I didn't say you could do that." He stops himself and breaks out the obnoxious grin again. "Okay, okay, I'll give you that one, considering I've done the same thing to you about a thousand times."

The smile fades as he watches my expression darken. Like I said, I've never had a good poker face, so I'm quite sure he's getting the full effect as my emotions pass across my features. Shock, followed by indignation, finally settling on rage. And I must be telegraphing loud and clear because he pulls back a fraction of an inch.

"Listen up, you James Bond wannabe," I hiss. "You're going to let me out of this car and I will *never* see you anywhere near me again. Because, if I do, *Kevin,* I'll call the

Washington Post and give them an exclusive, including how I was stalked by a rival paper. You don't think they'd just love to discredit you? To paint you as a lame little gossiping tabloid? And after the *Courier* has worked so hard to shake that image. Your editor won't be happy. And what would that do for your reputation, *Kevin*?"

Something shifts in his features and it's arresting. A cool hardness settles in his eyes and his mouth turns up into a sardonic smile. And just like that, the nice hot guy is gone. This is who he really is, right here. And it's pretty damn scary. I work hard to keep the edge to my own glare. I know his type, and if he gets even a whiff of weakness, I'm toast.

"Oh, Kate, Kate, Katie, Kate," he taunts me in a singsong voice. "Do you really think you can scare me? You have no power and, it would appear, you can't even make use of your father's. So, why don't you just give me something I can use and I promise not to bother you again? For a little while, anyway." He chuckles.

I don't say another word; I just pick up my phone and press nine-one-one. He's looking at me quizzically, thinking I'm bluffing, I'm sure. I put it on speakerphone so he knows I'm not.

"Hello?" I say when the operator asks the nature of my emergency. "My name is Katherine Brenner and I'm being held in a car against my will. I'm on the campus of Shepherd University in a white BMW, Washington DC license plate LVJ 2214. It's parked in the Arts Complex lot in the far northeast corner. Please hurry."

Before I can hang up the phone, the locks click open and he reaches over to unbuckle my seat belt.

"How the hell did you know my plate number?" he asks incredulously. When I don't answer, he decides he's had enough of me. "You want out? Fine. Get the fuck out of my car, you bitch," he says, giving my shoulder a rough shove.

My turn to smile now.

"Never mind," I say into the phone. "I'm out. No need to send a car. I'll come by the station later today. I have a picture of the guy and I think I know where he works." I end the call and start to get out.

He reaches for me again, but he stops short when I hold up a single finger and shake my head no. "Not unless you want an assault charge," I threaten.

"Oh, please." He sneers. "You won't do it. You won't even follow up with the police. We both know how much you hate the publicity. I mean you're already detested by your classmates and most of your professors. Isn't that right, *Katie*?"

I don't respond. Instead, I open the door and pull myself up and out, snatching the microphone as I go. It unravels in a trail of black wire that leads to a small recorder in the pocket of the passenger door. He lunges forward to grab it, but the seat belt holds him back as I scoop it up and stick it into my pocket.

"I'll be taking this with me," I say, slamming the door at the same instant that he erupts into a screaming tirade. I cross the parking lot at a jog, purposely dodging in and around other parked vehicles, just in case he gets any smart ideas about running me down. When I look over my shoulder again, he's still glaring at me and I can see his mouth moving. Now his window rolls down, and he's yelling something about freedom of the press. I flip him off and run into the building.

My heart feels like it's going to pound right out of my chest. Not because of the jackass I've just left outside, but because of the one who's waiting for me inside. And, God help me, I'm not wrong.

Chapter Two

Drew

It's easy to hate her. Much easier than liking her. I know it's wrong. I know *I'm* wrong. Katherine Brenner can't help that she's tall, with long, dark hair that falls around her shoulders in soft waves. It's not her fault that her blue eyes are specked with gold and that she has delicate, pale skin. Or that her lips are the color of fucking rose petals. I mean, what's not to hate?

Katherine Brenner is a dead ringer for the woman who absolutely obliterated my heart.

She doesn't think I know that she's there. After all this time, she's still under the mistaken belief that if she slips into the room quietly and takes a seat at the back, I won't even notice she's late. Oh, but I do notice, even with my back turned. I finish writing the details of the assignment on the whiteboard and turn around, my gaze scanning the back of the room until it lands on her.

"You're late, Miss Brenner," I say flatly. "Again."

A blush spreads across her face. "I'm sorry, Dr. Markham,"

she begins. "I was—"

"Miss Brenner, please spare us the excuses, you've already taken up enough class time."

She responds to my chilly tone by clamping her lips into a straight line and locking her jaw. She doesn't say a word. I cock an expectant eyebrow.

"Well? Don't you think you owe the rest of the students—the ones who bothered to get here on time—an apology as well?"

"I'm sorry," she mutters.

"How about you try that one more time?"

I can feel the resentment coming off her as she gets to her feet, her eyes never leaving mine. It's a dance we've done before.

"I'm sorry to have disrupted the class," she says to no one in particular.

"Fine. You may sit down," I say as I turn back to the board, confident my point has been made.

"Are you sure there isn't anyone else you'd like me to prostrate myself before?" she says just loud enough for me to hear. There is a collective gasp across the classroom.

With a sigh, I come around to the front of my desk and lean up against it, arms folded, head tilted. Her classmates fidget around us, torn between leaning closer to get a good look, and pulling back to avoid the impending explosion.

"No, Miss Brenner," I reply at last. "I can't think of anyone right now, but I'm sure I will. I'll get back to you when I do. In the meantime, why don't you bring your things and have a seat right up here by me?" I nudge an empty desk in the first row with my foot.

Someone snickers and a few others join in hesitantly, testing the waters to see if I'll call them on it. I don't. Without further comment, she picks up her backpack and wiggles her way through the rows of desks to take the seat that I have indicated. Once she's seated and I have a good look at her, I notice immediately that she appears disheveled, as if she's been in a tussle. And pale. Is that blood on her temple? Christ. I'm tempted to ask her what the hell she's gone and done now, but I ignore the impulse, instead reaching for the box of tissues sitting behind me on my desk. I pull out a wad and hand them to her, leaning closer so no one will overhear us.

"You have something on your forehead," I murmur.

"Oh. Thank you," she says in barely a whisper, her cheeks coloring. I watch while she dabs at the cut. After a few seconds, she looks up again and I continue, just as softly.

"I'd like to speak to you when class is over."

She gives me the slightest nod of her head.

I'm not supposed to hate students. Or like them, for that matter. I'm just supposed to teach them to the best of my ability. Yeah. Right. Easier said than done.

Temporarily satisfied, I stand up straight again and clap my hands together. "All right, please pass your homework forward to my desk and let's talk about the midterm projects, shall we?" I brighten up and walk back around to the board on the far wall behind my desk. I write a date at the top in red then underline it for emphasis.

"As you all know, they're due at the end of the week. And I've decided to cancel class on Friday so you can take the time for any last-minute preparations."

A soft murmur of excitement ripples across the classroom.

"You can have up until Friday to get your paper in. *But*," I say with emphasis, "I think you all know by now that I leave early on Friday afternoons. So, if you plan to take advantage of that extension and turn it in on Friday, you must deliver it to my home by five p.m. There is a cylinder attached to the bottom of my mailbox, where the newspaper goes. You can leave them there. Please do not put them inside my mailbox, that's against the law and I'd hate to have to sick the Postal

Inspector on you."

A soft chuckle from around the room.

"Please don't ring my doorbell," I continue. "Please don't slide it under the door, or give it to my neighbor or tie it to a brick and throw it through the window."

Some snickering and a couple of amused faces. Yeah, I know at least one or two of them who'd happily deliver their papers that way.

"I'm serious," I warn, scanning the room and making eye contact with as many of them as possible. "I'm going to walk out of my house on Friday at 5:01 p.m. and if your project isn't where it's supposed to be, then too bad for you. In fact, I *strongly* encourage you to get it in before Friday so you don't have to worry about that."

We spend the next half hour going over the details of the assignment until the clock strikes eight forty-five. I send them on their way. All, that is, except for Katherine Brenner. She's sitting silently, staring down at her hands and waiting for me to finish making notes at my desk. Her hair hangs down on either side of her head like a dark-brown veil. Finally, I take my glasses off, rub the bridge of my nose, and sigh.

"Miss Brenner," I begin wearily, "you and I have a long history. And not a very good one. You don't have much time left before you graduate. That is, assuming you *do* graduate."

She sits up straight, eyes widening. When I slip my glasses back on, I notice the nasty-looking gash on her forehead is bleeding again, a thin trail of sticky crimson wending its way from her hairline to down behind her ear. I hand her more tissues and she gets the idea.

"Ugh," she grunts in frustration.

"You might need a few stitches," I point out.

"Yeah, I know," she mutters in response.

"I want you to be crystal clear on this point," I say, poking the ink blotter on my desk with my index finger for effect. "I expect you to be on time every day between now and the end of the semester. No sneaking in after class has started. In fact, I want you in *that* seat for every class. Do you understand?"

"Yes, Dr. Markham, I understand," she says, keeping her voice soft and even.

I shuffle through the stack of papers on my desk—the assignment that they just turned in. When I come across the one with her name on it, I hand it to her. She looks perplexed.

"I'm not accepting your homework assignment," I explain and her eyes widen in disbelief.

"But it's done," she protests, her calm exterior cracking all at once. "The assignment is *done*, Dr. Markham!"

I shrug unsympathetically. "Then you should have made sure it was in on time."

I watch her take a deep breath, close her eyes for an instant, and start again. "Dr. Markham," she grits, "I was three minutes late to class. You hadn't even *asked* for the assignment yet," she reminds me.

I shake my head.

"Miss Brenner, I'm done discussing this. You might as well take those papers and dump them in the trash can, because I won't even consider them at this point. So, I strongly suggest you turn in a spectacular midterm project to help make up for the grade."

I can see the wheels turning. She's furious. I'm sure she wants to tell me off, but she knows how close she is to failing my class. And if she wants to graduate on time, if she doesn't want to spend another year waiting to take this class again, she doesn't dare risk pissing me off any more than she already has. I'm surprised by what she *does* dare do, though. Katherine Brenner leans toward me and locks cold, blue eyes onto mine and, for one disconcerting instant, I feel like she can read my thoughts.

"Why do you have to be like this? What's the point?" she

asks with more curiosity than animosity.

"What are you talking about?"

She shrugs.

"I'm a human being, you know? I have a complicated life outside of this classroom. What are you? Four, maybe five years older than me? You were in my shoes not so long ago and you know as well as I do that things happen, Dr. Markham. Things that are out of my control."

I feel a wave of irritation wash over me. I don't care how close in age we are. I don't like being lectured, especially not by one of my students. Especially not by this student.

"*Miss* Brenner, you are on extremely thin ice here," I say coolly. "I think you'd better go now before one of us says something we'll regret."

She gets up without another word, abandoning her assignment on her desk and walking out the door without so much as a glance back.

Chapter Three

Kate

People tend not to believe in things they can't see. That is, until they see them. That's how it was with *The Ghost* and me. Oh, I knew he existed. I just didn't believe all the crazy rumors about him. How could I? There were ridiculous tales about freshmen who'd gone missing, evil-eyed curses, and bodies buried in the quad.

His actual name is Russell Atherton and, once upon a time, he was the toast of the classical music world—the next great conductor. But, after the untimely death of his daughter, Russell wasn't much interested in toasts, conducting, or anything else. He became a hermit in a small cabin, not far from Shepherd University. And he probably would have stayed hidden away from society, had it not been for Maureen Clevenger, Dean of Music at Shepherd, and his ex-wife.

She convinced him to take a token position as Conductor-in-Residence. His worldwide reputation was enough for the university to sign off on the rather unorthodox employment offer. And that was the beginning of *The Ghost.* He'd walk the halls in the wee hours, startling the crap out of the music students who liked to practice late into the night. Like me.

And, it should be said, Russell Atherton *is* a creepy looking guy. He's tall and thin with skin so pale that it practically glows. He has long, silver hair that he wears in a ponytail down the middle of his back. And his pale-blue eyes are so light that they look creepily vacant.

But fear of ghosts wasn't a luxury I had as a freshman piano major. Not with classes and work taking up all my daytime hours. And, without my own piano at home, I'd spend hours in the practice rooms, occasionally getting to play the Steinway grand piano in the concert hall. That's where I was the night he caught me "air conducting" on the big stage. I just couldn't resist hopping up on the conductor's podium and pretending I was leading an orchestra in a performance of Beethoven's Fifth Symphony. I kicked off my sandals so that I was barefoot, and closed my eyes, hearing the music in my head as I played. When I felt a tap on my shoulder I jumped and gasped, my eyes flying open.

"What's your name?" he asked gruffly, taking an empty seat in the violin section in front of me.

"K-Kate," I stammered. "Kate Brenner…"

His eyes narrowed.

"You're the senator's kid," he said.

I nodded.

"Why aren't you a conducting major?" he asked.

"Because I don't conduct," I said, wondering why he would ask such an insane question. Hadn't he just seen for himself how little I knew about it? That I was just faking it?

He considered me some more before speaking again.

"You do conduct. You just don't know it. Yet."

Fast forward nearly six years and I'm standing on the conductor's podium—for real this time—in front of the

Shepherd University Wind Ensemble. Unfortunately, they're not making me feel especially welcome. In fact, they're snickering, and it's starting to piss me off. I pretend not to notice as I stand and flip through my score for the "First Suite" by Gustav Holst that we're working on.

I suppose I should have expected this after that debacle in Markham's class this morning. Half of the students who were there are playing in this ensemble. And the ones who weren't there have obviously heard about what went down. They don't even bother to hide their pointing and whispers.

I take a furtive glance over at Russell, who's sitting to the side of the stage, observing. He gives a slight smile and an even slighter nod. They serve as a reminder that, while I *do* have to take shit from Drew Markham, I do *not* have to take it from the Shepherd University Wind Ensemble.

Feeling my confidence level rise, I pull off my sneakers and toss them to the floor—something that looks weird but somehow seems to center me. Then, I take a deep breath and find the spot in the score where I want to start.

"Good afternoon, everyone," I say, trying my best to sound pleasant. "Let's work the final movement of the Holst Suite, please. Tyler?" My gaze travels to the section leader for the saxophones. "I really need you to hit the melody a little harder in the opening line. You guys are the main attraction there."

"Harder?" he echoes, trying to sound innocent. "You want it *haaaarder*?" He draws out the word like a moan. A sex moan.

What a little shit! I survey him for a beat before responding.

"Tyler," I begin with a sympathetic tone and smile, "I know you're used to things being...*softer* than you'd like, but, just this once, it would be great if you could man up and hit that section *Good. And. Hard.* Are you...*up* to it?"

Until this instant, I had no idea that someone could blush

and blanch at the same time. And yet here's Tyler doing it right in front of my delighted eyes. There are catcalls and taunts from the rest of the band, and the poor guy looks as if he'd like to slide right out of his seat and melt into the floor.

"Okay, okay!" I call out over the din, trying to put him out of his misery and out of my mind so we can get back on track. "We don't have a lot of time, so let's start this last section. Ready?"

Nothing. Nada. Zip. Zero. It's as if I'm invisible. Really? Why do they have to make everything so hard? I take another deep breath.

I can do this. I can do this. I can do this…

"*Ready*?"

This time there's considerably more edge to my voice, though not one of the musicians so much as glances my way.

"Screw this," I mutter under my breath as I raise my arms, baton in my right hand. I start to count down, pretending I have their undivided attention.

"One, two, one, two, one, two…ready…*AND*!" I start to conduct at the same time I start to sing the melody that the saxophones *should* be playing. I throw a cue to the trumpets, who aren't playing. They grin stupidly and look at me as if I'm nuts. But I keep going, my silver bracelet jangling with every downbeat.

"Flutes! This is you coming up!" I yell as if I'm trying to be heard over the band. This time, they're glancing at one another, clearly unsure of what to do. The first flute shrugs and raises her instrument with the others following suit and, when I cue them, they come in.

Well I'll be damned…

The oboes and bassoons are right behind them. By the time we're a minute into the score, they've all started to play for real and I can stop my singing.

This is where the fun begins. I close my eyes and let the

music take over my entire body. Conducting isn't just about waving a stick around and counting beats. Reading a score is like being an air traffic controller. I can see every flight coming in, going out, circling, taxiing, and parking at the gate. While each musician can only see his or her own "flight plan," it's up to me to see to it that everyone arrives at the correct destination safely. And on time.

I'm cuing sections with my left hand, beating time with my right. When my body folds in on itself and I grow smaller in stature, they instinctively play softer without me having to utter a word. When the lush part comes in and the melody drags like the drone of a bagpipe, I allow my arms to lead in long, broad strokes, as if I'm painting a canvas that's twenty feet tall. They respond in kind, with wide swaths of lush, vibrant sound.

Finally, when the jig returns, I start to dance. Dance! An actual little jig lifts my body up and down on the podium. This is how it feels to have the music take over every cell. When I open my eyes, I see my flutes and bassoons, horns and oboes, saxes, and brass. They're playing lighter and brighter. I see heads bopping and toes tapping as if they're enjoying themselves.

As I bring them to the spiraling conclusion and drop my baton, I'm breathing hard and smiling big. They stare at me, dumbfounded.

"Yes! Now *that's* how you play that piece!" I holler with a triumphant hop on the podium. I'm beaming as my eyes roam across the risers, meeting the gazes of every musician there. "Except for that shitty opening, you gave me, that is." I chuckle, and they join me. It's the first time they're laughing *with* me instead of at me and it feels good.

"Really," I say a little softer now as I lean over my podium toward them, inviting them into an intimate conversation. "You guys sound *amazing* and we're going to kick ass on this when we play it at the spring concert." I pause for a long moment, look down at the podium and then back up at them. "My job—my *only* job—is to help you sound as good as possible so we can remind people that this is one of the top music programs in the country. I am here for *you*. Please keep that in mind," I beseech them, getting my point across as several of my musicians look away from my gaze guiltily.

I let my face relax into a lighter expression. "Now get out of here! I'll see you for our next rehearsal in a couple of days," I say and they scatter to put their instruments away.

I'm making a note in my score when someone clearing his throat. I look up and see Russ standing there.

"Well played, Kate," he says now that we're alone on stage.

"I'll be damned," I say quietly but excitedly. "I might just get them to respect me yet."

"You might just," he agrees with a grin. "Seriously, you handled that very nicely."

"Thanks, Russ," I say as I start to pack up my things.

He takes a seat in front of me and I can tell he's got more to say. I don't have to guess what about.

"So, I hear that Drew Markham gave you a hard time this morning."

I swear this guy has ears everywhere in this school. "It wasn't a big deal." I shrug as I close my score and stuff it into my bag.

"That's not what I hear. What happened?"

I stop what I'm doing and take the seat next to his, recounting the morning's events with minimal emphasis on what an ass Markham was to me. But Russ isn't stupid. He knows there's more to this than I'm telling him and he's getting angrier by the minute. His ghostly white skin is growing crimson from under his collar up to his hairline. His hands have clenched into fists and he's trembling.

"He's got some fucking nerve, threatening to fail you," Russell spits. "Who the hell does he think he is? He's just a little shit who teaches music theory. Music *fucking* theory! Does he really think he has the authority to keep you from graduating?"

"Apparently," I say, a little taken aback by the venom in his tone. I don't often see this side of Russell Atherton, thankfully.

"Well, I think it's time I disabuse him of that notion."

I lean forward and put a hand on his shoulder.

"Please don't," I beg him softly. "Russell, it'll just make things worse if he thinks you're trying to protect me. Please."

He shakes his head either in disgust or disbelief. More likely both. "Stop it, Kate. You're not some frail, abused little girl. You're a strong, confident conductor. You *just* proved that in the way you handled that rehearsal."

My stomach tightens with the prospect of Russell confronting Dr. Markham about this—or anything involving me. After a long, uncomfortable minute, he stops his ranting and takes a good look at me.

"I'm sorry, Kate," he says after drawing a long, deep breath. "I didn't mean to upset you." And then there's concern in his voice and his expression. "You know, you don't look so good, kid."

Now that the conducting adrenaline has left my body, I realize that I don't feel so good. My forehead has stopped bleeding, but the aching throb has morphed into a dull pounding behind me eyes that makes me wince when I blink too hard.

"Yeah, well, it's been the day from hell. I think I'll feel better after I get a good night's sleep."

"Then I suggest we cancel our lesson for tonight so you can go home and get one."

"Really?" I ask, trying not to sound too relieved.

"Absolutely. Go and try to get some rest. The last thing you need is to get sick right now."

He couldn't be more right about that. I get back to my feet and snatch my sneakers from where I'd tossed them down on the stage.

"I will, thanks," I say, slipping them on without bothering to lace them. "And Russ?"

"Hmm?"

"*Please* don't go chasing down Dr. Markham. I just want to graduate and get the hell out of here."

A chilling smile crosses Russell's face and it makes me stop in my tracks.

"Kate, I was chasing Drew Markham a long time before you came into the picture."

I have no idea what that means. Something tells me that I hope I never do.

Chapter Four

Drew

"One grande, half-caf latte with almond milk and two sugars," Tessa Morgan says cheerily as she hands me a steaming white cup.

"Thanks," I say, trying to make a little more room for her as she slips into the seat next to mine. We're all shoehorned into the small conference room, waiting for our boss to arrive for the weekly faculty meeting.

"You're welcome. Thanks for saving me a seat."

"Well, I couldn't have you standing for the entire meeting in those ridiculous heels you wear." I grin, then take a sip of coffee.

"Just because it's cold outside doesn't mean I can't be fashionable, Drew Markham." She huffs with faux indignation.

And she is fashionable. From silky, golden-blond hair, to tan skin, to perfectly manicured nails, Tessa Morgan always looks as if she's just stepped off a runway.

I started teaching at Shepherd just after my fiancée—

scratch that—*ex*-fiancée bailed on our relationship. Tessa was a good friend when I needed one. And she still is.

"I got your email about Kate Brenner," she's saying now, dropping her voice so our colleagues won't overhear. "No, she hasn't come to see me about you. Or anything else, for that matter. What makes you think she might file a complaint against you, anyway?"

"She was late to class and I wouldn't accept her homework. Things got a little heated."

She raises perfectly arched blond eyebrows over perfectly shaped green eyes.

"How heated?"

I shrug. "I don't know. Just enough that I wondered if she'd gone crying to you after class."

"Well, tell you what, how about I call her in for a chat? I can feel her out on it— "

"Stop right there," I interrupt, shaking my head and holding up a hand.

"What?" she asks innocently. "Really, I don't mind facilitating for you— "

"Yeah, I'll bet you don't mind," I accuse with a knowing smile.

"What's *that* supposed to mean?"

Her tone is indignant now and I notice a couple of adjunct professors glancing our way.

"Just that I know you, Tessa Morgan. You're *dying* for a reason to get Senator Brenner's daughter in your clutches. A chance to get a little dirt on our local celebrity."

"Hey!" She gives me a playful shove. "I'm her advisor. It's my *job* to facilitate things like this."

"Am I wrong?"

"Drew!" she hisses at me under her breath.

"Am. I. Wrong?"

She glares at me before finally rolling her eyes.

"Fine. Fine. You're right. I'd love a chance to talk to Kate. She's been at Shepherd for more than five years and the only time I ever see her is when she stops in once a semester so I'll sign off on her schedule. She's very mysterious, that girl. I'd love to know what she's hiding."

"Uh-huh." I smirk. She raises her hand as if to smack my arm again, but I'm saved by the arrival of the dean of music, Maureen Clevenger. She bustles in, wearing her trademark no-nonsense suit and her trademark no-nonsense expression. Lagging behind her is her frazzled assistant, Mary. They take the two seats at the head of the table, which have been left vacant for them.

"Good afternoon, everyone. So sorry to be running late. And sorry for the cramped quarters. They'll be finished installing the new carpet in the main conference room sometime tomorrow. In the meantime, I promise to get through the agenda as quickly as possible so those of you who are standing don't have to do so for very long."

Between full-time, part-time, and adjunct professors, there are about two dozen of us on the music staff at Shepherd, and today we're all crammed into the small meeting room next to Maureen's office. Every square inch of the oval table is accounted for, and the overflow professors are standing in clusters along the walls.

"I've got several items on the agenda, so let's just get started. The first item is final exams. I know we haven't even gotten to midterms, yet, but I want to avoid the confusion we had last semester. Please submit your proposed schedule for exams and your preference for room assignments so Mary can start work on the master schedule," she says, with a nod in the direction of the fortysomething-year-old woman next to her. "No harassing Mary for special favors. Period. Everybody understand?"

We all nod. Last semester was a disaster with students in

the wrong rooms on the wrong days because half the faculty was fighting over early time slots so they could get out of town for the holidays. Clearly Maureen's not having that this time around. And, clearly Mary is under the impression that we're all going to swarm her, based on her terrified expression and darting glance.

"Excellent," Maureen says, ticking off an item on her meeting agenda. "We have about half a dozen senior recitals coming up, starting the week after next. Mary will get an email out to each of you sometime today. Drew and Barry, you're excused from adjudicating those because you'll have your hands full prepping for graduate oral exams at the end of the term."

We all nod our understanding and Maureen checks a second box.

"A reminder that the tenure committee has been considering applications since the beginning of the school year. As you all know, we have one opening this time around. I expect an official decision will be made in the next month or so."

"As if Drew hasn't got that all locked up," snorts my colleague Barry Green.

I shoot him the frostiest glare I can muster, but he's oblivious, as usual. Several of the adjunct faculty members in the room nod and mutter their agreement with his observation.

Maureen is not amused. "*Ladies and gentlemen*," she grits out. "I'll thank you to keep your comments to yourselves. We have more than one suitable candidate, and it's up to the committee to determine who gets the slot." She waits until silence again settles over the room and then she continues. "All right, moving on. If you haven't been keeping an eye on the weather in the last twenty-four hours, then you should know that what was expected to be just another early-spring snowfall, has turned into something quite a bit more substantial. As of right now, it looks as if it could get bad over the weekend. They're not calling for the snow to start until sometime Saturday morning, but the university is going to cancel classes on Friday."

"Snow day!" someone calls out from the other side of the room. Maureen ignores the comment.

"Please make sure your students know to monitor their email for that announcement. I know it's only Tuesday, and the weather's beautiful right now, but we all need to take this situation very seriously. If this thing is as bad as they say it's going to be, we could all be snowed under and stuck at home from Saturday into next week."

She puts her pen down and folds her hands in front of her on the table. Uh-oh. That's "Maureen Code" for serious business.

"I met with President Fitch this morning," she says. "He wanted to give me the heads-up that Senator Tucker Brenner will be on campus next month for a political roundtable discussion. There's some speculation that he'll announce his intentions to make a run for the White House at that time. That means we can expect a media presence in and around the music department in the days to come."

"Why?" asks Barry Green, whose seat is squeezed so close to mine that I can smell his Old Spice. "What do they want here?"

"What do they always want?" I grumble. "They're looking for a comment from *the exalted Miss Brenner*."

Maureen shoots me a nasty look.

"What?" I demand, spreading my palms up toward the ceiling. "Come on, Maureen, you know it's true. Honestly, I'm counting the days until she graduates and takes her paparazzi with her."

From the far side of the room, someone shuffles. The tall, pale figure of Russell Atherton emerges out of the crowd of professors standing in the corner, wearing his signature ratty T-shirt with a long-sleeved plaid shirt over it. I didn't even notice him back there. But then, that's what he's good at, isn't it? Appearing and disappearing like a goddamn ghost.

I'm not the only one surprised to see him as a low murmur makes its way around the small room. Russell hasn't attended a single faculty meeting in the time I've been teaching here. In fact, I'm not sure everyone in this room even knows who he is. Lucky bastards. Maureen twists around in her seat at the head of the table to see what everyone is staring at.

"Russell!" she exclaims, seeming genuinely happy to see him. "I didn't realize you were here. Come, pull up a chair next to me. There's no need for you to stand back there."

But he shakes his head, making his ridiculous white ponytail swing from side to side.

"No thank you, Maureen. I won't be staying long. I just wanted to be here in case someone needed to represent the interests of my student. And I can see now that someone does."

"Which student? Kate?" Maureen asks.

"Who else would it be, Maureen? He only *has* the one student," I point out and am met with a snarl from Russell.

"Russ…" Maureen cautions him quietly.

It's a warning he chooses to ignore as he stalks to the table. Two of my colleagues scramble to roll their chairs in opposite directions so they can clear a space for the fists that slam down on the glassy mahogany table. The conference room is still, without so much as a breath or a blink to tip the tension.

"You listen to me and you listen good, Drew. I will not tolerate anymore of your bullshit. I suggest you lay off Kate Brenner, or you'll have *me* to deal with. Understand?" he growls.

I wait a beat to see if Maureen will intervene. She doesn't.

"You're the one who doesn't understand, Russell," I say coolly. "I will enforce the policies of this university as I see fit. And I'll thank you to mind your own business."

All heads swing back toward Russell as if this is a round at Wimbledon.

"Yeah." He snorts. "Because being a few minutes late for class is such a serious infraction."

"It is in my classroom," I inform him, refusing to give him the satisfaction of raising my voice.

"Apparently, seeing as how you threatened to fail her in her last semester of graduate school. I have to say, I read the student handbook cover to cover today and, as far as I could see, the only non-academic infractions that cause immediate failure and dismissal are cheating, criminal activity, and any kind of hate rhetoric."

Now they're all back to staring at me. Maureen raises a curious eyebrow.

"Is that true, Drew? Did you tell Kate you'd fail her for being a few minutes late to your class?"

"Really, Maureen? *That's* the part of this exchange that you feel needs clarification? After he just came in here and threatened me in front of the entire music department?"

"That doesn't answer my question."

"Oh, come on!" I huff loudly, throwing calm and cool out the window. "She was late. I gave her a verbal warning. Isn't that what professors are supposed to do?" I turn my glare to Russell who looks as if smoke is about to come out of his ears. "And, Russell, if your girl can't manage something as basic as getting up in time for class, then maybe she's got no business graduating from our program anyway. These students are a direct reflection on us."

"Enough!" Maureen says loudly. She closes her eyes for a second, takes a deep breath, and starts again in a lower voice. "First, both of you, please refrain from calling our female students *'girls.'* They're women. Kate is a *woman*, not a girl."

"Oh, wonderful," I say to no one. "I guess I'm a misogynist now, too."

When I see the fire in Maureen's gray eyes, I realize I may have gone a step too far. She sits back and surveys the room full of teachers before speaking in a chilling tone.

"I want to make something very clear to everyone in this room. There will be no discussion of Kate Brenner to anyone. Not to each other. Not to students. Certainly not to reporters. And let me remind you that there are unscrupulous members of the press who will try to get information by any means possible. They might call pretending to be another department or administrator on campus. They might come right out and offer you cash for inside information. There are to be no comments *on* or *off* the record to anyone. If I hear so much as a whisper about an 'anonymous source' within the music department, someone is going to lose their job. And make no mistake about it. I. Will. Find. You. Is there anyone in this room who needs clarification on anything I've just said?"

Silence.

"Good," she says with a satisfied nod. "All right then, everyone, please be careful with the weather this weekend and let's plan on meeting next Thursday if the university is open. Thank you all for your time. Drew, Russell, please stay."

The room empties quickly as a few colleagues shoot sympathetic glances my way. Tessa is the last one to get up. But, instead of exiting, she stops in front of Maureen.

"I just want to say that I'm with Drew on this. As Kate's advisor, I've found that it's more trouble than it's worth to have a high-profile student."

I cringe for my friend. Way to kick a hornets' nest, Tess.

"Oh? And why is that, exactly?" Maureen asks.

Tessa looks a little taken aback. "What do you mean?"

"What about Kate's presence in this department has been 'trouble' for you?"

I can see the start of pink rising to Tessa's cheeks.

"Well, I—uh—I've offered my services to her on numerous

occasions but she's determined to..." Her voice peters out before she can find a suitable ending to that thought.

"To *what*, exactly, Tessa? To keep her business private? To handle her own problems like a grown-up?"

"I...I, uh, Maureen, I still don't..."

"Tessa, please stick to academic advising. Drew is more than capable of handling issues with his own students. Understood?"

Tessa nods with a sour face.

"Good. Now leave us. Please," she says in a tone that doesn't sound like "please" so much as "before I throw your scrawny ass out the door." Tessa practically trips on her five-inch heels in her haste to get out of the room. Once she's gone, Maureen turns her attention to a pissed-looking Russell.

"Russ, I'm so happy that you felt compelled to come out of your office and join us in the real world for a change. But I have a sneaking suspicion that Kate has no idea that you came here on her behalf. Am I right?"

"Maybe," he grumbles begrudgingly.

Maureen gives a long sigh of resignation and when she speaks again, her tone is considerably softer than it was earlier. "Russ, you know very well that Kate is not only perfectly capable of handling this situation on her own, she'd prefer to handle it on her own. If you want to help Kate, then please keep an eye out for those sneaky creeps who call themselves journalists. I don't trust them to leave her alone, and some can get very aggressive. All right?" she asks.

"Fine," he mutters grudgingly.

"Good. I'll come by and see you in your office before I head out for the day."

Russell takes the hint and leaves. And then it's just Maureen and me. When she looks at me expectantly, I get up from the far end of the table and sit at her other side. She sighs and takes her glasses off long enough to rub the bridge of her nose.

"Drew, I'm going to advise you to tread very carefully here."

"Why? Is the senator going to come after me next?"

"No," she replies dryly. "I'd just hate for any complaints to complicate your bid for tenure. They're not wrong, you know. Tenure *is* yours, so long as you don't burn the building down. So stop playing with the goddamned matches already!"

I'm taken aback by the hiss in her tone. It's very un-Maureen-like.

"Maureen, you don't understand—"

"Please, Drew. I'm not blind. You're not the only one who sees the resemblance. But Kate isn't Casey."

I feel my lungs suck in a breath that I didn't tell them to take.

"Is that what you think? That I confuse her with Casey?" I ask, trying for indignant but coming up short. Instead, my words end up sounding petulant.

She smiles at me now. It's a strange smile, though. Part pity, part fondness, and part insanity.

"I think that Casey still makes you furious even after all this time. And I think that Kate is a convenient proxy for your anger."

"Oh, please. You know what, Maureen? I'm sick and tired of being painted as the villain—"

"No, stop right there," she says, holding up her index finger in warning. "I am very fond of you, Drew. You know that. But do *not* make the mistake of thinking that you are above reproach. You harass, threaten, or coerce that young woman again and it just might cost you more than tenure. You might not have a job at the end of it. So get your act together and get over it. Get over *her*."

With that, my boss stands up, grabs her belongings, and leaves me sitting at the table, wondering exactly which *her* she's expecting me to get over.

Chapter Five

Kate

He's handing back the papers. One by one, he peels the manuscript pages off the pile in his hand and folds it in half, discretely delivering it to its owner. I try not to look too interested as I watch my classmates surreptitiously. Joanie the flute player grumbles and rolls her eyes. Not the grade she was expecting, I guess. From the desk next to me, pianist Craig lets out a long sigh of relief. Not the grade he was expecting either, apparently, but for different reasons.

Markham passes the assignments back until there are none. Despite my efforts to remain disinterested, I can feel my face heat with the embarrassment of being excluded. I make a point of pretending to be engrossed in the notebook on my desk, hoping no one will notice. Well, he did say he wasn't going to accept it. Just because I left it here doesn't mean he even looked at it. In fact, it probably hit the trash can before the door closed behind me.

"Ahem."

My head jerks up at the sound in front of me. He's standing at his desk, reaching across it with my assignment in his hand. My hand is trembling slightly as I take it from him. God, I hope he doesn't notice.

"Thank you, Dr. Markham," I mutter quietly.

"Don't thank me till you look it over," he says in an equally soft tone.

He walks behind his desk to the board and starts to write out a few bars of music. With his back to me, I decide it's safe to take a peek. Slowly, I pull the two ends of the folded paper apart, afraid of what I might find.

"Excellent inversion of the motif!" he's written next to a fragment he circled. Further down the page I get "Yes!" where I have given the bassoons an unexpected solo. There are a few other scrawling compliments in red ink as I get down to the bottom and flip to the second page. And there it is. I skip past a few other remarks he's made to get to the space under my last line of music.

"Overall, a very well-thought arrangement. I hope you'll continue along these lines as you complete the project. And I hope you'll bring it in on time.

Grade earned: 95. Grade Received: 0. –D. Markham."

When I glance up from the paper, he's watching me. Everyone else is so busy reading their own comments that they don't notice when he raises a single eyebrow at me. It's a question. And a dare. I don't answer, nor do I bite. I tuck the pages into the back of my notebook and pull out a piece of blank manuscript paper so I can copy down the phrase of music that he's written on the board. I suppose I should be grateful that I got the comments out of him.

"All right, enough ogling the papers," Markham says after a few minutes. "I've been getting a lot of questions in regards to the midterm assignment. And, quite frankly, I'm alarmed by them. You should be just dotting the i's and crossing the t's at this point. *Not* emailing me questions about basic music theory. So, I'm going to do some one-on-ones with you for the rest of the class, to go over a few key points that appear to be throwing several of you off.

"You are graduate students, not freshmen. Everything we're doing now is built on the foundation of the last three semesters. And the last four *years* before that. This isn't anything new that I'm pulling out of thin air. These are concepts we've studied in other composers' music at length. Now, I'm asking you to apply them here. Okay, if you're not doing a one-on-one with me, then please copy the measures that I've written on the board and give me a quintet orchestration of it."

When he seems satisfied that we're all clear, he sits down at his desk and pulls up a chair next to his, inviting each student to check in with him to address their questions. Time is almost up and I still haven't decided if I'll take a turn or not. Sitting so close to him, I have the advantage of hearing him speaking with my classmates. And, so far, he's been nice enough to everyone. Helpful, even.

"You can't have the violins playing a C-natural while the violas are playing a C-sharp," he's telling a bassoon player named Evan.

"I, uh—I don't understand," Evan replies, scratching his perpetual bedhead.

I try to keep from smiling as I work on the assignment in front of me. I can't help but notice that Markham doesn't give Evan a nasty lecture or a warning about failing.

"You're running out of time, Evan," Markham begins candidly, his concern obvious in his tone. "I think the best use of what little you have left is to just start over. Don't come at it from a twenty-first-century composer's perspective. Pretend you're one of Mozart's students. Write it the way he would want you to write it. The way it would have been written in *his* day. Does that make sense?"

"Uh, yeah, I suppose…"

Out of the corner of my eye, I see our professor pat my classmate's arm supportively. "Take another run at it tonight, then come see me during office hours tomorrow and I'll have another look. You can do this, Evan. I know you can."

I sneak a quick glance and see that Evan is as surprised by this offer as I am.

"You'd do that? You'd see me two days in a row?" he asks, clearly stunned.

Markham's expression is perplexed. "Of course. That's what office hours are for. That's what *I'm* here for."

A stunned Evan nods, taking his paper and shuffling back to his seat. I'm still watching him walk away when I hear my name.

"Miss Brenner?"

"Y-yes?" I ask and immediately berate myself for stuttering. What's wrong with me? Why do I let him make me like this?

"Did you want to go over your paper?" Markham asks.

"Sure," I say a little hesitantly. There are some furtive glances from my classmates as I put the staff paper on his desk and pull up a chair so we can both look it over.

"You really did an excellent job with this," he says quietly. "If the midterm assignment is as good as this, there's no reason you shouldn't score an A."

"Thank you," I murmur, keeping my eyes fixed on the paper in front of me.

"Do you understand why I gave you the grade I did?"

I'm on guard immediately. Such a simple question could so easily be a setup. I clear my throat to buy myself another couple of seconds while I consider my reply.

"I am disappointed that you wouldn't accept the assignment," I begin slowly. "But I appreciate the fact that you took the time to look it over and give me your comments," I conclude at last.

There. Diplomatic, polite, *and* the truth.

"But you *understand* my reasoning?" he presses.

Oh, come on, really? Clearly, he is not going to let this go. I sigh and angle my chair a little so I can look directly into his eyes. They're so brown that they almost look black when you get up close to them.

"No, Dr. Markham, I can't say that I understand it, because I don't. It seems unreasonable to me," I say with as much sincerity as I can muster. "That being said, I'll just have to respect whatever decision you make."

Markham's jaw clenches into a hard line and his dark eyebrows draw down into a harsh *V*. Clearly I will not be benefiting from the same kind concern that Evan just received. When my professor speaks again, I can hear the frost in his soft voice.

"Miss Brenner, if that were true, if you really *did* respect my decision, you wouldn't have gone crying to Russell Atherton about me."

I can actually feel the blood as it drains from my face.

"Dr. Markham, I swear to God I didn't say anything about our conversation. He'd heard about it from someone else. And I asked him—I pleaded with him—not to discuss it with you," I explain in a hushed tone.

For a long beat he seems to be looking for something on my face. Sincerity, maybe? I hope so, because that's what it is. That and abject horror. Finally, he gives a long sigh of reluctant acceptance.

"All right, Miss Brenner. But if he wasn't acting at your behest then you might want to have a little chat with him about letting you fight your own battles. He's not doing you any favors."

I'm not sure who to be more upset with—Russell for going

against my wishes and confronting Markham, or Markham himself for making sure that I knew about it. I sit back, closing my eyes and rubbing my temples. My headache just got about ten times worse.

"Yes, you're right. I'll do that. It's just…it's hard to make Professor Atherton do anything he doesn't want to do."

"Yeah. I know," he mumbles.

What? Is it possible that, for once, Dr. Drew Markham *gets* it?

I'm about to expel the largest, longest sigh of relief when he steals all the oxygen from my lungs.

"Of course, if you'd refrained from giving him an earful in the first place, we wouldn't be having this conversation now, would we?"

And just like that, my tiny drop of relief is replaced by a wave of discomfort so overwhelming that I know I have to get out of this room before things get ugly. Uglier.

I have to stop and swallow, fighting back a sudden, unexpected wave of nausea. Oh God. I've got to get out of here, and fast.

"Okay, you're right, Dr. Markham. I apologize. You're right, I never should have said anything to him and I'm sorry that he did that to you. May I please be excused? I'm really not feeling very well."

He gives a half snort, half laugh.

"Miss Brenner, if you think you're going to get out of your assignment by playing sick—" he starts to caution but I have to cut him off.

"I understand. May I *please* be excused?" I whisper.

"You don't have any questions about your project?" he asks.

"No, thank you," I mutter distractedly, wiping the sweat that's starting to form on my brow.

"All right, Miss Brenner. Go," he says, holding my paper

out for me to take. I grab it and my bag, and then make a run for the door.

In less than sixty seconds, I'm down the hall and retching in the ladies' room. When there's nothing left to come up, I sit on the cold tile floor with my back against the stall and I breathe until the urge to cry leaves me.

Chapter Six

Drew

I love my Thursday afternoons because I love order and organization. And my Thursdays are all about the order and the organization. After a few obligatory office hours, I've got the time to concentrate on my lesson plans and wade through the ever-growing piles of paperwork on my desk. I'm just about through with this week's mountain of minutia when there's a knock on my office door. Surprising, since everyone knows better than to bother me in my office on a Thursday.

"Come in," I call out from my desk, not bothering to get up.

When the door opens, I'm greeted by a tall blond guy, probably a little older than me. I'm certain I've never met him before, but there's something that's vaguely familiar about him.

"Excuse me, Dr. Markham? May I have a moment of your time?"

"Uh, sure, I guess. Come in."

"Okay if I sit for a minute?" he asks with a pleasant enough grin and I nod toward the chair in front of me.

"I'm sorry, I'm sure I've seen you before but I can't place you. Are you a Shepherd professor?"

"No, I'm not. My name is Kevin Kilpatrick, I'm a reporter for the *D.C. Courier*."

That's where I know him from. But not from his byline. I just saw his name and picture in an email being circulated by campus security. He's one of the press members who've been banned from campus. But I don't tell him that, because I'm curious to see where this is going. I put the assignments I'm grading aside and fold my hands on my desk. He's got my full attention now.

"Yes, of course. What can I do for you, Mr. Kilpatrick?"

He pulls a small notebook and pen out of his pocket, flipping pages as he's speaking.

"I'm hoping you can give me some insight into one of your students. Katherine Brenner?"

Seriously? Does he think I'm a fucking idiot? I stare at him, unwilling to respond to such an asinine request. Finally, he gets the idea and continues anyway.

"Yeah, so, maybe your thoughts on her as a student, the influence her father has at this university, how the other faculty and students feel about her. That sort of thing."

I tilt my head to the left just a hair, taking him in from a different angle, just to fuck with him. He shifts in his seat uncomfortably.

"Mr. Kilpatrick," I say at last, "surely you know that I'm not permitted to comment on any student at Shepherd University. So why are you here?"

He gives me a sheepish shrug. "I don't know. Something tells me she's not your favorite pupil."

"Excuse me?"

He flashes a cryptic smile. "Let's just say that word around campus is that there's no love lost between the two of you. And do you know what that tells me, Dr. Markham?"

I sit back in my chair. This should be good.

"No. But please, enlighten me."

"It tells me that you see something there. In her. You see a side of her that other people don't. Maybe the *real* Katherine Brenner. Now, I've met the girl, Doc, and I have to say, she's not all rainbows and sunshine, if you know what I mean."

"I don't," I say flatly, but he's unaffected by my tone.

"Do you find her to be difficult in your classroom, Doc? Because I'm curious to see if your observations are the same as mine."

I lean forward, over the top of my desk and he moves in closer, as if I'm about to tell him some deep, dark secret. For a split second, his eyes light up with anticipation.

"First, stop calling me 'Doc,'" I spit. "Second, I don't know who the hell you think you're talking to, Mr. Kilpatrick, but I have no intention of violating the privacy of any student—whether I like them or not."

"Okay, so you *don't* like her then."

He starts to scribble furiously in his little notebook.

"That is *not* what I said!" I protest.

"You didn't have to."

He grins. I scowl.

"Come on, don't be like that," he coaxes, waving his hand at me dismissively. "I can keep your identity a secret. No one will know you were the one who made the comments. I know you're a hard-ass in the classroom—it's not surprising that someone like her would rub you the wrong way. Well, here's your chance to tell the world about Senator Brenner's daughter. Is she an entitled bitch? Does she get a free pass cause her daddy's a politician? Go ahead, you can tell me *anything*. I'll make sure the whole world knows the truth."

I'd give anything to knock the obnoxious grin right off his

fucking face, but I can't. Instead, I take a deep breath, close my eyes for just an instant, and keep my voice as even as possible. "I think you should leave now, Mr. Kilpatrick."

He doesn't budge. In fact, he's looking downright comfortable in my office chair, as if he's some long-lost friend who's stopped by to reminisce about the good old days.

"She's quite the student. Did someone tell you to give her a pass or special treatment? Or maybe someone offered to pay you off to give her good grades?"

I can feel my face getting hot as my blood pressure starts to rise, but I just stare at him without so much as a twitch for a response.

"No?" the reporter asks, raising an eyebrow and then jotting something else down. "Well, what about romances? Have you seen her with any particular guy? Or, better yet, any particular *girl*?"

I get to my feet so fast that my chair rolls back and hits the wall behind me with a crash.

"Seriously? This is what you consider news?"

He shrugs without so much as blinking an eye.

"Doesn't matter what I think is news, Doc. It's what the people want to read. What they want to buy. Senator Tucker Brenner is going to announce his bid for the White House very soon. That's going to put him *and* Kate into the spotlight. I intend to be the one who's there with the scoop on the daughter of 'Senator Satan.'"

"Out."

"Oh, come on…"

"Get. Out. *Now*!" I growl.

The jackass doesn't move from his chair.

"If you're not gone in the next ten seconds, I'm going to call campus security. Then they'll call the police and charge you with trespassing, Mr. Kilpatrick. Hard to work from a jail cell, you know. And with a snow storm on the way, who knows how long you'd be stuck there."

Kilpatrick stands up, rolling his eyes and muttering under his breath.

"I'm telling you, Doc, if you don't talk someone else will. Don't say I didn't give you first crack at it!" he calls out over his shoulder as he exits my office.

I get up to close and lock the door behind him. What a weasely little shit! And who the hell has been telling him about what goes on in my class? I sit back down and consider what he's just said to me. I'm tough, sure, but a hard-ass? I've had my share of asshole professors in my time. Mean sons of bitches who'd fuck with us just to fuck with us. But that's not me.

I set a high bar for my students because they need to know what it's like out there. I've been out in the world of professional classical music and if they're not prepared—if they're not tough enough—they're going to get chewed up and spit out faster than they can call mommy and daddy to come get them. I refuse to do my students the injustice of letting them think it's going to be easy for them once they leave the safety and security of Shepherd University. It's not. And they need to be prepared for that reality.

And that includes Katherine Brenner. Even though she irks me. Even though she brings out the worst in me. Even though I know it's not her fault. It just doesn't matter.

Chapter Seven

KATE

"Let it go. Let it go. Let it go. Let it goooooo..."

Ughhh! That stupid song from that stupid movie is haunting my dreams. God! I wish whoever's playing that shit *would* just let it go. But they don't. The tune keeps playing and playing and playing. It stops at some point, only to return a short time later.

By the third refrain, my subconscious begins to accept that this isn't a dream at all. I'm really hearing this. And from close by. Groaning, I lift my head and, through bleary eyes, spot my phone on the table next to me.

I crossed the line between under the weather and sick as a dog somewhere in the middle of the night and I've been in and out of a hazy stupor ever since, not quite able to discern what's real from what I'm dreaming. This is definitely real. Not a dream, unfortunately. The image of a cartoon character is lit up on my display. She's got long, white hair, a bluish complexion, and a crown made of icicles. The Ice Queen is calling me, and that's never a good thing.

"Hello?" I answer, my voice hoarse from sleep.

"Hello, Katherine. This is Leandra Styverson, your father's press secretary?"

"Yes, Leandra. I know who you are," I mumble.

"Are you all right, Katherine? You don't sound so good..."

"I'm fine, thank you, Leandra. What did you need?"

"Uh, well, I'm calling on behalf of the senator. He's going to be in North Carolina next month, on the campus of Shepherd University. He's participating in a political town hall and he'd like for you to attend."

When I don't respond immediately, she continues.

"I've arranged to have a ticket held for you at will call. I would recommend dressing in something a little less casual than you're used to. There will be television crews and it's entirely possible you'll be picked up on camera."

"I see."

"So we can expect you to be there then?"

"No."

Long pause. This response can't have come as a surprise to Leandra. This is hardly the first time we've done this dance.

"May I ask why?"

"Leandra," I say on a long sigh, "we both know that the only reason he, or, more likely, *you* want me there is so there's someone in the audience for the camera to cut to when they're talking about him. The sweet, devoted daughter. It's all about—what do you call it? *Optics*, right?"

She doesn't respond for a long, uncomfortable second.

"Very well, I'll pass on the message."

"Great. Thank you, Leandra. Good-bye—"

"Wait, please, Katherine. There's something else," she squeezes in before I can hang up and resume my hibernation under the blankets.

"What?" I moan, unable to keep up the feeling fine facade.

"The senator would like to have dinner with you, even if you don't come to the event on campus."

Even in my hazy state, I know what a bad idea that is.

"No. Absolutely not. I'm not interested in being a photo op."

"Katherine, he wanted me to tell you that he's arranged a private room at Villa Romano. His security team will clear the venue beforehand and no one will know you're coming. He promises that it will be just the two of you. No photographers."

I consider this. My father is a lot of things, but a liar isn't one of them. If he's promising me privacy, he means to deliver it. The question is whether I want to have him all to myself.

"Fine," I say at last, in exasperated defeat. "What's the date?"

Leandra can hardly contain her surprise and excitement. "Wonderful! It's Friday, April seventh. That's exactly two weeks from today."

"Tomorrow," I correct her.

She pauses.

"No, actually, I've got the calendar right in front of me."

"But today is Thursday," I say, wanting nothing more than to stop talking. My throat feels as if I swallowed a gallon of gas and tossed a match in after it.

"No, afraid not, Katherine. Today is Friday, I'm quite certain of that."

And then it occurs to me—I have no idea how long I've been asleep. I know I've gotten up a few times to drink something and take a few pills, but I just assumed…

"Leandra?" I ask, my voice suddenly shaky.

"Yes, Katherine?"

I'm terrified to ask the question. Terrified to know the answer. "W-what time is it?"

"Four o'clock," she says. "On Friday."

What? No. No, no, no!

"I'm sorry, I have to go," I say breathlessly, even as I'm disconnecting the call.

That *can't* be right, can it? I scramble to bring up the main screen on my phone and there it is in big, glowing digital numbers.

4:04 p.m.

Shit!

I find the remote for my television set and scan through the channels until I find one that's twenty-four hour news. And there it is on a banner at the bottom of the screen.

Friday, March 24th. 4:05 PM.

Oh my God!

I've somehow lost an *entire* day. The day that I was supposed to spend recopying the midterm project before getting it to Markham. I should have just turned it in the way it was yesterday, when I was feeling better. Or was that the day before yesterday?

Don't panic, Kate.

Think, Kate.

Okay. Let's assess. I drag myself out of bed and hobble over to the table where the sheets of manuscript paper are spread out. The project is done, it's just a little messier than I'd like. He'll likely ding me for that, but probably not enough to lower the grade. I scoop up the pages, fasten them together with a paperclip, and stuff them into the big envelope I've set aside for them. Too late to drop this on campus. Markham's already gone for the day, so I'll have to get it to him at home.

I take a deep breath and concentrate on slowing my heart rate. It's okay, I've had to do this before and I know where he lives. I can be there in twenty minutes, if I leave right now. With no time to change, I just throw on a hoodie over the yoga pants and T-shirt I've been sleeping in. I look like crap, but I don't plan on getting out of the car so it doesn't matter. I'll just roll right up to his mailbox, stuff the envelope in the newspaper holder, and be on my way before he even knows I was there.

My headache is still a constant, and I'm a little dizzy, but I think I'm well enough to drive the ten miles or so. I'm going to have to be. I grab my keys and look around for my shoes. The first thing I see are the flip-flops I wear to go down to the laundry room in the basement of the apartment building. My toes will be chilly, but I can crank the heater in the car. Within five minutes of hanging up on The Ice Queen, I'm headed down the stairs and to the parking lot. Three feet out the front door I realize I can't see my car. It, like everything else in my line of sight, is buried under six inches of snow.

• • •

Winter storms in the mountains of North Carolina are nothing to take lightly. My little car climbs a hundred feet or so, then spins out and slides back down fifty of those feet. Luckily, all the sane people are already buttoned up tight in their nice warm homes and I'm the only lunatic braving this weather right now.

When I decided that there was enough time to get this assignment to Markham's house, I didn't consider the fact that his house sits higher up on the mountain. By the time I turn off on the steep, winding road leading to his neighborhood, I've fishtailed about a dozen times, spun out twice and, at one intersection, I did a slow-mo 360. But I'm almost there now.

With a little help from a wrench and YouTube, I figured out how to get the Corolla's battery cables back to their happy place. And thank God for that because just a few days later, the poor little engine is having to work unusually hard against gravity and ice as it climbs to the higher elevation. I have the accelerator pressed all the way to the floor and still, I'm barely inching along. Eventually the terrain levels out and the car settles down, along with my stress level.

I spot the turnoff for Windsor Court and make a slow, wide left to avoid gliding into the curb. As I drive past the big houses, I look at their sprawling lawns, now nothing more than blankets of fluffy white snow. A few people are out and about, bundled up tight as they shovel or snow blow. There are a group of teenagers having a snowball war on one property, while younger kids build a snowman across the street. They remind me of what it was like growing up at our home in Virginia.

Winter brought snow angels, sleigh rides, and sliding down the big hills on cookie sheets in our neighborhood. The memories make me smile. Then the smile promptly fades as I recognize the last house on the block. The log cabin-inspired house takes up the entire rounded end of the court. I glance at the clock on my dash. Four forty-eight. Twelve minutes to spare.

"Thank. You. God!" I breathe out loud as I maneuver my side of the car close to the mailbox. "Thank you, thank you, thank you!"

The wheels skid a little, but I manage to get close enough to slip my parcel into the brass cylinder reserved for the delivery of newspapers and probably take-out menus. There are three other manila envelopes inside already. Good. That means he hasn't been out to collect them. I slip mine into the middle of the pile so it doesn't look as if I was the last person to get my paper in.

A flood of relief washes over my exhausted, aching body. That's it. All I have to do now is make my way back down the hill and the few miles home. I'm going to crawl under the covers of my bed and stay there all weekend. I'm already envisioning my pillow as I shift the car into drive once again and give the accelerator gas. But nothing happens. That is, nothing except for that sound. The sickening high-pitched whine of tires spinning without any traction.

"Come on," I coax the little car. "C'mon, c'mon, c'mon. Please!"

When I try again, it's the same. Okay. Maybe reverse will get me some grip.

No dice.

I try again and again, realizing, too late, that I'm only melting the snow under the tires, causing it to refreeze instantly as slick ice.

"No!" I wail, pounding the steering wheel in frustration. "Dammit!"

The wash of relief is long gone, replaced by a wave of nausea and exhaustion that hits me like one of those anvils that falls from the sky in cartoons.

Shit. What the hell am I going to do now?

Okay. There are only a few options. I could go and knock on Markham's door.

Hell. No.

I could abandon the car for now and walk down the hill to the main road, and hope someone picks me up and gives me a ride back to town. Not ideal considering how I'm dressed, but still preferable to Plan A.

I could just stay put. Not likely Markham's going to come out in this weather to get the papers. Maybe if I just sit here for a little while, a snowplow might come by and help me. Yes. That's what I'll do. I'll just wait for the snowplow.

That decided, I take a long, shaky breath and turn on the radio. But even the classical station is broadcasting nonstop doom-and-gloom weather predictions. Finally, I just turn it off in favor of silence. The problem now is that I can barely keep my eyes open. I don't want to fall asleep and miss the snowplow. They're loud though, right? Hopefully I'd wake up for something like that.

I close my eyes, only to feel a fierce burning behind

the lids. Ugh. The fever must be back. And the chills. I twist around, looking in the backseat looking for something that I can use as a blanket. But there isn't anything. And, whatever adrenaline that got me here has now drained out of my body. Exhausted and frustrated, I set my forehead against the steering wheel. If I can just rest. Just for a few minutes, I'm sure I can figure this out.

Chapter Eight

Drew

It's taken my neighbor and me nearly an hour to get his snow blower up and running.

"Jesus, Joe, do us both a favor and buy yourself a new one next season, will you? I think I dislocated my shoulder pulling the starter on this thing," I complain as he rolls the machine back into his garage. "You're one cheap son of a bitch," I tease and give him a slap on the back. He's a salty old geezer who gets a kick out of busting my chops, so I like to give it back to him whenever I can.

"No, man, cheap is the shitty bottle of bathtub gin I'm going to give you for helping me out with this." He snorts, and then his leathery old face softens. "Seriously, thanks. It's starting to come down hard now. I'll be out here again in an hour, I'm sure. I mean, *fuck*! It's like we're in some goddamned snow globe or something."

Joe gestures to the rapidly appearing winter wonderland around us. Already, the neighbors' yards have lost their definition. The cul-de-sac is a pristine surface of white, powdery snow, making it hard to tell where one property ends and the next starts.

"You set for the storm otherwise? Anything you need before I'm snowed in?"

"Oh no, I'm good," he says, waving away my concern like it's an annoying gnat. "Wood. Food. Gas. Batteries. This ain't my first rodeo, ya know, Drew."

I look at him with a raised eyebrow. "I don't know, man, seems to me you've left the most important thing off that list. What about the liquor?"

He throws his head back and laughs. "Oh no. Don't you worry about *that*. I've got a stash that would make the Alcoholic Beverage Commission stand up and take notice."

"I'll bet you have, Joe." I grin and shake my head.

"Come on in and have a quick shot of bourbon with me. Just a little something to warm the gut before you head back home."

I'm about to accept the offer when I feel the vibration of my cell phone in my pocket. I hold up a gloved finger at Joe.

"I'm in. Can you just give me a second to take this call?"

He nods and wanders toward the garage while I glance down at the display.

"Tessa," I answer. "How are you doing with the snow?"

"Oh, I'm fine. That's the beauty of living in a condo, Drew, other people do the shoveling." She laughs. "What about you? You playing Paul Bunyan up there on the hill? Chopping your wood and churning your butter?"

"Churning my butter? Where the hell did you get that from?" I snicker.

"I don't know, it just sounded like something you'd do when your cabin is snowed in. Not that your place is a real cabin."

"Oh, now you're just being insulting."

"Please, Drew. How many cabins have a Viking stove and a mudroom and a sixty-inch flat-screen TV and—"

"All right, already! I give up. You're right, it's not exactly a little fishing cabin in the middle of nowhere. But it's not like I haven't stayed in those, too. They're just better suited to short-term stays. No hot water or heat gets old pretty fast when the temperature drops down into the single digits."

"Hmm, well, I suppose. So, if you're not churning butter then what *are* you doing up there on the mountain? All by yourself? Alone?"

My internal alarm goes off. This is a typical Tessa maneuver. She's looking for an invite to spend the weekend snowed in with me.

"Oh, well, it's *really* coming down up here already. I don't think I could get out if I wanted to, so I'm just staying close to home. Hunkering."

"Well," she begins, "it just so happens that one of my neighbors drives a snowplow and he's offered to drop me at your place. *I* could keep you company."

She says this last part a little slower and a lot softer. I pace to the end of Joe's driveway, out of earshot.

"Tess, you'd be stuck for days. It's a mess up here. Believe me, you're much better off in your own place. Why don't you throw a bag of popcorn in the microwave and watch one of those old musicals you like. What's the one you enjoy so much? Seven Guides for Seven Mothers?"

She snorts loudly. "Brides, Drew. Seven *Brides* for Seven *Brothers*. And I'd love to watch it with *you*. C'mon, Drew..." she coaxes.

Shit. I don't know how to get out of this, but I do know I sure as hell can't be stuck here with Tessa for the weekend. I'm trying to decide which lie will sound most convincing when I notice Joe. He's walked out past me on the driveway into the cul-de-sac and he's staring toward my house with obvious interest.

"Oh, hey, Tess, let me call you back later," I mutter, trying to see what he's looking at.

"How about I just come—"

"Tess, I've gotta go. It's too dangerous out. Maybe tomorrow if the roads are clear, okay?"

"Fine," she grumbles.

I say good-bye and walk to where Joe is still standing, looking toward my property curiously.

"Hey, man, what's up?"

"You expecting company?" he asks me, and I glance at him.

"No, why?"

"Look over there. By your mailbox."

It's dark now, but I follow the trajectory of his pointing finger and I can just make out the shape of a snow-covered vehicle.

"Huh, I don't know *whose* car that is," I mumble. "You know what? I'll bet one of the neighbors wanted to move it so they can plow their driveway," I offer up as a possible excuse.

"Nah, I don't think so. Look at all that snow, it's been there for a while. And—"

Joe stops short and cranes his head forward a little trying to get a better look from where we're standing down the street.

"What?" I ask, suddenly feeling uneasy.

"Drew, I think there might be somebody inside that car."

Chapter Nine

Kate

When the rap comes on the window, I'm so deep in a distorted dream that the sudden, sharp sound makes me sit bolt upright, breathing hard. Even through the cover of snow that's accumulated on the windshield, I can see that it's dark outside now. What? How long have I been asleep? My eyes fly to the dashboard clock. Just over an hour. I take a deep breath and turn slowly, reluctantly to my left, afraid of who might be standing there.

I'm right to be afraid.

Dr. Markham is wearing a huge navy blue parka and snow boots and he's motioning for me to roll down my window.

"Miss Brenner," he says before I can even explain my presence. "Why are you sitting in front of my mailbox in your car…sleeping?"

"I-I, uh…."

He raises an irritated brow over one of his dark-brown eyes and I try to pull myself together.

"I'm sorry. I dropped off my paper and now I'm stuck in the snow."

He seems confused for a second.

"You didn't check your email, did you?"

It's a question, but it sounds more like a pronouncement of judgment.

"Email?" I have no clue what he's talking about.

"Miss Brenner, the university closed today in advance of the storm. I sent out an email last night extending the deadline until our next class."

I stare at him, mouth agape. If I'd only taken two minutes to check my email, I could be home in a warm bed right now, instead of stuck in the snow in front of this jerk's house.

"No," I say in a near whisper. "No sir, I've been sick the last couple of days. I wasn't in classes yesterday…or today—I mean, I thought today was yesterday and I didn't go to classes. And then, when I woke up, it was today. Like, an hour ago. I was too sick to even look…I just got out of bed long enough to drive my assignment up here."

He considers me for a long beat without comment before squatting down to look under the vehicle. Then, he stands up again.

"Yeah, it looks like you might be stuck in an ice rut. Go ahead and start the ignition, I'll see if I can give you a push out of it," he says, leaving to walk around to the back of the car. I do as he asks and put the Corolla into gear. When I feel him pushing his weight against the trunk, I press the accelerator, hoping to catch enough traction to pull out. But the tires just spin and whine against the slick surface.

"Again," he calls out from behind me. I accelerate with the same results.

Finally, he comes back around to my window, breathing heavier and looking less than thrilled. "I'm afraid you're good and stuck, Miss Brenner," he says flatly. I watch as he looks off into the distance then sighs deeply before refocusing on me.

"Come on, you'd better come inside before the temperature really starts to drop."

Uh-uh. No way.

"Oh, thank you, Dr. Markham," I say with a polite smile. "That's really generous of you, but I'm fine here."

He looks perplexed.

"How are you fine here? This storm's just getting started. There's going to be another three feet by morning," he informs me, shaking his head the whole time. "No. You can't possibly sit here."

I keep the smile plastered to my face.

"I really do appreciate the offer, but I'll just wait here. I'm sure a snowplow will come along, and then I can hitch a ride down to the main road."

Now the eyebrows go up in skepticism.

"Miss Brenner, there *is* no snowplow. This development is the last to get plowed out, so you could be sitting here for the next twenty-four hours. *Easily*."

I just shake my head, still smiling. "Thank you, but—"

"Stop. Thanking. Me," he grits out.

"I'm fine. Good night, Dr. Markham," I say as I flip the toggle to roll up the window.

A strong, black-gloved hand blocks it from rising all the way, and I'm forced to roll it down again. He reaches inside and unlocks the car door, then yanks it open. I guess he's not taking no for an answer.

I roll the window up again, close my eyes, take a deep breath, and step out of the car. Even though I'm bracing myself, I can't hide the wince that crosses my face as soon as my feet hit the snow. He takes a long look at me, from head to toe. Lightweight hoodie. T-shirt. Yoga pants. Flip-flops. No coat, no gloves, not even a pair of socks. Markham's eyes grow wide.

"Are you fucking *kidding* me?" he asks incredulously.

Wow. I don't think I've ever heard him curse before, and it startles me.

"I…I was in a hurry to get the paper to you…" I stammer out, but before I can even finish the sentence, he leans down and scoops me up in his arms, like a bride in her groom's arms as they cross the threshold.

"Oh, hey! No, please, Dr. Markham, put me down!" I protest, kicking my feet.

"Stop struggling," he hisses at me. "If you think I'm going to leave you in your car to freeze to death, or let you lose your toes to frostbite, then you're even…"

He stops himself before he can say it, but we both know where he was going with that sentiment.

You're even dumber than I thought you were.

Oh yeah, I'd put money on that one. I'm so mortified that I stay perfectly still and keep my mouth shut as he carries me easily around to the back of the house and deposits me in what appears to be a mudroom. He quickly pulls his boots off and hangs his coat on a hook.

"Stay here," he says, disappearing through the doorway.

Oh my God, oh my God, oh my God!

Could this be any worse? I'm sick and stuck in a blizzard with a man who hates my guts. I actually groan out loud at the thought of it.

"Here, put these on," he says when he returns holding a pair of wool socks.

I sit on a boot bench and pull them over my freezing feet, unable to stifle the sigh of relief that comes over me.

"Come inside, I'll get you a hot cup of tea," he says, turning to leave again before he's even finished speaking.

I follow him silently out of the room and into a spacious kitchen. It's stunning, with vaulted ceilings and exposed beams. The countertops are butcher block and the appliances are top-of-the-line professional-grade stainless steel. He gestures to an island in the middle of the kitchen and I perch on one of the stools there.

"Your home is beautiful," I say quietly as I look around.

He mumbles an acknowledgement that may or may not be a "thanks" as I watch him make his way around the counters and cabinets, pulling out a cup and tea bags then lighting the gas burner under a copper kettle on the stovetop.

"Milk? Sugar?" he asks without looking at me.

"I'll take honey if you have it," I say, thinking of my throat, which is feeling raw again. He nods and pulls one of those plastic bear-shaped bottles from another cabinet.

"So, do you cook?" I ask, trying to find some neutral conversational ground.

He looks up from where he's squeezing the amber-colored guts out of the honey bear. "Why do you ask that?"

I gesture at the six-burner stove.

"This just seems like a cook's kitchen."

The kettle must have been warm already because it whistles after less than a minute. He shrugs as he pours water into the cup and sets the tea in front of me.

"Cooking was more my ex-fiancée's thing when she lived here. But I don't mind it. I was just going to make myself some dinner when I found you outside."

Great. So now I'm keeping him from his supper on top of everything else. Well, if he's trying to make me feel guilty for disturbing him, he's doing a damn fine job of it.

"I'm sorry to have inconvenienced you," I say softly as I take a sip from the mug.

Oh. So, so good.

I spend a long moment with my nose inside the rim, taking in the warm, moist steam coming off the liquid. When I look up, he's watching me a little too closely for my liking.

"Are you still feeling sick?" he asks suspiciously,

eyeballing me as if an alien might pop out of my stomach and scurry across the wide plank wood floor at any time.

"I'm still a little under the weather, but I'll be fine."

He looks unconvinced.

"You really don't look well at all," he informs me.

Gee, thanks, Professor Prince Charming.

"Yeah..."

"Are you hungry?"

"No, thank you," I say quickly. Food is definitely not at the top of my list right now and the last thing I want to do is hurl in his house.

"You look tired, too. Are you tired?"

I open my mouth to reassure him that I'm fine, but the truth is that I'm not. I'm not fine at all. I nod yes. Yes, I am dead tired. Markham points toward the far end of the kitchen.

"Go ahead and take the tea through that doorway and down the hall to the den. There's a big couch in there and I've got a fire going. Make yourself comfortable and I'll be right there."

I get up and follow his directions, coming out in a room that makes my jaw drop. The vaulted ceilings continue in here, but with a rich, wood plank surface to complement the beams. A river rock fireplace sits in the middle of one wall, flanked by built-in bookcases that go all the way up. On the other side of the room is a baby grand piano, set in front of tall picture windows.

"Wow," I murmur under my breath as I make my way to the plush, overstuffed couch facing the fireplace. I'm struck by the fact that there isn't a television in this room. Either he doesn't watch, or he's relegated it to some other space. Of course, with the number of books on the shelves and the small pile on the table by his rocking chair, I'm guessing he prefers to pass the time reading.

I sit gingerly on one end of the couch with my tea, making

a concerted effort not to gawk at my surroundings. It's just so strange to see Drew Markham in this context. No suit, no briefcase. No snarl.

Well, okay, maybe a *little* snarl.

But this is where he lives, where he spends his hours when he's not at work. It occurs to me that if I look hard enough, I might just stumble across a few clues as to why he's such an ass. I hear his footsteps in the hallway and when he appears in the den, he's carrying a glass of water.

"Do you have a headache?" he asks.

"Splitting."

He nods as if he suspected as much, taking the mug of tea from me and setting it on the end table to my left. He hands me the water and produces a couple of pills from his pocket.

"Some Tylenol. And finish the whole glass, you're probably dehydrated," he advises.

I gulp the water and hand the glass back to him. That's when he extends his hand toward my face. Before I can stop myself, my eyes are shut tight and I'm cringing into the couch cushion, as if bracing for an impact. When none comes, I open my eyes. His hand still outstretched, eyebrows arched in surprise.

Oh. Oh no! What the hell did I just do?

"I was just going to feel your forehead," he assures me very quietly.

"I—uh—I thought…" I stammer, unable to finish the sentence, because there's simply no tactful way to recover.

He straightens up, letting his arm drop to his side.

"You thought I was going to *hit* you?"

He sounds beyond incredulous. He sounds offended.

"No! No, of course not," I lie. "You just…you startled me is all," I say, summoning a little indignation of my own.

"Well, I'm sorry, Miss Brenner, if I startled you," he replies coolly. "That was not my intention."

Shit. I've really pissed him off. Or freaked him out. Probably both.

"I thought you might like to lie down for a little while," he says, handing me a thick, fluffy pillow. "There's a blanket over the back of the couch there. I'm going to have my dinner in the kitchen. Just call out if you need anything, I'll hear you."

He starts to walk from the room before I can speak.

"Thank you, Dr. Markham. For everything," I call after him.

He just looks over his shoulder briefly and gives me a curt nod.

Well, there's no un-ringing that bell. I take the pillow and lay it flat on one end of the couch, and stretch out before pulling the blanket over me.

Ugh. I'll just have to deal with the fallout from that mess later. For now, I can't keep my eyes open another second.

Chapter Ten

Drew

I'm not going anywhere anytime soon. And, while that had been a pleasant prospect when I was here alone, it's a goddamn nightmare now. I'm too pissed off to concentrate on cooking anything so I just stomp around the kitchen, fixing myself a sandwich. I sit at the island, tearing angry bites out of my sandwich, not even tasting them.

Christ, did she think I would—that I could—lay a hand on her? The idea that she'd think me capable of such a thing is beyond offensive. I think I'd better address this right here and now, because the last thing I need is her going back to school and telling Maureen that she felt threatened. Not only would that squash any chance I have at tenure, it could end my career.

I leave my half-eaten plate and stalk back down the hall, talking before I'm even through the doorway.

"You know, Miss Brenner, I have to say that I find it—"

I stop short. She's lying on the couch, blanket kicked to

the floor. She's breathing heavily, panting really, her head tossing restlessly from side to side.

"Miss Brenner?" I ask, moving closer.

No response. When I bend to pick up the blanket, I notice the perspiration pouring off her face, which seems quite flush all of a sudden. I put a hand to her forehead. She's burning up. One glance out the window tells me there's no way in hell I'm getting her to a doctor. And even if an ambulance could get through, the closest hospital is nearly an hour away. Her brain might be deep fried by then. No, I'll have to handle this myself.

"Miss Brenner?" I ask, giving her a slight shake. Watery, glassy blue eyes open. "We have to get your fever down, okay? I'm going to bring you upstairs."

Her eyes close again with no response. I bend down and pick her up easily. Somehow, she feels lighter than she did when I carried her in from her car. Has she always been this thin?

She moans in discomfort as we start up the stairs and to my bedroom.

"Shh," I say softly, trying to comfort her. "You're going to feel better soon."

When we get upstairs, I set her down on the edge of my bed and go into the connected bathroom. The big Jacuzzi tub hasn't been used since…well, since Casey used it. I push the memory aside as I bend over to close the drain and turn the faucets on. Once I'm satisfied that it's the perfect temperature—tepid, verging on cool—I leave the tub to fill and return to the bed. She doesn't look any better. In fact, she looks worse than she did downstairs.

"Miss Brenner, we need to get your fever down. I'm going to put you in a tub of cool water. But that means you have to take your clothes off. Can you manage that?" I ask hopefully.

Her lips are moving, but I can barely hear the words, so I

put my ear only an inch from her mouth.

"Please, I need help," she murmurs. "I can't…"

Okay. Time to get creative. I bend down and pull the socks from her feet. Then I help her to stand up. She leans on me as I unzip her hoodie and wriggle it off her sweaty body. I toss it onto the bed and we walk the few shaky feet to the bathroom. Once we're standing in front of the tub, I stop to consider how best to proceed.

"Okay, here we go, then," I announce, keeping a hand on her shoulder as I walk behind her. "Put your arms up," I direct and she obeys, lifting her trembling arms above her head as if she's been caught in a stick up. I tug the T-shirt up gently until it's over her head and past her arms. At this point I can only see her back, and that's the way I'd like to keep it, so I hand her a towel to cover her chest before walking around to face her front side again.

"Here, let's do this," I suggest, tugging the towel a little and arranging it so that it hangs down straight from where it's tucked under her armpits to her shins. I reach around the towel gingerly and tug at the waistband of her sweatpants. There's some resistance because of the chilling sweat on her body, but I manage to inch them off without seeing any of her pale flesh. Thankfully, her panties coming along for the ride so I don't have to do this twice.

As I toss her lightweight, sweat-soaked clothes into the corner of the bathroom, it occurs to me that she came out dressed like this because she was hot with fever. She was underdressed because she was overheated, not because she's the stupid, foolish girl I assumed her to be. Well, I can apologize later. For now, I have to figure out how to maneuver this. I can't just stick her in the water unless I'm sure she'll be able to sit up on her own. Otherwise she could just slip into the water and drown.

"Do you think you can sit up on your own in the tub?" I

ask her, even as she's swaying.

"I…I don't know," she mumbles, then shakes her head slightly. "I don't think so."

The realization of what I need to do hits me hard. I desperately rack my brain for a different solution, but I can't think of one.

"Katherine, you have to get into the tub so you can cool off. I'm going to go in with you to hold you up. But I'll keep my shorts on. Are you okay with that? I can't do it unless you're okay with that…"

She nods. "Yes," she says in barely a whisper. "Yes, please, help me."

Here goes tenure.

I help her wrap the towel so that it's all the way around her body, then I quickly strip down to my boxers. I pick her up again and carefully maneuver us both into the cool water, her in front of me so that I'm looking at the back of her shoulders. Her delicate, pale shoulders. They're speckled with tiny freckles. Beauty marks, my mother used to call them.

Wait. What?

I shake my head as if that will clear the random thoughts and try to focus on the task at hand.

"Are you all right? I just want to get your fever…"

Before I can finish the sentence, she turns herself around, scrambling into my lap and burying her face in my chest.

Oh. Oh, Jesus.

I hold my arms up and out of the water so as not to touch her any more than I have to.

"Miss Brenner?"

She whimpers and clings to me.

With a long sigh, I close my eyes and take a deep breath.

Okay. We'll do it this way then. I use my hands as a cup, gently shifting water over her back. Her long, narrow back with the alabaster skin and the…

Jesus Christ, Drew, enough of that!

I return my thoughts to the sick young woman in my arms.

"Okay, I'm going to lean you back so we can get your hair wet. All right?"

She nods slightly.

"You got your towel there?" I want to ensure there are no wardrobe malfunctions.

She nods again, her eyes still closed and I lean forward with her in my arms until the back of her head hits the water, as if I'm baptizing her. I'm able to dunk her just far enough back so that her long brown hair floats out around her head like some sort of halo. As the towel absorbs the water, it adheres to her body tightly, forming a perfect cast of her breasts.

Okay, okay. Look at something else.

With my hands underneath her shoulder blades, I bring her back up slowly. She immediately wraps her arms around me again and we sit like this in silence for another ten minutes, until I'm confident her temperature has dropped. It's a little trickier getting out of the tub now that both of us are soaked and dripping. Finally, having carefully extricated us, I set her down on her feet on the bath mat, one arm around her slender waist. With my free hand, I reach for a large, dry bath sheet, unfurling it so it acts as a privacy curtain for her, then I guide one of her hands to my shoulder to steady her.

"Okay, I've got you, go ahead and let go of the wet towel."

She allows the wet one to drop with a sloppy, soggy *smack* onto the tiled floor and I flip the one I'm holding horizontally so I can wrap it around her. "Do you need to use the…do you have to go to the…"

She shakes her head no, confirming my suspicions that she's dehydrated. I lower the lid on the toilet and help her to perch there while I grab a towel for myself.

"Wait here, I'll be right back," I call over my shoulder as I walk back into the bedroom, my sodden boxers dripping all over the carpet. I shuck them as quickly as I can, dry off, then pull another pair from the dresser along with fresh jeans and a sweatshirt. Once I'm redressed, I turn down the made bed and rummage for something dry that Katherine can wear, finally settling on a long-sleeved button-down shirt.

"Arms up," I say when I bring it back in the bathroom. She does as I ask and I slip it over her head and down her lean arms. Then I help her to her feet again, pulling the shirt down over the towel. I breathe a sigh of relief when the last towel hits the floor and she's cool, dry, and dressed—without me having seen a thing I wasn't supposed to see. As long as she remembers that when she's feeling better, I'm in good shape. Right now, she can barely keep her eyes open so I scoop her up and carry her to my bed, laying her down gently. She sighs contentedly when her head hits the pillow. I'm just leaning across the bed to pull the covers over her, when I feel a light touch on my arm. I look down into her heavy-lidded eyes.

"I'm sorry," she murmurs in barely a whisper. "I'm so sorry."

She's delirious with fever and there's no telling what she's talking about. That is, until she starts talking about it.

"I didn't mean it. Whatever I did to make you hate me, I didn't mean it," she says, struggling to keep her eyes open.

I stare down at her for a long beat.

"I don't hate you," I say finally, more to myself than to her. "Close your eyes and see if you can sleep. It's going to be okay. You're going to feel a lot better soon," I promise, and hope to God it's true.

She nods and obediently closes her eyes, her breath slowing into a deep, regular rhythm almost immediately.

I glance at my alarm clock on the nightstand and realize that it's been just a couple of hours since I found her out front, sleeping in her car. Well, this evening was just full of surprises, wasn't it? I go downstairs and throw her clothing into the washing machine and do a quick clean up of the kitchen. I consider sleeping down on the couch, but I might not hear her if she calls for me, so I put up the fire screen, grab my ereader, and head back up. She seems to be resting comfortably, but I check her temperature by putting the back of my hand to her forehead. She's definitely cooler.

In the closet, I find an extra pillow and blanket. I take them to the overstuffed armchair and ottoman that sit opposite the bed, making myself comfortable. I try to read some of my book, but I find I'm having trouble concentrating. I just keep going back to her words.

"Whatever I did to make you hate me, I didn't mean it…"

Do I hate her? I mean *really* hate her? I think so. No, I *thought* so.

What I know for certain is that I've spent the last six years tormenting her at every opportunity. If that's not hatred, then what is it?

I close my eyes before I can allow myself to make that final connection.

Casey is reaching out for me. She's so beautiful, her dark hair flowing, fanning out the way Katherine's was in the tub. Except Casey isn't in a tub. Her hair is flowing, but she's standing upright.

"Oh, baby, I've missed you so much," I murmur.

She gives me her sweetest smile.

"Come back to me," I plead. "We can make a go of it. I swear, this time will be different…"

She's reaching out for me, her fingers lightly brushing against my face. I lean in to her touch, reveling in the feel of her skin against mine. That electric current that's always connected us. I close my eyes. When I feel her pull her hand away, I open them again, just in time to see the twisted smile on her face as she slaps me.

I wake myself up gasping for breath and it takes a second for me to remember where I am and why I'm there. I'm sleeping in the chair because Katherine is in the bed. Katherine is in the bed because she's very sick. With this realization, my gaze swings to where she is lying. I'm startled to find her watching me with wide, unblinking eyes. Something is very wrong. I'm on my feet and by her side in a heartbeat.

"Miss Brenner?"

"S-s-so c-c-cold…" is all she can get out.

I see it then, even through the covers. She's trembling violently.

Dammit!

She's gone from being red with heat to blue with cold. I feel her forehead once again, but this time it's damp and clammy. I pull another blanket from the closet and lay it over the down comforter.

"P-p-please…" she begs.

"What? What can I do for you?" I ask, watching her face intently.

And then I know. I know exactly what she wants.

Oh, Jesus. Really? I can't *do that, can I?*

"Y–you want me to get under the covers with you?" I ask, hoping she'll shake her head no. But she doesn't. She nods.

I can only stare down at her as my right hand rakes through my hair. I can't. There's no way. It crosses more lines than I can count. But her eyes are begging me, wordlessly, to help her. I shake my head slowly.

"You're *sure* you're comfortable with that?" I ask her slowly, carefully, one more time, just to be sure.

"Please," she whispers. "Please. I'm so c-c-cold…"

I pull back the corner of the blankets and slide in behind her from the other side of the bed. Once I'm there, I can feel her trembling as it shakes the mattress. Before I can think too much about the logistics of this, she takes care of it for me, turning on her left side and scooting backward toward me until her back is against my chest. I hiss with the icy touch of her skin on mine. She really is freezing.

I forget about everything except getting her warm, my hands rubbing the outside of her arms from shoulder to wrist. At the same time, I snake my right leg over hers and allow it to move up and down, creating warmth in the friction between our two bodies. Her sigh of relief comes instantaneously. I continue to rub and rub and rub, occasionally allowing myself to run a warm palm from under her arm, along the outside of her chest, hips, and thighs. She groans her appreciation.

It takes awhile, but her violent shaking eventually subsides and I feel her skin warming a little. As I sense her lapsing back into sleep, I try to move back and away from her slowly, but even in her slumber she seeks the heat of my body, scooting with me, inch by inch, as if we are attached by some invisible seam. Finally, I give up, draping an arm over her waist and counting her breaths until I find myself drifting off.

This time, Casey is nowhere to be found. And, for that, I am profoundly grateful.

Chapter Eleven

KATE

The warmth seeps in from somewhere outside of me, through my skin and deep into my bones. I want to weep with relief as this soft, enveloping heat drives away the frigid chill. Finally, the convulsive trembling has subsided and I can breathe without shaking. I can let myself drift back into the welcoming embrace of slumber. This is where I go to find my mother. Sometimes she's there, waiting with open arms. Other times, I can only see her from a distance. Today I find her there, but she isn't alone.

My father is screaming at me, fist raised, eyes crazed with rage. I can't make out what he's so angry about, though. And then, my mother is standing with him, her hand on his shoulder. "Tucker," she says gently, "you mustn't get yourself so worked up, my love."

Her love. Yes, he was. And no one else's.

"Mama?" I whisper, reaching out for her. I haven't seen her in so very long. I'd almost forgotten how beautiful she is,

long dark hair hanging in waves around her face. Her eyes are the color of cornflowers, her skin like porcelain. "Mama!"

She smiles at me. "Katie, I'm so proud of you," she murmurs.

"Stop that!" my father yells at her. "There is nothing to be proud of. She's brought shame upon this family!"

My mother's brows knit together in concern. "Is that true, Katie? Have you shamed us?"

"Mama, please, stay with me," I whisper.

Now she's scowling at me, shaking her head. "No, Katie. It's your fault I'm gone."

"It's your fault!" my father agrees, pointing a finger at me, as if he's a wizard about to cast a spell.

I'm crying as I reach out for them. "Please, forgive me!"

And then they are gone in a flash of light, and I am standing alone on the porch of my childhood home. I bang my fists on the door, crying out for them.

"Mama, please, let me in. Daddy!"

I gasp, sitting bolt upright, fighting against the haze and the pain. My heart is pounding so hard that I'm sure I'd be able to see it thumping against my chest. If I could see anything, that is. But it's so dark in here that I can't even see my own hand in front of my face. It was a dream. Wasn't it? I'm looking around me frantically, searching for some clue as to the answer, when I feel a hand on the back of my arm.

"Get away!" I hiss into the darkness, afraid to turn around, afraid it will be one of them coming for me.

"Hey, hey, it's okay," says a voice in the darkness.

I feel the mattress shift and, suddenly, I'm bathed in light. It takes a little time for my eyes to adjust. When the blurriness clears, I realize I must still be dreaming. There's no other reason I would find myself in bed with Drew Markham.

"It's me. It's Drew," he says calmly. "Markham," he continues, just in case I've forgotten who he is.

"Wha—w-where am I?" I ask as I take in the unfamiliar room, my voice coming out in a whisper. I'm in a bedroom, in a bed. When I look down, I realize I'm not dressed anymore. At least, not in my own clothing. I'm wearing a white, button-down shirt that must belong to him. No underwear. And then it hits me.

I gasp when I find Markham is squatting down next to me. When did he get out of the bed? Did I dream that? Wasn't he just next to me?

"Miss Brenner, you're in my bedroom," he says quietly, moving his hand to feel my forehead. Oh, now I *know* I must be dreaming. Drew Markham doesn't have a compassionate bone in his body. At least, not where I'm concerned.

"Your fever broke, but then you got a terrible chill. You asked me to come into the bed with you. To warm you."

"Are you real?" I ask him softly, my entire face and body pulled tight in fear and anxiety.

"Am I *real*?"

"I mean—I…I can't tell what's a dream or a hallucination or…"

I think I see a glint of humor in his eyes.

"Yes, I'm real."

It occurs to me that if it is his shirt that I'm wearing, then it would follow that… Yes. He did. I remember it now. There were towels. Lots and lots of towels…

"Y–you…you changed my clothes," I say, with a slight tremor in my voice.

He takes a deep breath, and sits on the edge of the bed.

"Yes. You were burning up and I had to get your temperature down. Fast." He pauses and looks down at his hands in his lap. "I, uh, I put you in a tub of cool water to break the fever," he continues, not looking at me. "Then I put that shirt on you and moved you to the bed so you'd be more comfortable. I didn't see anything—I didn't see you. There was a towel on you the whole time, even in the water. I slept in that chair," he informs me, pointing his chin in the direction of a big chair and ottoman where a pillow and blanket are still lying. "I wanted to keep an eye on you. Then you woke up after a few hours, trembling with cold and you begged me to get into bed and warm you up."

The heat. Oh, I was on fire. And then the water was like a wonderful dream.

"I had to get in the tub with you because there was no way you could sit up on your own. But you were in a towel the whole time," he repeats. "I never saw you. And I was dressed—in my boxers," he's quick to tell me.

I nod my head, recalling this timeline.

And then there was the shivering. He's right, I was practically convulsing with the cold. That was when something warm wrapped around me.

Oh. My God. I begged him to get into bed with me.

I put a hand to my temple, which feels as if it's about to explode, and am struck by a wave of fatigue. It hits me with such force that I have no choice but to let my body drop back against the pillows. I grunt at the impact.

"Are you…are you all right?"

I consider him carefully. Even in my haze, I see what a risk he took in helping me. He touched me. Bathed me. Dressed me. And then he got into bed with me. We both know that I could spin this into something that would be very, very bad for him. I could probably have him fired. And wouldn't that be fine payback for every nasty thing he's ever said or done to me.

"Miss Brenner? Please don't be upset, I just didn't know what else to do," he's pleading.

Markham looks totally at a loss, staring at me as if I might burst into flames or worse yet, tears, at any time.

The sense of gratitude that I feel right now is so overwhelming that I gather what little strength I have left and sit up again. My arms wrap around his waist and my head finds his chest.

"Thank you," I say into his sweatshirt.

I feel him tense up for just an instant, and then he relaxes, using one of his hands to pat my back gently. I don't know how I would even begin to explain this to him. This overwhelming relief that's washing over me in waves. For the first time in more years than I can count, I'm not wholly responsible for my own well-being. Someone is taking care of me and it feels so good—my gratitude is so immense—that I can't control the sobs that rack my body as I cling to this man that I detest.

"It's okay," he says softly.

I'm shaking my head against his sweatshirt. "No, you don't understand... I...I just...I...*thank you*," I finally manage to spit out. "Thank you..."

"Shh," he comforts. "Nothing to thank me for."

After a minute, he wraps both of his arms around me and he's leaning forward so that I am leaning back. He lowers me slowly to the bed and then sits up.

"You're just exhausted," he murmurs. "You need to get more rest. Are you hungry?"

I nod. "A little...but my stomach..." I murmur.

"It's okay. We'll wait a little while and then I'll bring you some tea and toast. We'll see how you do with that and go from there, sound good?"

I smile up at him through my exhaustion. "Yeah, that sounds good," I say softly, finding it hard to keep my eyelids up now that I'm horizontal again.

"It's okay. You're okay."

His words filter into my mind just as I lapse back into a deep sleep. This time my parents are nowhere to be found. And, for that, I am profoundly grateful.

Chapter Twelve

Drew

I'm dumbfounded. Absolutely and completely at a loss for whatever it was that just happened in there. I was waiting for the other shoe to drop. The big, spikey one that's laced with threats and blackmail. I know there was nothing else I could have done in this bizarre clusterfuck of a situation. Still, I was so sure she'd seize this opportunity to throw me under the bus. But she didn't. I'll be damned if Katherine Brenner wasn't…*grateful*.

Downstairs now, I stir up the dwindling embers of the fire and toss in a few more logs. They ignite immediately. When I walk to the window and pull back the curtains, I can see the snow falling fiercely as it passes through the beam of the streetlight out in the cul-de-sac. I should get the snowblower out of the garage and hit the driveway. Or at least make a path to the street. But really, what's the point? There's so much on the ground already, and so much more to come, that I'm better off letting the pros handle it tomorrow or whenever they get around to digging us out.

Us.

It's been a long time since I've been an "us." Not that I am now, except that there *are* two of *us* in this house. Being alone has never bothered me, except for right after Casey was gone. I heard her footsteps everywhere. I imagined her figure in every shadow that flitted through my line of sight. But now, well, I prefer it, going solo. I have to say, though, if I were a young woman I might find the prospect more than a little daunting.

Will anyone notice that Katherine Brenner didn't come home last night? Maybe she has a roommate. Maybe she keeps in close contact with that imbecile father of hers. Who knows? Of course, none of this is my concern, either way. Or, at least, it wasn't until she rolled up in front of my house and crashed a perfectly fine blizzard.

What a bizarre and unexpected twist that she should end up here, on my doorstep. Sick. In a storm. I have yet to decide whether it's a good thing or a bad thing. I suppose I'll have to wait and see how we weather the rest of the storm. Literally *and* figuratively.

Chapter Thirteen

Kate

This time when I wake up, I'm not scared. I know where I am and how I got here. The digital clock on the bedside table reads 4:05 p.m. Can that be right? Dr. Markham brought me tea and toast at around six in the morning. If this clock is accurate, then I've been asleep for the last ten hours. Is that even possible? I don't think I've ever slept ten consecutive hours in my life. Maybe the clock's wrong. I feel around for the bedside lamp and switch it on, then I get out of bed carefully. I'm weak and my legs are a little bit shaky, but I'm able to get to the bathroom on my own without too much trouble.

I peer out the small window. Oh yeah, it's definitely late afternoon. I can tell by the low angle of the sun. It'll be dark in less than an hour. The amount of snow on the ground is staggering, and it's still coming down in huge flakes that resemble feathers falling from the sky.

I splash my face with some water and take a good look at my face in the mirror. "Ohhhhhhh God," I moan under my breath.

My eyes are deeply sunken and rimmed by dark circles. I've never had much color, but now I look downright chalky. Even my eyes, normally a bright blue, seem to be dull and pale. Okay, well, I may look like crap, but this is the best I've felt in a week. I spy a hairbrush on the counter and run it through the wild mane that comes along with sleeping on wet hair. I carefully remove my long, dark strands from the bristles, wrap them in a tissue and put them in the bottom of the trash can under a cardboard toilet paper roll and an empty shampoo bottle. Hopefully he won't know I've taken the liberty. I use a little toothpaste on my finger to brush my teeth, then turn my attention to what I'm wearing.

I'm swimming in this button-down shirt of his. I spend a little time rolling and tucking and by the time I'm done, it could pass for a fairly modest shirtdress. I'm tempted to see if he has a pair of boxers I can borrow, too, but I think that might be a little too intimate. For both of us.

Feeling slightly more presentable, I pad down the stairs. The den is empty and silent, save for the crackling of the fire. The room is even more impressive now that I'm seeing it in the full light of day. The baby grand piano is absolutely stunning—its glossy black striking against the stark white landscape behind it through the huge picture window.

I listen carefully, hoping to get a clue as to Dr. Markham's whereabouts. It comes in the form of footsteps in the direction of the kitchen. When I get there, I find him standing in front of the window, surveying the snow, just as I'd been doing upstairs.

"Hi," I say quietly from the doorway.

He turns around, brows arched in surprise.

"Miss Brenner, I hadn't expected to see you up and around at all today," he says, stepping away from the window and moving closer to me. He's seems to be examining my face carefully as he approaches. "May I?" he asks, extending his hand toward my forehead.

I give him an embarrassed smile and eye roll as I nod. This time I don't flinch, and his hand feels good on me. It's soft and warm. He flips it over so that he's testing my temperature with the back of his hand.

"No fever," he proclaims with a smile. "You look a little pale, but really not bad at all. Come, sit down at the table and I'll serve you some soup, if you think you can eat it."

I haven't been interested in food for hours, but whatever he's got simmering on the stove has awakened the hunger within me, and with a vengeance.

"I think I could eat," I say, taking a seat as he pulls open cabinets and sets up a fresh bowl for each of us. "That smells great. What is it?"

"*Stracciatella*," he says, ladling it out of a huge stockpot. "In case you're not familiar, that's an Italian chicken soup."

"I'm not familiar. But I'm looking forward to becoming better acquainted," I say, unable to take my eyes off the steaming bowl as he walks it carefully across the kitchen without spilling a drop. He places it in front of me and points to a small bowl on the table with cheese in it.

"It's really good with some grated cheese on top."

I take his suggestion and spoon some on while he fetches his own bowl and sits in the chair across the table from me.

"So, how are you feeling?" he asks.

"So. Much. Better," I say, pushing the soup around the bowl with my spoon so it will cool off. My eyes dart up to his and then back down again, so that I'm talking into my soup. "I can't thank you enough, Dr. Markham."

"It was nothing, Miss Brenner," he replies quietly. "I'd have done it for any of my students. I just hope you *are* okay. You know—with what happened…"

I guess he's still worried that I'm going to freak out on him. Fair enough.

"I—uh—I..." I begin awkwardly, then stop, setting my spoon down and sitting up to face him properly. "I *am* okay with what happened, Dr. Markham. And not just that. I need you to know how grateful I am. It's been a long time since anyone has taken care of me like that. I mean, don't get me wrong, I can take care of myself. It's just that I was so sick and I don't know *what* I would have done if I'd been alone last night. There's no way I could have managed."

He seems to consider me, his dark eyes shifting up and down, left and right as he examines my expression. He looks as if he'd like to say something about my declaration. He even goes so far as to open his mouth to speak, but then he stops himself.

"Try the soup before it gets cold," he says at last, gesturing with his chin.

Okay, then, so much for sharing. I take a spoonful and bring it to my lips. It's a salty, golden elixir as it spreads soothing warmth down my throat.

"Oh. Oh my God...this is *amazing*." I gasp, hurrying to slurp a second spoonful and a third. "I think this might be the best soup I've ever tasted in my life. Not that that's a high bar, mind you, considering how many cans of Campbell's Chicken Noodle I eat."

His face fills with a proud grin and I pause, spoon midway to my mouth. I don't recall ever having seen that kind of an expression on his face before. He's usually all business, all the time. That is, when he's not being a jerk.

"I'm glad you like it," he says. "And there's nothing wrong with Campbell's. They kept me fed when I was an undergrad."

It's strange to think of him like that—like me—an overworked, underpaid music student trying to make ends meet.

"Where was that?" I ask, spooning soup again.

"What? Where did I go to school?"

I nod and examine my spoonful closely. "Is there egg in here?"

"Yes. You beat some egg into the broth," he informs me. "I went to the New York Conservatory."

"For undergrad? I knew you'd done your doctoral degree there…"

"For all of it," he says, stirring some cheese into his own bowl of chicken yumminess. "Undergrad, master's, and doctorate."

I put my spoon down again and look at him incredulously.

"Seriously? All three? That's impressive. And really expensive."

He smiles. "I was lucky. Someone there took a liking to me. Sort of like Russ Atherton took a liking to you, I suppose."

"I was actually accepted there for undergrad…" I blurt and as soon as the words are out of my mouth I wish I could stuff them back into my mouth. And now, I know his question before he even asks it.

"You got into the New York Conservatory and you chose a tiny private college in North Carolina instead?" He's staring at me like I've just told him I'm a leprechaun.

"It's a long story," I mutter and turn my focus back to my soup. "I wish I could cook like this." I marvel, hoping to get him off the subject of schools. It works.

"You don't cook?" he asks idly.

I shake my head. "No, not really. We had a housekeeper when I was growing up. And now, well, my current living arrangements aren't the best for whipping up gourmet meals."

"Housekeeper, huh?" There's just a hint of accusation in his tone.

"Yeah," I say between slurps. "My mother died when I was seven and my dad…well, you know about him. He wasn't home much, so the housekeeper made sure I at least had a hot breakfast and dinner."

"Oh, I see. I'm sorry about your mother. I didn't realize you were so young when she passed," he says a little stiffly.

"Thanks," I murmur.

"And do you rent a room or something?"

"Excuse me?" I ask, looking up, confused by the sudden turn in topic.

"You mentioned your current living arrangement doesn't allow for you to cook. I thought maybe you don't have access to a kitchen."

"Oh, that. Yeah, I live in a little studio apartment on the south side of town. I have a small fridge, a microwave, and a little two-burner stove. There's barely enough room in there to make a sandwich, let alone cook a whole meal. So you can see why I'm so blown away by your kitchen." I smile as I gesture at the impressive room around us.

"South side? Where about?"

"Marquette and Twenty-Second," I say a little too quietly, clearly embarrassed by my address.

He clears his throat before he speaks again. "That's not a very good part of town, you know."

I hear the concern in his voice and it irritates the hell out of me because I've been here before, and I know what the next part of this conversation sounds like.

"Yeah, well, it's what I can afford. So…"

I brace myself for the next awkward question, the one concerning my father being a senator and the money he must have to help his only child. Surprisingly, that's not the question he asks.

"Have you thought about getting a roommate? Maybe you could swing something in a better neighborhood if you shared a place."

I'm caught off balance by this change in trajectory and I find myself stumbling to answer.

"I…I, uh, I did. I mean, I tried, you know, initially. It's just difficult finding the right person, you know? I mean, ideally, it'd be someone who either doesn't know or doesn't care about…you know…"

His brows furrowed together. "What?"

I look up and meet his eyes. Is he serious?

"Who my dad is. What he does. What he's like."

I see the light of understanding spark in his eyes. "Ah. Yes, I see," he says with a nod. "Is it still that much of a problem for you?" he asks curiously.

"Yeah, sometimes. It's better than it was back when I first got to Shepherd. I'm sure you remember all the fuss."

He nods his remembrance.

"Yeah, well, it's better now. Or it *was* until rumors started about him running for president. Now it's starting all over again. You know a reporter actually disconnected my battery cable to get me to accept a ride from him? When I figured out who he was, the jerk didn't want to let me out of his car. I had to call the police from *inside* the car to get him to let me out. Can you believe that?"

"What did he want?" Markham asks, sounding suddenly alarmed on my behalf.

"The usual. He was looking for a quote about my father. But, jeez, he seemed like such a nice, normal guy. He *almost* got me to go out with him."

"How did you figure out who he was?"

"God, it was just…just dumb luck." I shrug. "Remember when I came in with this cut on my forehead?" I ask, pointing in the general vicinity of the scab. "The one that was bleeding in class the other day? Well, I'd done it right before he offered me a ride and when I got inside his car, I just happened to pull down the visor so I could get a look at it in the mirror. I wanted to see if it was still bleeding. That's when I found this little microphone attached there. The jackass was recording our conversation." I shake my head, still in disbelief when I recall the events of that morning. "I felt like—I *feel* like such an idiot for trusting him. For getting into that car with him—"

"Wait, wait, wait," Markham says, holding up a hand to stop me before I continue. "This happened *that* day? The day you were late?"

I nod. Let's see if Dr. Drew can put together two plus two.

"Is that why you were late? Because some reporter was holding you hostage in his car?"

And there it is. Four.

"Kinda," I say, taking another spoonful of the soup so I don't have to look at him.

"Did he hit you? Is that why you were bleeding? Is that why you thought I was going to hit you?" he asks, his tone turning angry now.

My head whips up.

"What? No. Well, I mean, it was his fault, but he didn't do it, no."

When he looks perplexed, I explain the circumstances leading up to me banging my head on the hood of the car.

"Did you catch his name?"

"Oh yeah. I got a good picture of him, too. Kevin something from the *D.C. Courier*."

"Kilpatrick? Was his name Kevin Kilpatrick?" he asks me with sudden interest.

I shrug. "I don't know, he didn't give me his last name. Why? You know him?"

"Maybe," he says distractedly, like he's trying to piece something together.

"Yeah, well, anyway, he's like the rest of them. Always trying to get me to say something inflammatory about my father. And when they realize that's not going to work, they start digging around for skeletons in my closet."

"And do you?" he asks mildly.

"Do I what? Have skeletons in my closet?" I chuckle.

"Sure, if you call eating canned soup and ramen noodles skeletons."

He smiles and, once again, it transforms his face.

"No, I meant, do you say inflammatory things about your father? Is that why they keep chasing you around campus?"

I'm mid-swallow when he asks this, so I wave my spoon around in a hold-on-a-sec gesture. "No, the opposite, actually. I refuse to comment on him or his politics or our relationship. So they keep coming back again and again."

We're quiet for a minute, sipping *Stracciatella* until my spoon hits the bottom of the bowl with a noisy clank.

"Here, let me get you some more," he says, taking my bowl to give me a top-up. I don't stop him. In fact, I'd chug this stuff if I thought I could get away with it.

"It isn't that I agree with him."

Where the hell did *that* come from? What do I care what he thinks about me or my father?

Markham sets the newly filled bowl in front of me and returns to his own.

"Your father?"

I nod. "I hate his politics. I hate his attitude. But, he's my father, you know? How I feel about him is not for public consumption."

"That's perfectly reasonable," he agrees.

"I think so. But the press doesn't. And my classmates don't," I mumble and sip down some more soup. "Everyone assumes that if I'm not against him, I must be for him."

"But you're not for him. So why not just say so and spare yourself a lot of grief?" he asks.

"Because no matter what he's done or what he thinks or what he says, he's still my father."

"Does he know about the reporters?" he asks, frowning into his bowl.

"Probably. Though, I don't think he knows to what extent

they'll go to get to me. That last guy." I start, waving my spoon around animatedly. "That Kevin asshole—sorry, Dr. Markham, but that's what he is—turns out he's been watching me for *months*."

"You've seen him before?" he asks, a flicker of horror flashing through his eyes.

"No, and that's what's so scary. The fact that I hadn't *noticed* him. And then he was asking all kinds of questions like…why am I driving a car that gives me so much trouble? How can I live in an apartment that's so small? He even asked me why I don't have a winter coat. He *really* freaked me out."

Something seems to occur to him.

"Is that why you were out in a blizzard with nothing but a hoodie? Because you don't own a winter coat?" he asks incredulously.

"Umm…"

Chapter Fourteen

Drew

I've asked the question before I can stop myself and I immediately see it's a mistake by the look on her face. She's not offended, she's embarrassed.

"I'm sorry," I hasten before she gets a word in. "That's none of my business."

She looks at me for a long moment, then shakes her head. "No, it's fine," she says with a weak smile and a shrug. "The coat I've been wearing for the last five winters finally fell apart back around Christmas. I figured I could get through the season by layering my clothes. Who knew we'd have the coldest, longest winter on record?" She laughs a little, but I'm confused.

"Okay…the old car. The apartment. The coat. I have to ask—why don't you just ask your father? Surely he can help you with a coat…" I immediately regret this question even more than the other one. The look that passes over her face is some cross between sadness, regret, and mortification. "Jesus

Christ," I mumble. "I'm turning into Tessa."

I'm startled when she suddenly bursts out laughing. "You mean Professor Morgan? Hah! So I'm not the only one who thinks she's nosy."

I smile, but I can't quite bring myself to laugh with her.

"Yeah, well, we're kind of friends," I let her know. I'd hate for her to say something that she'll regret when she realizes the connection I have to Tess.

She slaps a hand across her mouth. "Oh, I'm so sorry, Dr. Markham. I…I didn't know. I didn't mean to—to be offensive…"

She looks so horrified that I feel myself soften. I shake my head.

"No. Don't be sorry, Miss Brenner, you're right. Tessa is very… Well, she's just… She's…" I don't know what makes me stop defending Tessa, but I do. "Oh, for fuck's sake," I say, throwing down the napkin that I've been holding. "You're right. She just can't mind her own goddamn business," I say and then we're both laughing. It's nice, the sound of laughter in this kitchen again. "Of course, we're just friends."

Now why, for fuck's sake, did I feel the need to go and say that?

"Oh, I, uh, of course…" she stammers, the sentence hanging there.

"Well, yeah, so we're just friends," I repeat for some inexplicable reason. "She was a big help to me when…when my fiancée…"

Now I'm the one having trouble finishing my sentences.

"I'm sorry," she says, meeting my eyes. "I'm sure that was a really difficult time for you. It's good that Professor Morgan was around to help you get past it."

Did she seriously just say that?

I suddenly feel my face harden and, when I speak, it's chillier than even I expect it to be.

"Yes, well, Miss Brenner, it's hardly the kind of thing one *'gets past.'*"

She blinks hard and looks down into her bowl. I get up from the table abruptly and busy myself loading the dishwasher. When I spin around, she's standing so close that I nearly crash into her.

"*Jesus Christ,*" I hiss. "Did you need something else?"

"I—uh—I just wanted to apologize, Dr. Markham. I'm sorry if I overstepped."

I can only glare at her, our short-lived thaw replaced with that familiar sense of irritation. She speaks again before I have a chance.

"I—um—I think I'll go back upstairs and lie down for a bit, Dr. Markham," she says, her voice tight and small, like she's trying not to cry.

Oh, hell…

"Miss Brenner…" But I'm too late. She's out of the kitchen. I move quickly to catch her in the den, but she's already a blur of white cotton shirt and long dark hair on the staircase.

Chapter Fifteen

Kate

How could I be so stupid? Why on *earth* had I let myself get comfortable enough to tell him about myself? And why, for God's sake, did I have to go and bring up his ex-girlfriend? Fiancée. Whatever.

When I get to the master bedroom, I close the door behind me as quietly as I can and contemplate locking it. No, that's just stupid. It's his house. Besides, it's not as if he's going to come up here after me. He's probably grateful for the break from me.

It isn't until I take a long, shaky breath that the tears start to fall down my cheeks. I go into the bathroom and shut that door before walking to the shelf that holds a stack of clean towels. I take one and push my face into it, allowing the plush cotton to swallow my sobs as they rise from within my chest.

My rational mind tells me that I'm overly emotional because I'm exhausted and weak. My irrational mind tells me that I have conflicting feelings about *him*.

He hates me. But then he took care of me. And now he hates me again. And why do I care anyway? Another wail escapes my lips and I sink down until I'm sitting on the cold tile floor, my back against the vanity. My arms come around to hug my legs and I rest my face on my knees. I wish that I could just sink right into the earth. But I'm not that lucky.

"Miss Brenner?" comes the muffled voice from inside the bedroom.

Oh no…Really?

I try to stifle my crying, but I can't. He knocks on the bathroom door. I don't answer. I'm certain he can hear me, but I don't know how to stop, and I just don't give a damn anymore. What's he going to do? Laugh at me? Yell at me? *Fail* me?

I hear something against the door. Like he's sliding down next to it onto the floor.

"Miss Brenner?"

The direction of his muffled words confirm my suspicion about his position.

"I—I'll be out in a sec," I manage to say in a small, shaky voice.

"May I please come in and talk to you?"

I don't know what to say, so I don't say anything.

"Please?"

Well, shit, it's his bathroom. I can't exactly keep him out, can I?

"O-okay," I sob at last, turning my back so I don't have to see the look of disgust on his face when he comes in.

I hear the creak of the bathroom door behind me and there's a palpable shift in the room as he enters. Then I feel his hand on my shoulder. It just makes me cry harder. And then he is there, on the floor with me, pulling me up against his chest with strong arms. I shake my head no. I don't want this. But I do. I don't need this. But I do. And, somehow, this awful, mean, arrogant man seems to know this already.

With my face buried in his sweatshirt, I just cry and cry until the only thing left is the sound of my dry, hiccupping, heaves and sniffling nose. He's patting my back, rubbing my arms and shushing me softly.

Oh. My. God.

This is my worst nightmare, and then some. I sit up, abruptly, trying to wipe my sodden face with my hands, not looking at him. I can't look at him.

"I'm sorry," I say in a hoarse whisper.

Drew Markham gets to his feet and holds out a hand for me to take. I do, still not able to meet his gaze. When I'm upright once more, he turns away from me and briefly runs the water in the sink.

"Here," he says, cupping my chin in his hands gently, trying to direct my face to his. I stare at the floor and shake my head. "Please? *Katherine*?"

When he says my name, it's so unexpected that my head jerks up. He reaches toward my face and I just close my eyes, allowing him to press the wet, cool facecloth to my skin. When I open my eyes again, he's smiling. But not any smile I've ever seen in his limited repertoire of pleasant expressions. It's shocking. And disarming. And sexy as hell.

Wait. What? Where the hell did that *thought come from?*

He's gently leading me back into the bedroom. That's when another fleeting thought hits me.

Is he trying to seduce *me?*

I mean, is it all that far out of the realm of possibility? He's my professor, but he's barely five years older than me. If he wasn't such an uptight jerk so much of the time, I probably would have been considering the scenario sooner. In the end, he holds the covers up for me to climb under. Alone. And I'm not sure if I'm relieved or disappointed.

"Come," he says quietly. "You're beyond exhausted and

far from well. I'm sorry I didn't remember that myself."

I slowly walk past him and slip under the blankets. He pulls them up to my chin and looks down at me. "I don't, you know."

"Don't what?" I ask, already feeling the heavy pull of my eyelids.

"I don't hate you, Katherine."

No more pulling. My eyes fly open like a pair of shades snapping up to the top of a window.

"Excuse me?" my voice is barely a whisper.

He sits next to me on the edge of the bed.

"When you were delirious—with the fever? You apologized. You said you were sorry for whatever you did to make me hate you. I don't hate you, Katherine. I never have."

I feel my face grow hot, though not from the fever this time. I don't want to believe him, but there's no reason for him to make up something like that. And it does sound like something ripped right out of my subconscious. I stare at him in horrified silence.

"Can I show you something?" he asks. When I nod dumbly, he pulls his phone from his pocket, pokes at the screen a few times, and turns it around for me to see.

I'm looking at a picture of a woman sitting on the front steps of this house. It must be summer because she's wearing what looks to be a yellow sundress. Her hair is dark and it falls in long waves down and around her shoulders. Her eyes are bright blue and her smile is wide and easy. And, if I didn't know any better, I'd swear that she and I were related.

"Who—who is that?" I ask in a shaky voice, though I have a feeling I might already know.

"That's Casey. We had just moved into this house that summer."

I stare back at the screen and then up at him again.

"Anyway," he continues, "you might have noticed that

you bear a striking resemblance to her. I…I think that's why I have such a hard time with you in my classes. When you were a freshman, she had just…well, she was gone and I was so angry. I'm still angry," he admits. "And I'm so sorry that I took that out on you."

"It's been a long time," I say slowly. "Are you…have you two…?"

His brows knit together in apparent confusion.

"I mean, did she marry someone else or something?"

He's staring at me so intently that I think I've pissed him off again. He opens his mouth to say something, then closes it. Finally, he closes his eyes, takes a deep breath, and tries again.

"Katherine, what do you *think* happened to my fiancée?"

I shrug. "I heard you had a bad breakup. I just assumed that's why sometimes you seem so—" I stop short. Not because I'm afraid to offend him anymore, but because he staring at me with wide, disbelieving eyes. Shit. Something's very wrong here.

"Who told you that?" he demands.

"Well, uh, I'd hear other students talking about it—about you—in class." I shake my head. "You know it's amazing the things people will say in front of you when they don't like you. It's like I cease to exist because they don't want to see me…" I can see he's not interested in my little digression so I get back to his question. "Um, yeah, so I would hear people commenting on it all the time back then. Ugly breakup. She left you heartbroken. That kind of thing."

We just look at each other for what feels like a long time until, finally, he speaks again.

"Katherine, Casey didn't leave me. She died."

And just like that, I feel the air get sucked right out of the room.

Chapter Sixteen

Drew

Is it really possible that Casey's been gone so long that people don't know? Don't know her, or what happened? Christ, it was all over the news in the beginning. But I can see clearly that Katherine had no clue. I suppose just because I couldn't get away from it doesn't mean other people couldn't.

"Tell me about her," she says from next to me.

It's the first time anyone has asked me to do that. I have to think for a second.

"Uh, well, her name is—*was* Cassandra. Casey, we called her. We met as graduate music majors in New York. She was a pianist. And she was just this kind and gentle soul. It's like her heart was bigger than other people's. She cared about everyone. Worried about everyone. And she looked…a lot like you. But she was very different."

"Not a bitch then?" she says with the hint of a grin in her voice.

"I *never* said you were a bitch," I object.

"Yeah, well, you didn't have to," she concedes so quietly that I'm not even sure I was meant to hear.

"Difficult. You can be *difficult,* Katherine. But that's not what I meant anyway. She wasn't strong like you are. She was delicate. Fragile, really."

"How so?"

"Well, when I say she worried about everyone, I mean everyone. She was empathetic to the point of being overwhelmed by other people's problems. She worried about global things like world peace. She worried about local things, like her teacher's brother's daughter's cancer. And then she struggled with depression—maybe because of all that empathy, but then again, maybe not. It's hard to say. The crazy thing is that she had so much. She was a gifted pianist. Her family adored her. *I* adored her. This profound, constant sense of worrying—it was just part of who she was, you know?"

I sense her nodding next to me but she doesn't comment, just keeps listening with the utmost attention to every word. It feels good, having someone hear me for a change. No greeting card platitudes or awkward glances. Just an ear. It gives me the courage to share more than I've shared in a very long time.

"Anyway, I was in love with her. So, so in love with her. We got engaged and then we found out she was pregnant."

Katherine takes a sharp breath from next to me. But still, she doesn't comment, so I continue.

"We were over-the-moon happy. She wanted to come back here to North Carolina—this is where she grew up—so she could be closer to her mother. And I could work wherever. We had a little money between us, and her parents helped us out, too, so we bought this house. We planned a wedding for after the baby was born. It was a wonderful time, we were really happy," I say, hearing the wistfulness in my voice.

"What happened? To the baby, I mean," she asks when I've been silent for a long while.

I sigh heavily. No one ever asks about him, either.

"She lost him. *We* lost him."

She gasps and I feel her eyes on me, but I can't bring myself to look. I don't want to see the pity that I'm sure must be there, waiting for me.

"They don't even know why, really. It was just one of those things. Apparently it's not uncommon to lose a pregnancy in the first trimester. But for us, well, it was just so devastating. All of our plans for the future were wrapped up in that baby."

When I hear a sniff, I can't help myself, I cast a quick glance at the woman next to me. She's swiping at the tears that are threatening to spill onto her cheeks. I'm shocked. Not by the tears, but by the sentiment. It's not pity in her face. What is it? Sympathy? No, more like sadness, I think. Pure, utter, profound sadness for a couple who lost their child. A couple she never knew. I turn away from the raw force of her emotion. When I finally speak again, my tone is more composed.

"Yeah, so, there was no coming back from that. Not for her, anyway. I was heartbroken, but I thought maybe, someday, we'd try again. But Casey, well, she wasn't strong enough to weather that particular blow. Her parents and I tried so hard, but Casey knew. She knew what we were doing and she played along, pretending to be okay so we would relax a little. So that we wouldn't be watching her so closely. And then, one day…she was gone."

"*What*?" Katherine breathes next to me and then catches herself. She puts a small hand on my arm. "I'm sorry, you don't need to tell me…"

I shake my head and give her a pained smile. "No, it's okay, I understand. Um, well, she drove up to Andersonville Township and hiked up to Pikes Peak. She loved it there, especially in the fall when the leaves were red and yellow and orange for as far as the eye can see. At some point, she climbed over the guardrail and she just…let go. She didn't even jump, really. She just let go of her life."

There is nothing. Not a single breath between us. It's as if time has stopped and we're suspended in this cloud of my memories. At last, she is the one to break the spell and send us plummeting back to terra firma.

"I'd say I'm sorry, but that doesn't make it any better, does it?"

I shake my head, somehow not surprised that she understands.

"And her parents?"

"Ah, well, her mother is wonderful. Her father hates me. He blames me for what happened. I'm surprised he never told you that himself."

"What do you mean?"

When I look at her face, I realize what I've done. Again, she has no idea.

Fuck. Me.

This just gets worse by the second. I take a deep breath and meet her eyes steadily.

"Katherine, Casey's mother is Maureen Clevenger."

She looks completely perplexed now, unable to fashion together the pieces of the puzzle that she's holding in her hands.

"But, Maureen is Russ's ex-wife, isn't she?"

I open my mouth to solve it for her, but I see it on her face the instant it all snaps into place. She gasps again, her eyes growing large with her understanding.

"Oh my God," she whispers hoarsely. "Casey was Maureen and Russell's *daughter*? You were engaged to *their* daughter?"

I nod grimly as I watch her try to process this information; try to fill in all the blanks.

"Okay," she begins again slowly, "so how did you end up

teaching at Shepherd, then?"

"Maureen. The same way she brought Russell on staff, she hired me. It was the only way she could think of to help either of us. Maureen always seemed to know something like this might happen. But Russell—he was in denial. He kept telling her Casey was fine, that it was a phase. I think it's what ultimately led to their divorce. And then, he was on the road all the time, conducting orchestras all over the world. Maureen was here. She helped me with Casey during the worst of it and we got to be very close. I just—I fell apart…after…and I didn't want to do anything. I didn't want to leave this house. Hell, I didn't want to get out of the goddamned bed. And then, one day, she just showed up at my front door with a syllabus and a textbook. She hired me to teach a freshman theory class. Just one. Just enough to get me out of my own misery for a few hours a week."

"My class," she whispers, more to herself than to me.

"Yes, your class. It forced me to get out of this house and out of my head. I'd never taught before, so I had to concentrate on that. But I liked it and, before I knew it, I was teaching several classes."

"So, you'd lost a child, your fiancée committed suicide, her father blamed you, and when you showed up for your first day of work, you found me sitting there," she summarizes.

That's exactly how it happened, but I don't want to come right out and confirm it.

"I didn't tell you all this to make you feel guilty. Or even to make you understand why our…*association*…all these years has been so tense. I only tell you this so you have the story right, so you're not depending on thirdhand, overheard gossip from those idiots in class with you."

She snorts and immediately looks horrified. I feel the corners of my mouth twitch up as I try to fight back a smirk of my own.

"I know. I'm not supposed to think they're idiots, let alone tell *you* I think they're idiots." I say before my face morphs into a full-on grin. "But, Jesus Christ. I've never seen a bigger bunch of idiots in my life."

She bursts out laughing and I'm right there with her.

"Well, there's something we agree on," she says.

I nod and stand up.

"Something else we agree on is that you're tired. You've got some serious circles under your eyes and you're still pale. Are you okay with sleeping in here alone? Or would you prefer that I stay close by?"

She gives me a smile that's…what? Sweet, maybe? Yes. Sweet. Not sarcastic. Not a sneer. Not even a grin. Just a soft, sweet smile. I shake my head a little to dispel the thought.

"No, Dr. Markham, thank you. I think I'm over the worst of it. You're right, I'm just really, really tired."

I reach over to the nightstand and pull a remote control out of the drawer.

"Here," I say, tossing it onto the bed next to her. "It's early yet and you may want to watch a little TV. I've left a bottle of Tylenol on the dresser for you, in case your headache comes back. Do you want anything else to eat or drink?"

"Really, I'm fine. Thanks. But what about you?"

"What about me?"

"Where are you going to sleep? I'm in your bed," she reminds me, looking suddenly alarmed that she's kicked me out of my bedroom.

"Nah. I'll crash on the couch. I do that a lot, anyway. I like to sleep by the fire. But you come downstairs—or, better yet—call down to me if you need anything. Otherwise, you just sleep in as long as you like tomorrow. Okay?"

She nods her understanding and I walk to the bedroom door. My hand is already turning the knob when I stop and turn back.

"And, Katherine, you can call me Drew."

Chapter Seventeen

Kate

It's close to ten in the morning when I finally feel rested enough to wander downstairs. Either that, or my body just can't resist the amazing smells that are wafting up from the first floor. When I follow my nose to the kitchen, I find him standing in front of the big stove, cracking eggs on a griddle in the middle of the burners.

"Hey," I say.

He looks at me over his shoulder and smiles.

Nice.

"Hey yourself. How're you feeling this morning?"

"Much, much better," I assure him. "That extra ten hours of sleep seems to have done the trick."

And it has. I was too exhausted—and confused—to continue our conversation last night. To discover that Drew Markham was engaged to Russell and Maureen's daughter and that the poor woman was so distraught that she killed herself… It's just more than I could process. And, I think, more than he wanted to continue discussing.

I walk to the window, taking in the winter wonderland outside. Except, it looks more like the frozen tundra. There are only flurries blowing now, but there must be more than four feet piled up in some spots.

"No way you're getting out of here today," he says, reading my mind. "Or anytime soon, for that matter."

He's not kidding. I can't even distinguish the hump that was once my car. It's just part of the huge snowdrift that contains the curb, the mailbox, and the hedges. I give a long, low whistle.

"So I slept through the whole blizzard?" I marvel.

"Well, yes and no," Markham says, flipping some bacon. "Why don't you have a seat at the table? How about some eggs and toast? Do you think your stomach can handle that?"

As if on cue, it growls loudly enough for him to hear it across the room. His eyebrows go up and he smiles again.

Double *nice.*

"Or maybe you'd like something more substantial? I can throw in some bacon and home fries if you want."

"I want." I smile broadly and sit where he's already placed a carafe and a mug. I pour myself a cup of tea while he starts pulling items out of the fridge. "So, what do you mean, *'yes and no'?*"

"Ah, well. Yes, you slept through the first blizzard. No, you haven't slept through the second blizzard."

I set the carafe down with a dull *thunk* on the table.

"Wait. What?"

He nods as he empties a bag of potatoes, peppers, and onions on the other side of the griddle.

"Yup. The only thing worse than a storm of the century is two of them. We're getting a quiet day today, but there's another blast heading our way early tomorrow morning."

"No, *not* possible!" I squeak in dismay.

"Oh, possible. Very possible. Hey, would you mind popping some bread in the toaster for me?" he asks, nodding toward a fancy looking four slicer and a loaf of multigrain on the counter.

I get up and do as he asks.

"So, I could be here, with you…"

"For a while yet," he finishes my thought. "You okay with that?"

I glance at him over my shoulder, but his back is to me as he flips the bacon and pushes the potatoes around. Am I? I don't have a choice either way.

He reads my thoughts.

"I'm sure the snowplow will be through here today, just to get a jump on clearing before the next hit comes. We won't be able to get your car out, but I've got a four-wheel drive truck in the garage. It wouldn't be easy, but I could probably get you home this afternoon. If you really wanted to go."

I consider this. I consider *him*.

"I don't know which would be less of an inconvenience to you," I admit, grabbing a plate for the toast and setting it on the table. "Having me *here* or asking you to go out *there*."

He doesn't say anything as he offloads the cooked food onto platters and brings them all to the table. He nods for me to have a seat while he serves us both. Once he's sitting, he faces me again.

"Having you here isn't inconvenient. It's a little awkward, all things considered, but not entirely unpleasant. That being said, I will find a way to get you back to your apartment if that's where you want to be."

"Oh, huh," I consider. Do I want to be there? All alone with no supplies?

"Do you have food at home?" he asks, reading my thoughts. "You could be snowed in for another few days, easy. And nothing's open right now."

"I think a couple cans of soup…" I mutter, trying to visualize the contents of my tiny kitchenette.

"Does your building have an emergency backup generator if the power goes out? Otherwise you might be without heat. And you've been sick."

"You think I should stay here," I deduce.

He nods.

"I do."

"Okay."

"Okay?"

"Yes, okay. What? You expected a fight?" I snicker.

He grins as he spears a potato with his fork.

"Well, yeah, actually. You're never this accommodating. In fact, I think you enjoy being a pain in my ass during class."

I feel my face grow warm with the blush that I know is spreading across it.

"I can neither confirm nor deny that statement, Dr. Markham," I say enigmatically and take a sip of tea.

He smiles and we chew in companionable silence for a minute.

"Can I ask you something?" he asks.

I shrug, picking up a piece of bacon with my fingers. "Sure."

"Why didn't you just walk up to the door when you got stuck?"

Oh. I pause, bacon halfway to my open mouth.

"Seriously?"

"Seriously."

I put the bacon back on my plate, clear my throat, and swallow.

"Uh, well," I begin, stalling for some divine inspiration. The last thing I want is to go back to square one. The nasty square. The square where he's mean and I'm defensive and angry and we hate one another. But The Divine leaves me hanging, so I cock my head to the side and scrutinize his expression.

"Oh, come on," I say at last. "You *know* why."

"I assure you, Katherine, I do not," he says, suddenly rigid.

And there it is. That formal, tight-ass tone that I know so well. I sigh and shift my mindset back into guarded mode.

"*Dr. Markham*," I begin, my tone letting him know that two can play this game. "Had I not fallen asleep in my car, I would have walked down the hill to Main Street and tried to hitch a ride closer to home."

He stares at me, unblinking, for what feels like an eternity.

"In flip-flops? Really?"

I nod soberly. "Yes. Waiting for a snowplow was Plan A. Walking down the hill was Plan B."

"And asking for my help…?"

I sit back in my chair and cross my arms over my chest. He wants to know? Well, then I'm going to tell him.

"Truthfully, I'd have asked every single one of your neighbors on every street in this development before I would have come to your door."

"But that makes absolutely no sense." he murmurs, looking baffled by this confession.

"Doesn't it?"

"I mean, I know we've had our differences…"

It's all I can do to keep from snorting in his face.

"Our differences?" I echo disbelievingly. "Dr. Markham, there is nothing that you have said or done over the last five-and-a-half years that would lead me to believe you would help me. You can say what you like now—now that we've shared a few intimate moments and had our little heart-to-heart last night, but we both know that you would have found a reason to fail me had that paper not been in your mailbox by five o'clock. I could have been banging on your door, begging you to accept it, and you probably would have left me standing on your porch in the cold."

He's shaking his head, opening his mouth to object, but I hold up a finger for him to stop. He does.

"Come on," I say softly, conspiratorially. "You know it. I know it. It's just the two of us here now. Let's call it what it is for once." I sit back again and take a deep breath, putting a lighter expression on my face. "I can't blame you. Even if I didn't look so much like your—like Casey—it's like you said. I can be prickly and defensive. I can be a difficult person. I'll own that. But I guess I just never did understand what it was I'd done to make you have so much..." I cast around my brain for the word and then find it. "...*disdain* for me."

With that, I pick up my cup and look down into it, not wanting to see the expression on his face. Bracing myself for the blowup that is sure to come. Maybe I'll get lucky and he'll loan me boots and a coat when he kicks my ass out of here.

But he doesn't speak. Unable to keep my head down any longer, I finally look up to find him staring at me, brows drawn together in supreme confusion. At last, he takes a deep breath and stands up, taking my now empty plate from the table.

"Did you have enough to eat?" he asks over his shoulder.

Oh shit.

I nod curtly. "Uh, yes. Yes, thank you."

I put my elbows on the table, close my eyes, and rub my temples with my fingers. The headache is starting to resurface.

"Are you all right?"

My eyes fly open and I jump at the sound of his voice right behind me. My breath picks up. It's unnerving having him so close to me.

"I'm sorry. I didn't mean to startle you," he rushes to apologize.

"No, no," I say quickly, twisting around in my seat to look up at his concerned face. "*I'm* sorry. I didn't mean to... That was incredibly rude of me."

He sighs as he sits back down again.

"No. It's okay. I've said it before and it bears repeating. We have a complicated relationship, you and I. You don't have to apologize, Miss Brenner—Katherine. But how about we try and keep things a little lighter for the rest of the time you're here?"

"Lighter?"

What? Like puppies and rainbows?

He smiles at the confusion that must be evident on my face.

"Yes. Lighter. I have a big DVD collection. We can watch some movies. Or play Scrabble. Or you can take a book and find a comfortable spot to read. I'll make us a nice dinner. Does that sound all right?"

"I…I think that would be really great, Dr. Markham," I respond, my voice barely above a whisper.

"Good." He nods resolutely. "I think maybe you should go upstairs and take a long, hot shower." He grabs my mug and refills it with the hot, sweet tea. "Here, take this up with you. There are clean towels on the shelf in the bathroom. I washed your clothes from the other night, I'll leave them on the bed. Okay?"

I nod and take a good look at my professor. His face is soft and open, his hair messier than usual and his casual clothes are a stark contrast to the slacks and dress shirts he wears when he's teaching. Taking it all in at once, I'm struck by how different he looks. Younger. Much more like the "hot teacher" all the girls were talking about on my first day of freshman Music Theory.

Yes, something is different about the way Drew Markham looks. Or, maybe there's something different about the way I'm looking at Drew Markham.

Chapter Eighteen

Drew

She's crying but, thankfully, it has nothing to do with me. We're watching one of my favorite movies, *Truly, Madly, Deeply,* about a cellist who comes back from the dead to be with his pianist lover. And, while it has its amusing moments—like the undead orchestra—it's a poignant story about letting go. Something I could stand to do more of.

"Oh. It was so beautiful," she says now, turning to me as she wipes her damp face with the sleeve of her hoodie. "I haven't really ever seen Alan Rickman in anything but the Harry Potter movies."

"What? No." I'm incredulous.

She nods.

"Oh no, Katherine. You have no idea what richness awaits you," I say dramatically as I drop onto my knees and root around the DVD cabinet, pulling out one case after another. "I consider it my personal responsibility to educate you on the finer points of Mr. Rickman's career. We can start with his early stuff. Let's see, there's *Die Hard,* of course, and *Quigley Down Under.* Then *The January Man,* oh, and *Closet Land.* That one's just fucking disturbing…" I nod and laugh at the same time as if to confirm my own point.

"What? I haven't heard of *any* of those. I mean, *Die Hard*, yeah, but not the others." She slips down onto the floor with me so she can examine the DVD cases for herself.

"Listen, I want to go out and take another pass at the driveway with the snowblower before we get clobbered again tomorrow morning. Then, maybe we can watch another movie? I've got pizza dough in the fridge. We can eat in here," I say, gesturing to the TV room. It's considerably smaller than the den, but it's got a big, comfortable couch and a big, impressive flat-screen TV.

"Yeah, I'd like that." She nods enthusiastically and then hesitates. "Um, Dr. Markham?"

"Drew," I correct her. "You'll have to go back to Dr. Markham when we're back at school, but it's insane for you to call me that in my own house."

"I'll try, it's just a little weird. You know?"

"Please." I roll my eyes. "Weird doesn't even begin to cover it. What did you want to ask?"

She looks a little uncomfortable.

"I was wondering if I could play the piano a little? Just while you're outside?"

That's it? That's the big "ask" that she looks so worried about?

"Of course, but I have to warn you, it hasn't been tuned in a while."

Her face lights up.

"Oh, I don't mind. I don't get to play on a baby grand very often."

I get to my feet and offer her a hand up, which she accepts. She follows me back into the kitchen.

"Do you have a piano at home?"

"No, not now. There's one in my father's house in Virginia. That's the one I learned on. And sometimes I can use the grand piano in the concert hall at school. But, usually I'm stuck with the uprights in the practice rooms. I kind of forfeited my time on the 'good' pianos after I switched from being a piano major to conducting."

"I'd forgotten you'd been a piano major," I say as I grab my coat and boots from the mudroom and sit at the kitchen table to lace-up. "Why did you switch?"

She rolls her eyes.

"Russ. He can be very…persuasive."

This makes me laugh. She's right, he can be. But not in any conventional way.

"What did he do?" I ask, knowing there's more to this story.

"He caught me 'air conducting' Beethoven one night and informed me that I was a conductor. I got a whole speech on how concert pianists are a dime a dozen, but a conductor like me— " She stops abruptly, her face reddening.

"What?"

"I'm sorry, it just sounds so vain when I say it out loud."

Now she's got me curious. I know Russ Atherton well enough to know he only says what he means—whether you want to hear it or not.

"It's okay. What did he say?" I coax.

She clears her throat and looks down at the floor, studying her feet as she recounts the conversation.

"He told me that concert pianists are a dime a dozen, but that a truly gifted conductor only comes along once in a generation. He compared me to Bernstein and Toscanini. I mean, I know I'll never be like that—like them—but he was so convincing, I just had to drop everything else and study with him."

"Katherine," I say, waiting until she raises her cool-blue eyes again. "Russ is one of the greatest conductors I've ever seen and his instincts for music are spot on. So, I've got news for you, if that man says you're the next Leonard Bernstein, then you're the next Leonard Bernstein."

I head for the door before she can respond. "Okay, I'll be outside for a while. Enjoy the piano," I say with a wave as I shrug my parka on then head out the back door, leaving her stunned by what I've just said, and me stunned that I said it.

• • •

It takes me a good forty-five minutes to get through the snow and back down to the asphalt and I'm sweating my ass off by the time I'm done. I lose the coat before I can even get the blower back into the garage. By the time I'm stamping the snow off my boots, I'm also minus my hat, gloves, and scarf. I'm just heading back into the kitchen when I hear it.

At first, I'm not sure what it is that I'm listening to. The tune is so familiar that it stops me in my tracks. But still, I can't quite place it. I find myself drawn from the kitchen, down the hall and into the den, where Katherine's sitting at the piano, playing. I watch her left hand walk across the keys while her right hand flips to the next page.

That's when I realize what the music is. That's when she realizes that I'm standing there, watching her. I'm not quite sure what she sees, but the music stops abruptly and I catch a shadow of fear cross her face. She jumps to her feet and steps away from the piano bench as if it were scorching hot.

"I…I'm sorry, Dr. Markham," she stammers and I can see she's poised to run up the stairs again.

"Drew," I correct her absently as I walk to the piano and glance at the handwritten pages she's just been playing. "I, uh—it's just that I haven't heard that piece in a long time.

Years, actually."

I watch the color drain from her already pale face.

"Please don't be angry. I—it was the music. I couldn't help glancing at it and then I just had to hear it," she breathes. "I never should have…"

Whatever my expression is, it's clearly scaring the hell out of her. I will myself to calm down and I force a smile on my face.

"No, really, it's fine. You just took me by surprise. That's all."

But Katherine Brenner doesn't look convinced. "You know, maybe I should go read upstairs. Give you your space. I've disrupted your whole routine and now I've gone and stuck my foot in it…again."

She's shaking her head, rebuking herself internally even as she's talking to me. She starts to walk around the piano, but I stop her, reaching out and gently grabbing her upper arm as she tries to pass me.

"It's all right, Katherine," I say quietly. "It was actually kind of nice to hear it again."

"Did she…" she begins and hesitates. "Did Casey write it? Is that why you don't play it anymore?"

"What? Oh no. I wrote it. That's what I did before. I was a composer."

She looks stunned. "Really? A composer? I just assumed you were a Music Theory major."

I smile at her surprise. "Nope. I was a composer. Maureen thought that would make me a good Theory and Orchestration teacher."

"That piece is *so* beautiful. Would you…would you play it for me?" she asks a little tentatively. Her expression is so earnest and open that I find myself drawn in.

"I like the way you played it, actually. Why don't you give it another go?" I prompt her back toward the piano bench with a raise of my eyebrows.

"Are you sure?" she confirms, her voice excited and hesitant at the same time.

"Yes, I'm sure."

She returns to the bench and I watch in fascination as she spreads the music out on the bridge of the piano. Then, without so much as a glance down at her hands, she begins to play the notes I wrote so many years ago. I'd forgotten how much I love this piece.

I didn't write in any tempo markers or accents because I was the only one who played it and I knew exactly what it was supposed to sound like. But under her fingers it comes to life in a way I never imagined. She pauses where I played through. She uses the pedals to soften and sustain passages that were meant to be bold and jarring. When she gets to the intricate section in the middle, she leans in a little closer to the music, as if she's afraid she'll miss a note. But she doesn't. She sight-reads the rapid-fire figures with perfect fluidity. By the time she's finished the last line of the last page, I'm standing there watching her like a fool with a ridiculous grin on my face, shaking my head.

She looks up at me, clearly anxious about how I'll respond to her performance. "Was that okay? Did I get the gist of it?" she asks quietly.

I try to keep myself from laughing.

"I'd say the gist and then some."

I notice she's looking at me strangely all of a sudden.

"What?" I ask, still smiling. "What is it?"

She shakes her head slightly.

"I just—it's just, you never…"

"I never what?"

"You never smile like that. It's a good look on you," she murmurs, almost to herself.

Suddenly, it's as if my world has flipped upside down, I

can feel the heat creeping up from under my collar. I clear my throat and look down at the floor briefly. When I look up again and meet her eyes, I'm back in check, emotions locked safely away.

"Okay, well, I'm going to get started on that pizza," I say, extricating myself from her orbit and taking a step toward the kitchen. "Oh, and I remembered another Alan Rickman classic. *Robin Hood: Prince of Thieves.* You haven't lived till you've seen him upstage Kevin Costner."

She's still looking at me strangely when I turn my back and walk out of the room.

Chapter Nineteen

Kate

"Are you feeling up to some wine?" he asks me, bringing a pair of glasses and a bottle into the den, where we've relocated post–Alan Rickman movie marathon.

"Um, sure, I guess," I say, not doing a good job of hiding my discomfort. He notices.

"Would you prefer something else? This is a riesling. But, if you like red, I think there's a shiraz in the basement," he offers, clearly thinking I'm put off by his wine selection.

"I…I don't really drink much," I say a little sheepishly. "And when I do, I hardly ever drink wine. But I'll try it."

I see the confusion register on his face. For him, this does not compute.

"I know. You probably assumed I was a big drinker, right? Because I look tired and hung over all the time?"

"I, uh, well, no. I mean…"

I try not to giggle as he struggles to find an appropriate response.

"It's none of my business either way," he says, finally, pulling the cork and filling each glass.

"You're not the only one. I know I look like crap when I'm tired. And since your classes always seem to be first thing in the morning, you're not exactly seeing me at my best."

He doesn't comment as he hands me a glass with just a splash in the bottom.

"Oh, you know what? I've had wine before. Wine *coolers*," I offer, suddenly remembering my wayward high school years.

"Wine coolers?" he repeats, looking as if he's just smelled something bad.

I nod and he shakes his head.

"Yeah, well wine coolers are a little…" He pauses, seeming to search for the right word. I decide to help him out and spare him the embarrassment.

"Juvenile? Cheap? Tacky?" I offer with a grin.

"*Sweet*," he says as if the other adjectives had never even crossed his mind. "Sweet. But, if you like that, then I think you'll like this. It's sweet, by wine standards."

I take a tentative sip of the straw-colored liquid.

"Mmmm," I say after I sample it. I can't help licking my lips and nodding. "It's kind of appley. Crisp. I like it."

When he's topped my glass, I take a longer gulp.

"Whoa, hey, slow down a little," he warns with a laugh. "That's not a wine cooler, you know. It'll knock you flat on your ass if you're not careful."

I shrug and watch as he settles onto the opposite end of the couch from where I'm sitting with my legs tucked up under me. I had changed out of my sweats and into another one of his shirts that he left out on the bed for me to sleep in. We sip in companionable silence for a minute or two.

"So, you don't drink much. Does that mean you're not a frat party kegger kind of girl?" he asks out of nowhere. There's something about his tone that makes me think he's only half teasing.

“Not so much.” I smile. Two can play this game. The “fishing for info” game. “Is that what they all think? The faculty, I mean? That I’m some party girl coed?”

“Oh…” He seems to give this some thought. “No, I don’t think so. There’s speculation of course, because you’re very high profile, but you keep to yourself. And that kind of exposure paired with that kind of secrecy is always going to pique people’s curiosity. And that curiosity is going to breed rumors.” He shifts his gaze forward so he’s looking at the fire.

“May I have some more wine?” I ask, realizing my glass is empty. Did I drink all of it already? God, I don’t even remember doing that.

He takes my glass and gives me half a pour. “I wasn’t kidding before,” he says, catching my eye when he hands it back to me. “This stuff goes down easy, but it’ll hit you like a freight train later.”

I nod my understanding and take the glass from him as he pours some more for himself, too.

“I don’t—” I begin and then stop. He waits. I continue. “I don’t know what I ever did to give anyone a bad impression of me.”

He doesn’t miss my hesitation over which pronoun to use. I don’t want to point the finger at him. Or at his friend Tessa, Town Crier and President of the Shepherd University Gossip Coalition.

I watch him take a deep sigh and he turns back to lock his eyes on mine over the rim of his wineglass. I can see the licking flames of the fire reflected in them, giving him a little hint of the satanic. A chill runs down my spine.

“Katherine, from my end, it’s you being late all the time and coming in with bloodshot eyes. Some days you reek of smoke, like you’ve been in a bar all night and just stumbled into class. It feels disrespectful to me and it’s that kind of thing that makes people think the worst of you."

Despite my best efforts, I blink hard at his honesty. It's not exactly mean, but it's certainly not kind. I pick up my glass of wine and drain it. I can see he wants to say something about it, but he's holding his tongue. Yeah, well, I'm not going to hold mine.

"So, those things made you think what? That I'm some party girl? Or lazy, entitled, rich kid, or…or worse?" I demand.

He shrugs and considers the fire again.

"Well, they don't exactly make me think you're an honors student," he mumbles.

"And yet, I am."

He looks at me with confusion. "You're *what*?"

"I'm an honors student. President's Honor Roll every semester since I was a freshman," I inform him in what should be a strong, proud voice. But it's not. It's a small, weak voice that sounds as if I might burst into tears.

No. I'm *done* crying.

"You know what, let's not talk about this now," he suggests.

But I'm not finished with this conversation—not by a long shot. It's unlikely I'll ever have the opportunity, or the courage, to speak to him this candidly again.

"You know why I don't tell anybody anything? Because when I do, I find personal details of my life in the newspaper."

He starts to reply but I hold up a finger to silence him. He nods and takes a sip of his wine instead.

"I'm tired all the time," I continue, "because I'm a grad student with a heavy class load. And I also happen to work two jobs."

His brows go up in clear surprise.

"I have classes all day, go home, and grab a quick bite to eat. Then I clean offices in a professional building in town. I get off at ten, then I sit up and study till about one. My alarm goes off at five in the morning and I head over to the North Dining Hall on campus, where I work the breakfast shift until seven thirty. I try to change my clothes, which always smell like the smoke from the grill, but there isn't always time. If there's a spill that needs to be cleaned up before my shift ends, or if I get stuck hauling out the trash, I might be running fifteen or twenty minutes late. Which doesn't give me a lot of time to get all the way across campus, find a parking spot, and hike the stairs to your class before the stroke of eight a.m. *And*, Dr. Drew, if I argue with you in front of the class, it's because you won't give me a chance to speak. To explain myself or answer a question…or *anything*."

His stunned expression is so intense that I look away, into the fire. But I can see in my peripheral vision that he's still staring at me.

"So there it is," I continue. "Tired, bloodshot eyes, late all the time, smelling of smoke, grumpy. I think that pretty much covers it all, doesn't it? Sometimes, when people don't know the truth, they just make shit up," I conclude, thinking about my misinformation about his fiancée.

"I'm sorry, Katherine. I really am. I've been jumping to conclusions. But you just get on my nerves sometimes. I feel like you're always judging me."

"What?" I yelp, my voice suddenly too loud for this conversation. I sit up and glare at him incredulously. "You think that *I* judge *you*?"

"Well, *don't* you?" he asks, genuinely interested in what my answer will be. "I feel like you're always trying to show me that you're smarter than I am; that you don't need to learn anything from me."

The room feels chillier all of a sudden.

"What? Are you insane?" I argue, my pitch rising to match my volume. "I mean, really, you're the one who's constantly trying to trip *me* up!"

"Trip you up? What the hell is *that* supposed to mean?" he counters indignantly. A little too indignantly, in fact. He knows I'm right, I can see he does. And it's pissing him off. Yeah, well it's pissing me off, too.

"You ask me harder questions than everyone else. You deliberately try to embarrass me. You offer the rest of the class an open invitation to your office for help, but me… God, it's like you *want* me to fail your tests and your assignments."

"But you *never* do," he says, jumping onto my wave of accusations. And then he stops, cold, as the realization of what he's just said—what he's just done—sinks in. He's just admitted his guilt.

"No. No, I don't," I spit back at him as I shake my head, a triumphant smile spreading across my face. "I *can't* fail, you self-serving jackass! I can't afford to make a single mistake because you're just waiting; watching every little thing I do and say. Everyone gets a pass except for Katherine Brenner, the senator's daughter, right?"

He starts to answer, but I won't let him get a word in. I'm getting worked up now and my cheeks have gone from pale to flaming.

"I don't have the luxury of not passing your class. Not if I want to graduate. So I stay up all night studying and doing your assignments. I read ahead. I study in and around and beyond the composers we're studying because you have never *once* asked me a question that involved the material we were currently covering."

"Oh Christ," he grumbles, rolling his eyes. "That is *not* true."

"It is!"

"Please, Katherine. Paranoid much?" he scoffs.

"Copland."

"What?"

"Copland. We were talking about the correlation between

Mahler's Fourth Symphony and Beethoven's Ninth when you asked me a question about Aaron Fucking Copland. And then the discussion on the baroque concerto grosso style. The entire class is knee-deep in the eighteenth century with Bach and Vivaldi and you ask *me* about Béla Bartók. A *twentieth* century composer. Dude, don't even get me started on that assignment last semester when you asked us to write a—"

"Okay, enough, already!"

His volume startles me and I feel my heart pick up pace under my shirt. His shirt.

"You're right," he mumbles after a long, awkward silence.

"I'm what?"

"You heard me. You're right. I'm harder on you than everyone else. But let me ask you something. Has it made you think on your feet? Study more, study deeper? Has it made you a better student?"

Holy fucking shit. My fingers twitch with my desire to throw this wine in his strong-jawed, dark-eyed, sexy-stubbled face. Bastard. No fair looking sexy when I'm so pissed off.

"Fine." I huff petulantly. "Yes. You've made me a better student and you've made me a better conductor, and it makes me *absofuckinglutely* furious!" I roar with irritation.

I register just the hint of a slur in my words. And the profanity. Slurry profanity. Must be a hallmark of my tipsiness. I nod to confirm my own statement and promptly drain the glass of riesling I'm holding before reaching over to pour myself another glass, draining the bottle before he can.

"Good," he says in an obnoxiously calm tone. "I'm glad you're a better conductor because of me."

I try to eviscerate him with my steely stare. It doesn't work. He just looks at me, unfazed and amused.

"Oh no, no, no!" I yell, wagging my finger at him. "Don't you *dare* say that like it's a good thing!"

"Well, isn't it?" he challenges.

"Yes!" I shout. "Wait, I mean no! Christ—I mean, don't pretend you do it for my benefit when all you want to do is fucking torment me!" I'm shaking with rage. "God! You are such. An. Ass!"

Uh-oh.

Even in my woozy state I realize I might have just gone a step too far. I cringe a little, as if bracing myself for the ugliness that's about to spew forth from my professor. But ugliness isn't what spews. It's riesling. A mouthful of it when he snorts with laughter.

"Oh! Oh, Jesus." He howls, much to my confusion. And dismay. "You're right, Katherine, I *am* an ass!"

I can't resist. I abandon my pissiness in favor of laughing, too. "I *know*! Right? You are *such* an ass!"

He nods, tears starting to stream down his face, wine soaking into his sweatshirt. "But to be fair," he says, holding up his index finger, "you bring out the ass in me."

I consider this for a second as our laughter subsides.

"Yeah, okay. I'll give you that," I say, considerably more reasonable than I was just a bit earlier. "Hey, did you say there was more wine somewhere?"

Chapter Twenty

Drew

We're halfway through the third bottle. It's chardonnay and she doesn't seem to like it as much as the riesling, but I only had two bottles of that in the house. That's okay, though, because it makes her slow down a little. I, on the other hand, pick up her slack.

"So, your project," I begin.

"The one that's outside, encased in ice and snow?"

"Yes, that one."

"What about it?"

"When it thaws, is it going to be as good as what you turned in the other day?"

"Better," she informs me.

"I see."

"No, you don't."

"Is this you *not* being difficult?" I tease.

"Okay," she concedes with a giggle. "Maybe just a little." She uses her thumb and index finger to indicate "a little."

"Yeah. That's what I thought." I roll my eyes. "What I want to know is how you *do* that? How do you know exactly what the orchestration calls for? I swear to God, you seem to know every performance practice incorporated by every composer in every period. What keys they worked in. The tempos they liked to use, the instrumentation. You don't miss a single detail," I declare, the wine making me a wee bit dramatic. And loud. "It's as if you've memorized every characteristic ever used."

Her brows pull together as she seems to consider this. I'm guessing her brain is even foggier than mine is right now. And mine is pretty fucking fogged-in.

"Oh," she says, finally grasping what I'm talking about. "You mean when you ask us to arrange something in the style of Mozart or Bach?"

"Yes, exactly," I nod enthusiastically.

"Evan!" she suddenly shrieks with peals of laughter. "My God, could he be anymore *clueless*? I mean, he's a kick-ass bassoon player but Jesus Christ—crack open a book once in a while!"

I snort and she points at me.

"Aha! You think so, too," she accuses.

"I'm not really supposed to say..." I leave the sentence hanging, but it's clear I agree with her assessment of poor, dim Evan who doesn't have a snowball's chance in hell of passing my class this semester. Good thing he's got another year to sort it out before he graduates.

We're both laughing for no good reason now, other than the fact that we are well on our way to hammered. I reach for the wine bottle, put it to my lips, and take a long swig before passing it to her. She looks at me like I have three heads.

"Seriously? Did you not just nurse me back to health? Dude, you do *not* want my cooties all over your wine bottle."

"Oh shit, you're right." I grab a half bottle of zinfandel

sitting in front of us on the coffee table. I hand it to her and she pulls a swig. "There—your own personal bottle. Now, back to the subject at hand, *Miss* Brenner," I say, trying to sound serious with limited success. "You *always* know the answer. How do you do that?"

"Ah, well," she begins, lowering her voice and leaning in closer to me, as if she's about to share one of the best-kept secrets of the ages. "That's easy. I cheat."

I frown. That makes no sense.

"You cheat? How the hell can you cheat? You have no idea what question I'm going to ask. Not unless you're a mind reader. Wait, are you a *mind* reader?" I turn on her with the faux accusation. "That's it, isn't it?" I declare triumphantly.

She grins and giggles, shaking her head at me. "No, it's cheating because I know *all* the answers."

"Huh?" is the best I can muster in my increasingly inebriated state.

"I read *all* the books. Cover. To. Cover."

"What? The textbooks?"

She nods.

"Yuh-huh. And other books on music history. Sometimes I read t-t-thesissis that other students have done. I've read both of yours, you know," she says proudly.

"No fucking way!" I say with a half grin.

She purses her lips and raises her chin in an attempt to look scholarly and aloof.

"'At the heart of post-World War II American society was the drive to get the men back into the workforce and the women back into the home. As a result, there is considerably less compositional output from the women of this period which roughly mirrors the Abstract Expressionist movement.'"

My jaw drops to the floor. "How the hell did you…?"

"Holy shit!" She points at me and giggles. "I wish I had a camera so you could see your face. Where's my phone?" she mutters to herself and goes digging into the couch cushions. "Huh. Hmm," she mutters when she comes up empty.

Okay. Something totally insane is going on here, and it has nothing to do with the drinking. I reach out a hand and put it on her wrist.

"Really, Katherine, you read the whole thing?"

She smiles. "Yeah, I did. And it was pretty perfect, you know. Just the one wrong date on page fifty-six, down in the fourth paragraph—" She slaps a hand over her mouth, as if to stop anything else from slipping out.

I feel my eyes narrow as I go from impressed to suspicious in two seconds flat.

"How could you possibly know that?" It comes out as more of an accusation than a question.

"Okay, fine. I'll tell you," she says, rolling her eyes with exasperation. "I have a synthetic memory."

"A *what*?"

She concentrates and tries again. "A pornographic memory. No, that's not right either." She giggles at her inability to spit the word out. Whatever word it is she's trying to say. "I have an *eidetic* memory. There. That's right."

"A *what*?"

"You know, *phonographic*. I have a phonographic memory," she explains, the tiniest hiccup escaping her lips at the end of the sentence. It makes her giggle again.

My eyebrows go up in sudden understanding and supreme surprise.

"D–do you mean you have a *photographic* memory?"

"Isn't that what I just said?"

"Hold on a sec," I say, waving one hand at her while putting the other to my forehead, which feels as if it's stuffed with cotton candy. "Are you telling me you've memorized my master's thesis?"

"Yup. And your doctoral one, too. And every textbook

you've ever assigned, and all the scores I read. I can't help it, I pretty much remember everything I see."

"What? No fucking *way*! You're shitting me, *Miss Brenner*," I accuse with a light elbow to the ribs.

"Hey," she complains, elbowing back. "I shit you not, *Dr. Drew*."

"Prove it," I say with a firm nod, as if it's been decided.

"Huh?"

"Show me how you do it," I command, twisting my head to look around us. When I spot the novel she was reading earlier in the day, I snatch it up and flip to a random page. "Okay," I say as I look down at the page, then back up at her again. "Page two hundred and sixteen. Paragraph two."

"Oh, come on," she whines. "I'm not a trained seal, you know."

"Oh-ho! Did you want to maybe retract your previous statement about having a—a what was it again? A synthetic memory."

"Ei-d-d-ethic," she stammers and slurs at the same time, and it's fucking adorable.

"Exactly."

"Jesus Christ," she hisses. "You are *such* a pain in the ass! Fine, fine, fine. Get ready to have your socks knocked off, Dr. Drew…"

Katherine closes her eyes and puts her fingers to her temples, as if she's channeling some long-dead spirit. But she's only channeling the spirit of a third-rate romance writer named Whitney Larabee Lovelace.

"Ahem. Okay, here we go." She takes a deep breath and squishes her face together in a dramatic facsimile of melodramatic lust.

"'He leans down, his fingers playing gently along the line of my jaw. I can't help but lean in to his touch. It burns a fiery trail everywhere that his skin connects with mine.'"

She's recited the paragraph verbatim. Suddenly her eyes pop open. "And the word 'connects' is missing an *n* by the way."

I'm staring at her now, mouth agape, eyes wide, book dangling precariously from my fingertips.

"Jesus fucking Christ," I murmur in stunned appreciation.

"I know. *Right*?" She cackles with a grin, reaching for her wine bottle. When she does, my hand somehow lands atop of hers.

At first, she thinks I'm trying to stop her from drinking anymore, which wouldn't necessarily be a bad thing. And, although I *am* removing her hand from the bottle, that's not why. I take her hand in mine and use it to pull her forward, off her couch cushion and onto mine. She doesn't fight me.

My head is spinning with conflicting emotions. I want her. I want this. But there's that nagging part of me that's screaming "*What the hell are you doing?*"

And I can't blame that part of me. This has disaster written all over it. But I just don't care.

Chapter Twenty-One

Kate

I'm melting into him. It's the only way I can describe it. For the first time, I'm not fighting against Drew Markham. I'm moving toward him, with him. It happens slowly for the first few seconds as we're hesitant in our actions and unsure of one another's intentions. But somewhere within those inches we both draw the same conclusion. I lurch toward him and he catches me in his arms, both of us falling backward onto the couch. Our lips connect with a ferocity that is jarring.

His hands are in my hair and we're like two starving wretches who have stumbled upon a feast. My hands are under his shirt, feeling the smooth plane of his back, absorbing his warmth through my skin. We're both gasping and panting, pushing and pulling. And then he stops. I nearly fall off the couch when I no longer have the resistance of his body to push against. I pull back and look up at him, confused.

"W-what? What is it?"

His eyes are closed and he's shaking his head. His face is

a mask of regret.

"Drew?"

"I can't. I'm sorry, Katherine. You...me..."

He gestures toward the four empty bottles of wine on the coffee table. "We've both had way too much. You're still not a hundred percent well. I'm your professor. You're my student. There are a million different reasons why we need to stop this. Why *I* need to stop this. Right now. Right. Now."

I take a deep breath and extricate myself from what's left of his embrace.

"Umm, okay," I say quietly as I readjust my shirt and scoot down the couch a few feet so I can get a better look at him. "It's okay. Really." I nod and give him a slightly confused but reassuring smile.

Still, he doesn't look convinced. He stands up abruptly, his right hand raking through his dark hair while he paces behind the couch. I twist around to watch him.

"I don't know where that came from," he's muttering, more to himself, than to me. "What's wrong with me? I *know* better."

With a sigh, I wonder the same thing about myself. We hate one another. Don't we? Apparently not. But even I, with my limited knowledge of psychology, recognize that there's a very fine line between love and hate. Not that I love him or anything. But I certainly wouldn't mind another one of those kisses.

"Please don't make yourself nuts over this," I say, desperate to pull my thoughts away from his lips. "It's just one of those things. You said it yourself—we had too much to drink. So I propose that we *keep* drinking. And we pretend nothing ever happened. Jeez, it's entirely possible we won't even remember this in the morning. What do you think?"

He only waits a split second before replying.

"Yes. Absolutely." He nods. "I think there's another bottle of chardonnay in the wine cooler."

Chapter Twenty-Two

Kate

"What's so funny?" I smile up at him, from where I'm lying on the floor by the fire. He's in his chair, the sound of the wooden runners creating a hypnotic rhythm as they rock back and forth, back and forth against the slate hearth. He glances down at me, still rocking.

"You know, at first, I couldn't believe my bad luck—to have you, of all my students, stuck here with me. Now, I realize what incredibly good luck it was. And I *still* can't believe it."

"What? Are you saying you wouldn't have had just as good a time with Evan and his bassoon?"

"Hah! No, you're considerably more attractive than Evan. Or his bassoon, for that matter." He wrinkles his nose in distaste. "And, I've got to say, I'm just not really a fan of the scraggly goatee look."

"But I look like Casey."

"Yes, you do," he admits. "But not the same." He takes me by surprise when he leans over to tuck a rogue strand of hair behind my ear. I fight the urge to lean in to his touch. "The fact that you remind me of her isn't the attraction. In fact, it's been a deterrent all these years. I've been so angry with her for so long."

"Because she killed herself?"

"Exactly." His face clouds with concern. "Is that totally screwed up?"

I shrug. "I don't think so. But then, I'm not the best person to ask. I'm still angry at my mother for dying on me and that wasn't even her fault."

Despite our best efforts at increased inebriation, we've both sobered up fast after our aborted attempt at ill-advised romance. Gone now are the delicate wineglasses, replaced by green and white Shepherd University mugs, full of steaming hot chocolate. He hands me his to hold, so he can slide from his chair to join me on the floor.

"So," he begins, taking the beverage back into his own hands when he's settled on the rug. "Your father."

I look down into my own cup, as if there might be a secret message for me in the bottom, telling me how to avoid this unavoidable conversation. Unfortunately, there's nothing but warm, milky goodness looking up at me.

"My father," I repeat on a sigh of resignation.

"Are you close?"

"Hardly. I haven't seen him in years."

"Seriously?" I hear the incredulity in his tone; I see it on his face. I almost wish he'd stayed up in his rocker so I could avoid the uncomfortable intensity of his dark eyes.

"Uh-huh."

"But the way those jackal reporters hound you… What do they think they're going to get out of you if you're not even in contact with the guy?"

"They don't know I'm not in contact with him. Nobody knows."

"Well why the hell not? Maybe if they did, they'd finally leave you alone."

"Look, Drew, here's the thing. It's not what's true that matters. It's what people *think* is true that matters." I can see from the way his brows are furrowed that he doesn't understand what I'm getting at. "My classmates. My professors. *You*, Drew Markham. You don't know a damn thing about me, but none of you is willing to cut me an inch of slack because of the kind of person you *believe* me to be. No matter what I say to them, or to you, or to the press, everyone is going to believe what they want to believe. That I'm entitled. That I'm rich. That I support my father's ridiculous bill to defund the arts."

"Well that's pretty jaded, don't you think? Maybe if you actually explained to us—to them—what the situation really is, things would be different for you," he suggests and the sincerity on his face tells me that he believes it could really be this simple. Unfortunately, I know better.

I give him a patronizing smile. "Or maybe they'd take what I said and twist it."

"Oh, now you're being paranoid again," he scoffs dismissively. But I won't be put off.

"Think about it, Drew. Imagine someone finds out I was stuck here like this with you. The two of us, alone, for days. Suddenly you're being accused of an improper relationship with a student and I'm being accused of sleeping with my professor for a good grade. That's not at all what happened. And, even if the truth came out after the fact, do you think people—your boss, my peers—are just going to erase their initial impressions? Hell no! That's one bell you can't un-ring."

I'm thinking this is a good analogy, until I notice Drew Markham looking very pale suddenly. He's verging on green, in fact.

"You wouldn't tell anyone, would you, Katherine? About this? That I kissed you before?"

The question is wrapped in thinly veiled panic.

"What? No! God, no!" I gasp. "Are you insane? That was just an example. My point is that I can't say anything about my father to anyone because there's no guarantee that the truth is what will be printed. So, unless I decide I hate him enough to invent some scandal that'll hurt his career, I won't be saying anything."

He looks visibly relieved and I try not to giggle as the color gradually returns to his face. For a few seconds the crackling of the fire is the only sound in the room.

"Would you do that to him?" he asks.

I glance at Drew, who's watching me intently.

"You would," he determines from my split-second hesitation.

"Not now. But there was a time when I was so angry that I might have. Remember when I told you I got into the New York Conservatory?"

"Ah, yes, the 'long story,'" he recalls from our earlier conversation.

I smile. "Yes, exactly. So, when I was getting ready to graduate high school, I told him I was going to visit my aunt in New York City."

"And you didn't go?"

"Oh no, I went all right. Except, I didn't *just* go to visit my aunt. I also went to audition for the New York Conservatory. I was so careful not to tell anyone anything. I even auditioned under a pseudonym. As luck would have it, though, there was a reporter there doing a fluff piece about the musicians who come from all over the world to audition. He recognized me and snapped a picture with his phone. Next thing I know, it's in the papers. And on Twitter. And Instagram, and Facebook, and—"

Drew gives a long, low whistle.

"Shit. I'm guessing Senator Dad wasn't too thrilled by

that," he surmises.

"Not so much," I confirm. "I was so sure I could convince him to let me go, but he saw the whole thing as a personal betrayal. Oh God, he was *so* furious."

I close my eyes as an involuntary shudder runs through my body at the memory. They fly open again when I feel the press of warm flesh. Dr. Drew Markham gives my hand a supportive squeeze. I don't comment. Nor do I pull away.

"What happened then?" he asks, his eyes glued to my face.

"I was given the choice between studying something that he approved of, like political science or business or premed with his total backing…or continuing with a music degree without his financial or emotional support."

He inhales sharply and his hand tightens around mine.

"He—he kicked you out?"

"Pretty much. I got to keep my car and he gave me a little bit of money to start with, but I was told not to come home. Not to call home. Not to write home. He said I had embarrassed him so deeply that I might very well have cost him his career."

"He really thought you studying music could have that kind of an impact on his career?"

My eyebrows go up and I shake my head slightly. "In all fairness," I concede, "he did get a lot of shit from his opponents when word got out. Here he was all '*We don't need the arts. The arts take food out of the mouths of starving children.*' and then suddenly his own kid is studying music. Some people accused him of being a hypocrite. Others talked about how it was easy for him to oppose arts education funding and scholarships when his kid didn't have to worry about who would pay for her education."

"But, wait—I have to ask this question again, Katherine. If you got into the New York Conservatory, and you were *determined* to study music regardless of your father's wishes, why come to Nowhere, North Carolina? Why not just take your acceptance letter and go to New York City?"

Good question. And one that pains me to answer.

"Ah, well, it was the last card my father had to play. I wasn't eighteen yet, so he declined the admission on my behalf. I tried to undo it when my birthday rolled around a few weeks later, but it was too late by then. They'd given my spot, and my scholarship, to someone else." I try to sound neutral as I tell him all of this, but there's still a tinge of sadness to my tone. "I was pretty heartbroken. But, I didn't have a lot of options. Shepherd was my safety school and I got just enough of a scholarship to cover tuition and books."

"But not housing or food."

I shake my head. "No. That's when I picked up a job working mornings in the North Dining Hall. And that office cleaning job I told you about. That's not all the time, though. I pick up per diem shifts when things aren't too crazy at school, like they are now. It's tight, but if I'm careful, it's enough."

He's silent, but I can feel the anger coming off him. How strange it feels to not have it directed at me for a change.

"He's not a bad guy, you know. My father," I hasten to say.

No reply.

"I know it doesn't look that way from where you're standing—"

"From where *I'm* standing? Katherine, how can you not see?" He drops my hand and rakes it through his dark hair, leaving it nicely tousled. "I mean, I thought the guy was an ass because of his politics. But now..."

"Now what?"

"Now I see that he's abandoned you for not sharing his political views. You! His own daughter! *Who does that?*"

I consider how best to answer this question and finally decide that honesty is my best tack here.

"Drew, he wasn't always like this. It was after my mother died. He got so angry. The music…and the way I played it was just a constant, painful reminder of her."

"Still, to take *her* death out on *you*—"

He stops abruptly and I'm indescribably relieved that I won't have to connect the dots for him. Because, thankfully, he connects them for himself.

"Oh. Oh, fucking hell," he mutters, closing his eyes and shaking his head at his own hypocrisy.

"Yup."

"Did I really just say that?"

"You did."

"Oh my God. Katherine, I am sorry. So not only am I a dick for treating you like that in the first place, I'm a dick for doing to you *exactly* what your father has done."

"Kinda," I say, looking up at him with a smile.

He's staring at me with such intensity that I want to look away. But I don't. Instead, I scoot the short distance between us until my face is just inches from his.

"But I might let you make it up to me."

Chapter Twenty-Three

Drew

"Okay, okay, wait. Let me see if I'm understanding this. You went to school with *Daniel Gillies*?"

"Yes," I confirm for the third time. "He was my roommate for undergrad. We shared an apartment in Brooklyn. I was best man at his wedding a few years back."

"We're talking about the same Daniel Gillies? The one on the conducting faculty at New York Conservatory?"

I get up on my feet unsteadily and stand in front of a tall bookcase, perusing the shelves until I spot what I'm looking for. I reach up, grab the thin volume, and take it back to the couch with me. "Making it up" to Katherine turns out to involve her picking my brain about my time at the New York Conservatory. She's peppered me with a dozen questions about the curriculum and professors. And, the truth is, I'm only too happy to walk down memory lane with her. Those were the good old days for me. And Casey.

"Come here," I say, patting the cushion next to mine. She

gets up, blanket still wrapped around her, and sits where I've indicated. I flip through the plastic-coated pages until I find the one I'm looking for. "There," I say, pointing to the picture of myself in a black cap and gown, pink tassel hanging. I've got an arm around a tall, goofy-looking guy with a ridiculous amount of hair.

"Look at you! You're so young!"

"Gee, thanks," I retort, my tone dripping with sarcasm. "'Cause, you know, I'm such an old fart now."

"Oh, stop it." She giggles, giving me a gentle jab with her elbow. "You know what I mean. What's he like?"

I shrug. "He's a good guy. An exceptional conductor. We all knew he'd be going straight to the top."

Katherine reaches over and flips to the next page of the photo album. Looking back at us are Daniel and his wife, Vivica, a spectacularly beautiful black woman who looks as if she just stepped out of a Victoria's Secret commercial. She's wearing a wedding dress and clutching a bouquet of flowers with one hand and Danny's tuxedoed arm with the other. I'm standing to the right in my own tux. Casey is standing to Vivica's left in her silvery maid of honor gown.

"Wow," Katherine says from next to me.

"Yeah, I know. All the girls thought he was hot. I never saw it myself…" I chuckle.

"No," she says, shaking her head. "Not him. You."

"Me what?"

"You. You look so happy. I don't think I've ever seen you look even close to that in the years I've known you. It's a…" She pauses and looks up at my face. "It's a really good look on you."

"Huh. I guess I'll have to find more things that make me happy," I murmur as I close the distance between us with my lips.

"Well, Dr. Markham," she purrs against my mouth, not

an inch from her own, "I can tell you from having taken your classes for so long, when you're happy, everyone is happy."

I tilt my head back to laugh, but I don't get away for long. Katherine reaches up and takes my face in her hands, gently but firmly pulling me back down to her and her waiting lips.

She's right, I *am* happy. It's been so long that I'd almost forgotten how good it can feel. But, as I pull her into a tight embrace, something tells me I won't be forgetting again anytime soon.

Chapter Twenty-Four

Kate

My neck is stuck at a weird angle. When I reach behind me to adjust my pillow, it groans.

What?

My hand moves farther down and it takes me a second to realize I'm not lying on a pillow, I'm lying on an arm. Drew Markham's arm. We're nestled together, squashed up against one another on the big, soft couch in his den. We must have fallen asleep like this. I think. I'm a little fuzzy on the details of last night and there's a wicked throb behind my eyes that isn't from being sick this time.

His big, warm hand wraps around my waist from behind, pulling me into his chest. I feel his cheek against the top of my head.

"Good morning, Miss Brenner," he murmurs in my ear. It makes me smile.

"Good morning, Dr. Markham. I wonder, sir, could you enlighten me as to our…activities last night? I'm not sure I recall everything that went on."

"Oh, well, let's see," he begins, pulling the blanket farther down around us so I'm completely covered. "We drank too much. We kissed. We confessed our deepest, darkest secrets. We kissed again. We drank hot chocolate and kissed some more until finally…we fell asleep on the couch."

"We didn't…?"

"No. We didn't," he assures me. "You were a perfect gentleman."

I snort and then we're both silent for a long minute.

"Drew?" I ask, plucking up my courage.

"Hmm?"

"What does this all mean? For us?"

I feel him take a long, slow, deep breath from behind me. "I don't really know, Katherine. Not exactly, anyway. I think we don't hate one another."

"I'd agree with that statement." I chuckle.

"Good. I think we have some unexpectedly strong feelings for one another."

"I'd agree with that statement, too." I don't chuckle this time.

"*Very* good," he comments with a smile in his voice. "But I also think that we both know that there's not much we can do about those feelings for right now. Not without one or both of us getting into a world of shit."

Time for me to take my own deep breath. God, I'm so glad I don't have to look at his face right now. "But, Drew, I don't want things to go back to the way they were. Before."

He sits up suddenly, and I find myself flat on the couch, looking up at him. His face is crumpled with confusion and concern.

"What? Of course not. Is that what you think, Katherine? That I want to go back to…to *that*?"

I blink hard. "I don't really know what to think, Drew. I

don't really know what this is."

The tension leaves his face all at once, raising his brows, softening his mouth and opening his dark eyes. It's a reminder of just how devastatingly handsome this man is. And how I've been ignoring that fact for a very long time.

"I do," he whispers as he leans down and kisses me. "It's just got to simmer on the back burner a little bit longer. Do you think you can wait for me, Katherine?"

His breath is a soft breeze against my lips. It tickles me and I giggle a little.

"I can wait. But can the waiting wait until I leave this house?"

"Oh, I insist," he says and I feel his hands on my rib cage. If he'd just move up a little. Or maybe down a little.

He shakes his head, as if reading my mind. "Same rules apply in the meantime. This is as far as it goes for now. Agreed?"

I see the conflict in his eyes. He believes what he says, but it's a struggle for him. Somehow that makes me feel better. I'm not alone in my confusion.

"Agreed."

He hunkers back in behind me and I sigh contentedly at the feel of his arms around me. I think we're going to drift back asleep again until I feel the rumble of his voice in his chest.

"Katherine, why didn't you audition for the New York Conservatory this year? You could have started their doctoral program in the fall."

I consider lying to him, but I just don't have the energy. Or the desire, for that matter.

"I couldn't afford the application fee," I admit softly. I don't know why, but this makes me feel ashamed. He senses it.

"Oh, Katherine. I'm sorry. Was it very expensive?"

I feel unbidden tears pricking at my eyelids and I blink

rapidly to stave them off.

"It was two hundred dollars."

The words come out as a whisper and I feel his arm tighten around me even more.

"It might as well have been a thousand, right?"

I nod, not trusting myself to speak without choking up. The truth is that I *am* embarrassed. Embarrassed that I work so hard and still, in the end, it came down to a choice between applying for the opportunity of a lifetime…and eating. A month's worth of ramen noodles and Kraft mac and cheese.

"Did you ask for a waiver?" he pries gently.

I nod. "Yes."

"And they turned you down," he surmises.

I nod again.

He doesn't ask again so I swallow hard and offer. "It's the name. My name. No admissions office is going to believe that I have financial challenges so long as I'm the daughter of a senator. Especially that particular senator. They weren't going to do me any favors, even if I provided proof of financial need, which I didn't. I couldn't do that to my father—air our dirty laundry like that. Let people know how disconnected we are."

I feel Drew stiffen behind me but he doesn't comment.

"So," I continue, finally managing to swallow the lump in my throat, "I decided I'd finish up here and take the summer and fall to work as much as I can. I'll take lessons with Russell privately and—so long as the Corolla keeps running and I don't run into any unexpected expenses—I should have the cash to audition in the fall or early spring. It's a good plan. A sensible plan," I inform him, though we both know I'm just reassuring myself that I've made the right decision. "Not that it matters at this point, my window of opportunity has passed. Even if I could, by some miracle, get into the program, the scholarship funds have all been allocated by now."

"Did Russ know about this?"

"Yes."

"And he didn't help you?" I'm surprised by the harshness of his tone.

"Help me what?"

"Katherine, he could have easily loaned you that money. Two hundred dollars is nothing to him."

I flip over onto my back again so that he's looking into my eyes. I need for him to hear this.

"He did offer, Drew. He offered to cover it. He offered to loan it. He offered to call on my behalf and get them to waive it. I refused every offer he made."

He looks stunned. "What? Why would you do that?

"Because I can take care of myself," I say simply. "If I couldn't pay for it on my own, or get a waiver on my own, then it just wasn't going to happen."

He nods his understanding and I'm relieved that I don't have to lay out all the reasons why it has to be this way.

"Well, Miss Brenner, I have to say you've done a damn good job of taking care of yourself so far," he says as he reaches down to stroke my cheek with his thumb. "Very, very impressive."

This makes me smile so wide that I feel my eyes crinkle.

"Dr. Markham, I think that's the nicest thing anyone's ever said to me."

And I mean it.

Chapter Twenty-Five

Drew

The second storm hits hard, but fades fast as some unexpected warm front blows across the mountains. By Sunday, Katherine's car has finally emerged from its polar ice cap. I'm looking from it to her and back again, my expression skeptical.

"Are you sure you can get back home in that thing?" I ask her over my shoulder. She's sitting behind me, on the couch, curled up with a book in front of the fire.

"That *thing* has been getting me back and forth for a long time now," she informs me without looking up.

"Yeah, I know. That's the problem. Too long," I mutter.

She sighs as she puts the book on the coffee table and comes to join me in front of the big picture window.

"Look, it runs—when sneaky reporters aren't messing around with it," she says with a teasing smile, hooking her arms around my waist and pulling me close to her. And then she looks up at me with those incredible eyes. They're the color of the Atlantic and just as tumultuous, I've discovered.

"Drew, I don't want to go back to the real world any more than you do, but we don't have much of a choice. Classes are back in session tomorrow. I've got to work the breakfast shift and you've got to hand back all those midterm projects. You know, the ones you have yet to grade?"

"Ugh, don't remind me." I groan and roll my eyes.

"Drew, you know we can't. That we, you know…"

"I know. I know. This has to end here," I agree, speaking the words that she can't.

She nods.

"Can we revisit this in a couple of months after you graduate?" I ask hopefully.

"Absolutely. That is, assuming I do graduate. I have it on good authority that I'm on 'very thin ice.'"

"Hah!" I snort. "Yeah, well, I hear the ice has firmed up quite a bit with the recent cold temperatures. So, I wouldn't worry too much about that," I murmur and lean down to kiss her, but her firm palm on my chest stops me in my tracks.

"Hey, I'm serious, you *cannot* show me any special treatment. None. If I'm late, I'm late. If I pass, I pass. Anything else is unfair, not to mention suspicious to anyone who's paying attention."

She's right and I give her a curt nod of understanding.

"I know," I whisper, unable to take my eyes off her soft, pink mouth. "Miss Brenner," I say, leaning down again to kiss her, "I expect you to follow all the rules. Or you're going to be in some serious trouble…Miss Brenner."

She puts both palms to my chest and holds the distance between us.

"Oh, Dr. Markham," she chides me with one incredibly sexy raised eyebrow, "you're not doing anything to discourage my bad behavior."

I rest my forehead against hers and close my eyes. When I open them again, she starts to giggle.

"What? What could possibly be so funny during this incredibly, tragically, romantic moment?" I ask with a teasing grin.

"You really need to step back. You've got this one big freaky looking eye when you get that close to me. It's gross," she says, wrinkling her nose.

I straighten up and look down into her smirking face. "Seriously? I'm here baring my heart and soul to you and you're envisioning a Cyclops?"

Her smile fades into something much different.

"No sir. I'm envisioning a lot of things and a Cyclops is definitely not one of them," she murmurs, standing on her tippy-toes to put a soft, warm, frustratingly chaste kiss on my cheek.

Chapter Twenty-Six

Kate

It's not lost on me that we're exactly where we were on Friday, me in the driver's seat of my car, him hanging in the window. Only this time I'm not trying to keep him out. In fact, I'm wishing I could just take him home with me. Or stay here with him, in this perfect little bubble we've created for ourselves. But we both know that's not possible. Not now, anyway.

"So, tomorrow morning…" he begins.

"I know, don't worry. No touching. No long looks, no sappy smiles."

He continues my list.

"No first names, no one-on-one meetings in my office or anywhere else. And," he says, eyebrows going up now for emphasis, "it goes without saying that neither of us utters a word to *anyone*. Not Russell. Not Tessa. And, for God's sake, not Maureen. Even a whisper of a relationship with a student is enough to get us both in some seriously hot water."

"Don't you worry about me, *Dr. Markham*," I assure him.

"Good morning, Dr. Markham. That's a dollar thirty-five, please," says a young man I recognize from my freshman Music Theory class. Maybe I can get him to tell me where she is.

"Good morning, Liam," I say with a smile and hand him a couple of dollars. "I didn't realize you work over here."

He nods. "Yup."

Stunning conversationalist, this one.

"Does anyone else from the music department work here with you?" I fish.

He scratches his head under the university baseball cap and appears to think hard.

"Uh, yeah, Javier Moncayo. The violinist? He's a line cook for the lunch shift."

"Okay…"

"Oh, and that girl. The graduate student? She's over there," he says, thrusting his chin toward the dining area.

I thank him and turn around, spotting her at last. Her back is to me as she busily wipes down one of the empty tables. Feeling a little conspicuous among all these students, I take my coffee and move across the room to a spot against the wall, where I can hide in the shadow of a soft serve ice-cream machine. Not likely anyone will be looking for a swirly cone before lunchtime, and from here I can wait for a good opportunity to slip the phone to Katherine.

She moves quickly, silently, from table to table, picking up trays and trash that other diners haven't bothered to dispose of. She disappears into the back for a minute, returning with a broad broom so she can sweep the floor. To most of the students around her, she's invisible. They shuffle around her, oblivious as they walk through a pile she's just gathered from under the tables. But she isn't invisible to everyone.

At one table, several young men are snickering and pointing at her. One of them makes a lewd gesture simulating oral sex. She just goes about her job as if she can't hear them. I feel my face reddening with the urge to kick their scrawny little undergrad asses. But my attention shifts as I notice six students from my eight o'clock Orchestration class at another table. The same class Katherine will be attending in less than an hour. She's clearly trying to avoid them, but they're making it difficult, "accidentally" dropping things on the floor and then cackling wildly. I watch in horror as flutist Joanie Dolan holds up her container of orange juice and empties it onto the tabletop.

"Oh, Kate!" she calls out across the cafeteria. "Kate? Please come and clean this up."

To my utter amazement, Katherine simply picks up a roll of paper towels and a sponge then makes her way over to the table. She's silent as she mops up the mess. Unfortunately, they are not.

"You missed a spot," teases Ken Logan, a tenor in the opera program.

"Yeah, Kate, you missed a spot," echoes his girlfriend.

Still, Katherine cleans the mess, her head down, without comment. She's about to walk away when Joanie pushes her coffee cup over, splashing it across Katherine's apron and sweater in the process.

"Oops!" she says, either unable or unwilling to hide the grin that spreads across her face.

My hands are balling into fists and my breath is coming in angry puffs through my nostrils as I watch from my spot in the corner.

"Oh no, Kate!" Joanie exclaims with false dismay. "You're all covered in coffee! You'd better change before class!"

"Don't be late for Markham, Kate. You know he'll *fail* you if you're late," teases the girl. "He wasn't happy when you were late last week, was he? Oh, but it wasn't *my* fault that bowl of cereal spilled right before your shift was over..."

I'm done. If I stand here another second, I don't know what I might do to those little shits. I slip out the door before I can be spotted and make my way quickly back across the parking lot, shaking my head and muttering obscenities the whole way. Not just at them, but at myself.

Once I get to my office, I shut the door and lock it behind me before sitting heavily behind my desk. I look at the clock. Graduate Orchestration starts in a half hour. There's no way she can finish cleaning that mess, change her clothing, and run all the way to the Music building in time. She'll be at least five minutes late and, thanks to my frequent public shaming of her, there's no way I can ignore it without causing suspicion.

Is this what's been going on all this time? She mentioned she might be late if "something spilled" at the end of her shift. She neglected to tell me that there were people helping her to be late. Why the hell didn't she just say something? I know for a fact that woman is not a doormat. That's when it occurs to me, she doesn't comment, because she *can't* comment. Fighting back isn't an option Katherine has most of the time. Not if she wants to keep herself out of the news.

Luckily, *I* don't have any such concerns.

Chapter Twenty-Eight

Kate

I know there's going to be trouble the second I spot them sitting at their usual table. Damn! I was so close to getting out of here on time. But I know, even before they start their crap, that there's no way I'm getting to Drew's class on time. I'm already glancing around the huge hall, looking for the closest mop when I hear Joanie calling me. She's just dumped her orange juice on the table. Again. You'd think she'd get a new party trick by now. This one's getting pretty old.

I grab the nearest roll of paper towels and rush over to clean up the mess before it seeps over the edge of the table and onto the floor. Maybe I can skip the mop after all. But that hope is short lived once the coffee goes airborne, landing in equal parts on me, and on the floor. With a silent sigh, I grab the mop and start to clean up, ignoring the taunts of my classmates as I do.

It doesn't hurt anymore, this little game they like to play with me. In fact, I've invented a game of my own. Every morning that I cross paths with them, I time myself to see how long I can go without uttering a single syllable. They sneer, they taunt, they insult, and I just pretend I can't hear it. On the days when I can pull it off, they leave the dining hall pissy because they couldn't get a rise out of me. I *love* those days. Today, unfortunately, is not one of them, though.

When the coffee splashes all over my clean clothes, I realize I'm going to spend the next fifteen minutes in the ladies' room, rinsing my sweater out and then drying it with the hand dryer. I'm tired of this. I'm tired of them.

"Really?" I hiss at Lisa. The soprano gives me a huge Cheshire cat grin that I'd like to smack right off her face. "What, are you ten years old? Haven't you got better things to do than harass me?"

"Sure, but none of them are as fun as watching you on your hands and knees cleaning the floor," Ken Logan pipes up and they all laugh.

I'm about to say something else when I feel a tap on my shoulder.

"You go on ahead and get cleaned up before you're late," my supervisor whispers softly in my ear.

I nod gratefully and hand her the mop. As I walk away, I hear my classmates giggling and wonder if the last few days ever happened. Or were they just a dream? I guess I'm about to find out, because there's no way I'm making it to class on time today.

Chapter Twenty-Nine

Drew

Seven minutes. That's how late she is when she slips into the back of the classroom, breathing heavily, sweater covered in large, still-damp water spots where she'd obviously tried to clean it. I make a point of turning to write something on the chalkboard as she makes her way to her desk at the front of the room. When I turn around, I spot Joanie and Ken exchanging knowing looks and snickering.

"Something funny, Mr. Logan? Miss Dolan?" I ask with a glare in their direction.

They both turn serious in an instant and shake their heads no.

"Huh," I say, pretending to consider them carefully. "Because I'm fairly certain you were just snickering. Were you snickering at *me*?" I accuse pointedly.

"No! No, Dr. Markham, it was just…just a joke," Joanie says, quickly trying to convince me of what I already know to be true—but don't care about.

"You think my class is a joke, Miss Dolan?" I twist her words and watch with satisfaction as the color drains from her overly made-up face.

"No sir," she whispers, eyes widening.

"I think I'd like you to leave," I say.

She stares at me in disbelief. "But I didn't do anything!"

My glare stops her dead. I raise an eyebrow.

"Out, Miss Dolan. You, too, Mr. Logan. Now."

The two gather their things quickly and make their way toward the door at the back of the classroom. Unfortunately for them, they pass by my desk to get there. They're almost directly between my desk and Katherine Brenner's when I pick up the coffee mug I've brought in special for this class and "knock" it on the floor in front of them. The liquid splashes up, covering both of their pants legs.

"Oops!" I say, and catch sight of Katherine's head snapping toward me out of the corner of my eye.

Ken *The Coward* Logan sprints for the door, leaving Joanie Dolan standing there, staring at me.

"Miss Dolan, I believe you just knocked over my mug. I think you'd better clean that mess up before you leave."

She starts to protest but one look at me and she shuts her mouth. I pull a roll of paper towels out of my desk drawer and toss it at her. The girl drops to her knees reluctantly and starts to sop up the mess. The entire class is watching wordlessly in stunned disbelief. Well, not the entire class, unfortunately.

Katherine springs out of her chair and joins Joanie on the floor. She grabs the paper towels and unfurls a couple of sheets.

"Go ahead, I'll get this," Katherine says, shooing her away. Joanie nods dumbly.

Without so much as a glance in my direction, the flutist scurries out of the room, leaving her classmate to clean up the mess I made in an attempt to drive a point home.

Fuck me.

This is *not* the way I imagined this would go.

I drop to my knees and join Katherine on the floor, mopping up the soggy mess. With her back to the class, she gives me a *what the fuck?* look. I answer with an almost imperceptible shrug.

"Thank you for your help, Miss Brenner," I say as coolly as I can muster so as not to sound out of character. "Go ahead and take your seat."

I spend the rest of the hour returning assignments and fielding questions about the upcoming oral exams. When I excuse them, everyone leaves. Except, of course, for Katherine.

"What the hell *was* that?" she hisses, barely above a whisper.

"What?" I ask innocently.

She considers me carefully before speaking again.

"Is it safe to say you saw what happened in the dining hall this morning?" she asks with some irritation.

Deny, deny, deny.

"I don't know what you're talking about, Miss Brenner," I inform her coolly.

"Oh, please, I was late. You can't tell me you didn't notice *that.*"

"Whatever happened to delay you this morning, I'm sure it won't happen again, Katherine," I continue. But suddenly I can't hold it together for another second. I burst out laughing. "And I really *am* sure. In fact, it wouldn't surprise me if those idiots start going to the cafeteria on the other side of campus from now on." I chuckle. "They will if they know what's good for them, anyway."

But Katherine does not look amused.

"You can't do this."

"Do what?"

"You know what. Just because they can be nasty doesn't

mean they're stupid. You don't think it's going to strike one of them as strange that you did your little accident re-creation in here? When one of them puts two and two together, they'll be wondering why you would do something to defend me. It is just *so* out of character for you, that someone is bound to notice sooner or later," she scolds me.

"Katherine..."

"Stop it! Stop calling me that," she hisses softly as if someone out in the hallway might here us. "You know as well as I do what a risk you're taking every time you call me by my first name. Huge red flag there, *Dr. Markham*."

I can't suppress the grin that creeps across my face as she grows more frustrated with me. This only makes her angrier.

"Listen to me," I say, trying to sound more serious. "You're absolutely right. And, yes, I saw what happened this morning."

"Why were you even there?"

I reach into my pocket and pull out her phone, holding it out for her to take.

"That's where it is! I've been looking all over for this!"

"I found it under my bed last night when I called you to see if you got home okay. I thought it might be better to get it to you in the dining hall rather than in the music department... but, well, you see how that turned out."

She looks down at the phone then up at me again.

"Why does this say I have text messages? Did someone text me last night?"

"Yes," I inform her. "I did. I wanted you to have my number in your phone. But I did take the precaution of entering my name as D in your contacts. Just in case someone sees your phone. Or mine for that matter—I've just got K for you in mine."

She's rolling her eyes but I can tell she's trying to hide her smile.

"Well, thank you, Dr. D. I don't suppose you've come across a silver bracelet in your travels? I thought maybe I'd left it somewhere in your house."

"Yes, actually. I've got it out in my truck. I can go and get it now, if you like..."

She shakes her head. "No, I just don't want to lose it. It was a gift from my mother. Just hang onto it for me until we can find a safe time for you to get it to me."

"All right," I agree.

There's an awkward beat of silence between us.

"How long has this been going on?" I ask.

"What?"

"You know what. How long have they been screwing around with you like that?"

She doesn't reply, just stares at me. My eyebrows go up.

"Katherine..."

"*Dr.* Markham, it's fine. I'm fine. I can take care of myself," she informs me stubbornly.

"Funny, didn't look like that to me."

Her voice drops down to a level that's barely audible.

"You know what? Just because we...we...*you* know... Doesn't give you the right to—"

"To what? To worry about you? To defend you? To care about what happens to you?"

"Exactly. You never had any interest in doing any of those things *before.*"

Before we can finish our heated exchange, the classroom door opens and Tessa sticks her head in.

"Drew? I was wondering... Oh, hello, Kate. I'm sorry, I didn't realize the two of you were having a discussion."

"Nope," Katherine says as she spins on her heel and walks out of the room. "I was just leaving."

"We're not done discussing this, Miss Brenner," I call after her. She gives a little wave with her hand, not bothering to turn around.

When the door closes behind Katherine, Tessa gives me a quizzical look.

"Everything okay there?" she asks.

"Yeah. Just the usual."

"You know, maybe you should consider having her finish this semester as an independent study. I'll bet Barry Green would take her."

"No," I say, a little too quickly. And a little too loudly. "No," I repeat in a softer voice. "She really did an exceptional job with her midterm project. I'd like to see her finish the semester with me."

"Well, okay," she says, looking at me a little oddly. "Whatever you think is best. I just wanted to see if you'd like to grab some coffee?"

I glance at the sopped-up mess in my trash can. I never did get that second cup.

"Yeah, absolutely. But let's go off campus. I don't need to be back for an hour or so. Feel like a drive to Ruby's Café?"

Tessa's face lights up like a Christmas tree. "I'd love to. Let me get my coat and meet you downstairs."

She scurries away and I walk out to where I've left my vehicle in the parking lot. By the time I drive around to the front of the building, Tessa's waiting for me in a very stylish and feminine-looking parka. I didn't think they made those things to look *girly*. It gives me an idea. One that Tessa can help me with—if I'm careful.

"Hey, Tess?" I venture once she's buckled in and we're on our way in my truck.

"Hmm?" she replies, applying lipstick in the small mirror behind the sun visor.

"I'd like to get my mom a nice winter coat, but I don't know where to begin…"

"Foal and Fernham," she says before I can even finish

the question. She turns to look at me with her newly perfected pucker. "Beautiful outerwear that's functional and fashionable. Unfortunately, the closest store is in Charlotte. But I'd be happy to go with you sometime. Are your folks finally coming out this way? Because you know I'd love to meet them," she offers enthusiastically.

"Nothing for sure, but I'm working on it," I mumble, making a mental note of the store with the ridiculous name. "Foal and Ferman?"

She giggles and rolls her eyes at me. "You men are all the same. Here, I'll text it to you," she says, already typing into her pink phone with her pink-nailed thumbs.

"Thanks, Tess." I smile her way and consider when I can get away to Charlotte for the day, taking careful note of her coat so I don't inadvertently purchase its twin.

• • •

TUESDAY MARCH 28TH 11:15 A.M.

D: ***Hi***

K: ***Hi***

D: ***Where are you?***

K: ***In Dr. Green's Jazz History class.***

D: ***Zzzzzzzzz***

K. ***We just got our midterms back. I got an 89 :^(***

D. ***Seems low for you.***

K: ***I was sick last week. Or don't you remember?***

D: ***Ohhhhhh I remember. Where did you drop the points?***

K: ***Hard Bop.***

D: ***But not Bebop.***

K. ***No.***

D. ***How about swing?***

K. ***Swing was fine.***

D: ***So, just the Hard Bop.***

K: ***Again, yes.***

D: ***Hmm. I like my Bop hard, too. Maybe I can tutor you…?***

K: ***Face-palm***

D: ***WTF does that mean?***

K: ***Go ask one of the cool kids.***

D: ***You're the only cool kid I know.***

K: ***Aw sweet!***

D: ***Yes, you are. And I miss you. You've got great lips, you know.***

K: ***I do?***

D: ***Oh yeah. My lips think very highly of your lips.***

K: ***Do they now?***

D: ***They're looking forward to seeing them in class tomorrow.***

K: ***Hey! Keep your eyes off my mouth! No wonder your Bop is Hard!***

D: ***Yeah, about that…***

K: ***DEGT***

D: ***WTF?***

K: ***Don't. Even. Go. There.***

Chapter Thirty

Kate

I'm humming the Aria from Bach's Goldberg Variations as I walk into the concert hall for my evening lesson.

"Ah, Bach. Someone's in a good mood," Russell observes when I drop my things on the stage.

"Maybe," I say with a sheepish smile as I pull my shoes off and hop up onto the podium.

"Oh yeah?"

"Mm-hmm." I nod.

"What's his name?"

My head whips up before I can stop myself, confirming his suspicions.

"Uh-huh. That's what I thought," he says, pointing at me.

"I don't know what you're talking about…"

"Oh, please, Kate. I know you too well. Humming? Smiling? *Relaxed*?"

"Russ," I say on a long sigh, "I can't…"

He waves a dismissive hand in my direction.

"I'm just busting your chops, Kate. You don't have to tell me anything about your *trysts*," he says, making the last word sound naughty. I try to object but he stops me. "No, no, really. It's none of my business. And besides, we don't have time for chatting today."

"Oh, and why is that?"

"Because you've got some Dvořák to learn, my dear Katherine."

I'm confused.

"There is no Dvořák on the Wind Ensemble concert program."

He grins up at me.

"No, there isn't. But there *is* on the *Symphony Orchestra* concert program."

I hop off the podium and walk forward to the front of the stage so that I'm standing directly in front of him, but three feet higher.

"What does the orchestra have to do with *me*? I'm conducting the Wind Ensemble for my final jury grade."

He's still smiling.

"What?" I demand. "What aren't you telling me?"

He stands up and walks to the edge of the stage, where the footlights give him an especially ghostly look. The threads of silver in his hair are glistening and his face has taken on a bluish tint. It's really, really creepy, but I try to ignore it.

"Dr. Giovanni slipped on the ice and broke his leg over the weekend."

"Oh! I'm so sorry to hear that," I say, an image of the tiny Italian man flashes through my head.

"Don't be. He'll be fine. And…he asked if *you* might be willing to take over for him on the spring concert."

"Wait. *What*?"

I get down onto the floor of the stage and let myself drop over the edge so that I'm with him in the house.

"You heard me. Someone else will conduct the Wind Ensemble. You'll start with orchestra rehearsals on Wednesday."

I feel my breath catch in my throat.

"Oh my God… This is amazing!" And then I think about it. Did he just say Wednesday? My hand goes up to my forehead as a try to process. I shake my head down at him. "No, Russ, this is terrible… I can't get an entire program together in three weeks!"

He scowls his disapproval up at me.

"Stop it, we both know that's bullshit."

I close my eyes and try to settle the churning in my stomach. When I reopen them, he's smirking at me.

"Just because I can memorize the score in a night doesn't mean I'll know how to conduct it in a night," I whine.

"Are you through with your panic attack?"

"No. But that's beside the point. Which Dvořák?"

"The New World Symphony."

"The *Ninth*?" I ask, as if another symphony has that nickname.

He nods.

"But that can't be the only piece on the program…"

"No, it's not. There's an overture to start, and the Mendelssohn Violin Concerto."

I open my mouth to freak out on him, but he swiftly holds up a hand to stop me from imploding.

"I said *I'd* conduct those. You'll only have to worry about the symphony."

Okay, forget about imploding, I'm about to *ex*plode. Far and wide.

"Wait, wait, wait. So you're saying that not only will I get to conduct the big piece on the big symphony concert, but that *you*, Russell Atherton, world-class, renown conductor, are going to come out of retirement and conduct on the same program?"

"One night only, baby," he says, doing a mildly disturbing take on jazz hands.

"Holy fucking shit…"

My expletive makes him laugh, but I'm dead serious. The implications of this are huge. Russell conducting publicly for the first time in years is going to cause a major stir in the classical music world. Add to that any curious lookie-loos who'll come to get a look at *Tucker the Fucker's* daughter…

"I can't," I say, shaking my head resolutely. "No way."

Russell puts his hands on my shoulders and gives them a squeeze.

"This is it, kid. This is your chance to blow them all away and shut their mouths once and for all."

But I don't look convinced. Probably because I'm not.

"And hey, you can invite your new guy. That is, if you haven't kicked him out of bed for eating crackers by then." He grins.

"What? What do crackers have to do with anything?" I ask, head spinning with everything that's just happened.

He throws back his head and laughs, but I have no clue why. Clearly I'm missing something.

"Don't worry about it, it's just an old expression." He chuckles, then reaches behind him for something on one of the chairs. "Here," he says, handing me a score for Dvořák's Symphony Number Nine. "Come on, get back up on stage. We've got work to do."

I take the heavy manuscript from him and run my hand over its smooth paper surface. When I look up at him again, his gaze tells me everything I need to know. I can do this. I *will* do this.

"All right," I agree finally. "I'm in."

I get back up onstage and take my place on the podium. It feels good. It feels right.

...

Wednesday March 29th 11:35 p.m.

K: ***OMG OMG OMG!!! I'M going to conduct the Dvk9 with ShepU Orch!***

D: ***Doesn't Gabe Giovanni conduct that concert?***

K: ***He tripped on the ice and broke his leg :)***

D: ***Umm… Schadenfreude much?***

K: ***Didn't mean it like that!***

D: ***You didn't "help" him fall did you?***

K: ***What? No! I'm just PDH because he wants ME to conduct in his place!***

D: ***PDH?***

K: ***OMG buy a glossary or something. Pretty Damn Happy. UR the 1 who wanted to text!***

D: ***IKR?***

K: ***Oh-Ho! Look at you, Mr. TextyPants :)***

D: ***I miss you.***

K: ***Me, too.***

D: ***I'd like to see you.***

K: ***You will. In class on Friday.***

D: ***Couldn't you manage to come by for office hours tomorrow?***

K: ***Danger! Danger! Flashing lights, screeching sirens! Armed men with dogs!***

D: ***Oh, for God's sake. Just say NO next time.***

...

Saturday April 1st 3:35 p.m.

D: ***Are you hearing this?***

K: ***What? The out of tune clarinets or the dragging bassoon player?***

D: ***I was talking about the couple sitting next to you. She***

won't shut up.

K: ***So move.***

D: ***But I want to be near you.***

K: ***You're sitting in the row behind me. It's not like we're together.***

D: ***How can you say that, K? I'm gazing upon your silky tresses…***

K: ***Oh, please.***

D: ***The way they fall in those soft waves down the back of that sassy little sweater.***

K: ***Sassy?***

D: ***Grrrrrrrrr.***

K: ***WTF was that?***

D: ***Me. Cyber-growling when I think of how long and lean your neck is under that hair.***

K: ***Oh. My. God. Please, make it stop…***

D: ***Holy shit! He just whispered something naughty in her ear.***

K: ***Who? Whose ear?***

D: ***Girl next to you, who else?***

K: ***How can you tell?***

D: ***Because he whispered and smirked and the back of her ears turned beet red.***

K: ***That's it. No more pseudo-cyber dates for you.***

Chapter Thirty-One

Drew

It's standing room only at the Shepherd University Theater. Every seat is filled, every spare inch covered with camera, sound, and lighting equipment. Television crews are stationed around the perimeters. I've managed to squeeze into a row reserved for faculty and staff, sandwiched between a poetry professor in need of a shower and a mailroom clerk in need of a haircut.

Seated around a semicircular table onstage are three politicians who could not look, or be, more diverse. Annemarie Pugliesi, a congresswoman from New Jersey is first in the lineup. Her no-nonsense demeanor is reading as abrasive to the genteel southern audience she's addressing right now.

Next to her is James Little, the first black governor in the history of North Carolina. He's fairing slightly better than Congresswoman Pugliesi in that he knows his audience and has no trouble appealing to their southern sensibilities.

And finally, on the far end of the table is a distinguished

looking man in his early fifties. He's tall and lean, with dark hair and blue eyes. There's no mistaking who he is, and not just because of his reputation, but because of his striking resemblance to his daughter. I pull my phone out of my pocket and type in a text message.

I can't believe how much you look like your father

Katherine isn't here tonight, afraid that her father's campaign people might take advantage of her presence for a family photo op. And, by the look of this three-ring circus, she was smart to skip it.

The man's got 30 years and 60 lbs. on me. If that's supposed to be a compliment, it's a pretty lame one.

I chuckle at her response. This is about as intimate as we can be these days. We've managed to keep ourselves out of trouble mainly by avoiding one another—in person, anyway. Of course, I can't avoid her in class. And that's where we must be extra vigilant. So I keep my distance and act like the jerk that I am so no one will be the wiser.

I glance at my watch. This thing is about to get going and I won't be able to text her once the lights go down.

I have to sign-off for now. Are you ready for your big dinner? Call me after?

I get a thumbs-down emoji as a response to the former, and a smiley face blowing kisses to the latter. She's stressing about having dinner with her father later tonight. It'll be the first time they've been alone together in a long time. Longer, I think, than she's willing to admit to me. I'm starting to wonder if this asshole has spoken to his daughter at all since he kicked her out of the house at eighteen. Before I can get my blood pressure up thinking about it, the house lights dim and the moderator comes out on stage. I recognize him as John Lipinski, the Dean of the Shepherd University College of Political Sciences.

Lipinski throws out a few softballs to get the three politicians comfortable. But after that, all bets are off and he's pulling out the big guns. This guy does *not* mess around. He stumps Congresswoman Pugliesi on her plan to address unemployment in Appalachia, one of the areas hardest hit by the economic downturn of the last ten years. One mention of her newly planned programs to extend unemployment benefits have the audience hissing. What she doesn't get is that this community wants jobs, not handouts.

Lipinski moves on to Governor Little, confronting him about his multimillion-dollar highway project that's had traffic outside of Charlotte snarled for close to two years, with no sign of relief on the horizon. More boos and hisses.

And then our moderator turns his attention to Senator Tucker *the Fucker* Brenner of Virginia. Having seen John Lipinski go right for the jugular with the previous two candidates, I know exactly what he's going to ask before he even opens his mouth.

"Senator Brenner, you're sitting in a theater. A theater on the campus of a university that has a strong tradition of arts education. How do you justify your stance on arts funding?"

The senator acknowledges Lipinski with a nod and then faces the cameras. He obviously knows what the other two don't, that this town hall may be *held* in North Carolina, but his audience is much, much broader. He knows that his appeal has to be not just to this region, but to this entire country. Judging by the TV cameras, this little get-together is likely to end up on CNN, MSNBC, PBS and a dozen other configurations of alphabet soup.

"It is time," he says, pounding his fist on the table for emphasis, "to stop wasting our limited resources on pretty pipedreams when so many more important departments need that precious funding. How can we support ballet dancers in tutus when there are children in this country who go to bed hungry every night? How can we fund pornographic so-called art work when so many of our citizens are without basic medical care? And what is the point of throwing money at an orchestra attended by the rich elite, when our schools are in crisis all over this nation?"

Even as a large contingent of the audience hisses and boos, I can see how this guy has managed to gain traction for his plan to discontinue all public funding of arts organizations. Dance companies, orchestras, theaters, and museums. None of them is safe under the Tucker Brenner Bill for Arts Funding Reform. The senator seems to be unfazed by the negative response to his words.

"Okay, I'm just going to come right out and ask you this, Senator," Lipinski says. "Are you here to announce your bid for the presidency?"

The senator looks genuinely surprised by the question, though I'm sure he's not. Good actor, though.

"No, I am not."

Lipinski shrugs. "Then what are you doing here? On this tiny campus in the North Carolina mountains?"

"Well, it seemed to me to be a good opportunity to discuss my bill and my platform. And, as I'm quite sure you're aware, my daughter is a student here."

I sit up and lean forward, resting my elbows on my knees as if this will get me closer to the stage somehow.

"Yes, I am aware. Katherine is a graduate student here at Shepherd University."

"Yes. Yes, she is," Brenner confirms with a smile and a nod.

"And, as it also happens, she is about to graduate with a master's degree in *conducting*. Is that correct, Senator?"

"Yes, John, she is."

Lipinski holds up his hands toward the ceiling in a *WTF*? gesture.

"A tad hypocritical, don't you think? Turns out your own daughter's one of the 'entitled dilettantes' you like to shame so publicly."

Oh. I do not have a good feeling about where this is headed.

"And, Senator, isn't it true that she did this against your wishes?"

Suddenly appearing on a screen behind the three politicians is a picture of a newspaper article. There's a horrific picture of Tucker Brenner caught during one of his fiery public appearances. His mouth is open, his eyes are wild, and his dark brows are drawn into almost a point. Whoever unearthed this particular photo chose well, it makes him look like Senator Satan himself.

And then there's Katherine, in the adjacent picture, looking positively angelic as she plays the piano on what I recognize to be the stage at the concert hall of the New York Conservatory of Music in New York City. This must be the picture that got her into so much hot water with her father. The image has captured her with eyes closed and head back, totally immersed in whatever she was playing at the time.

The headline screams SENATOR'S DAUGHTER TO DADDY: TUCK OFF!

A ripple of giggles makes its way through the audience. Still, Tucker Brenner sits there, calm and cool, the hint of a smile on his lips.

"Was there a question somewhere in there, John?" he asks the moderator.

"Yes, Senator. What is your relationship with your daughter now, and how has her decision to pursue a career in music impacted your credibility in the senate?"

"Well, first of all, let me say that my relationship with

my daughter is no one's business but our own. We are a very private family. I respect Katherine's choices just as she respects mine. You'll find no disparaging comments from her in any publication. Ever. As for my credibility in the senate—well, there are those who questioned my dedication to this cause in light of these circumstances, but I have demonstrated, again and again, why my bill will have a positive impact."

"But, Senator, surely this must be a sore point between the two of you—"

"Not at all," Brenner cuts him off. "You must keep in mind that Katherine grew up in a very comfortable lifestyle. She isn't really impacted by the constraints I'm discussing…"

Wait, wait, wait. Did this guy just imply that he supports Katherine? I snort and get a nasty look from the poetry professor to my right.

"Senator, why isn't your daughter here tonight?"

"As I mentioned, we are a very private family. And I respect my daughter's wishes to stay out of the spotlight."

"Yes, but—"

"John, I believe that's the last comment I'll make on this particular subject. Now, if you'd like to discuss the bill…"

I've heard enough. I've seen enough. I stand up and shoehorn my way past the long line of legs in my row and to the main aisle so I can slip out a back entrance. Outside, the frigid air is a relief from the oppressiveness inside the theater. I look up at the cloudless sky, nothing but a vast black expanse cluttered with twinkling stars and the moon. It makes me think of Casey and how she used to lie on her back on the lawn, looking for shooting stars to wish upon.

I'm glad I don't see one right now, because I have no idea which wish I'd make. The life behind me, or the life ahead of me?

With a sigh, I walk back to the parking lot, careful to keep my eyes on the ground so I don't have to decide.

Chapter Thirty-Two

Kate

When the black Town Car shows up, I've already been sitting in the restaurant parking lot for forty-five minutes. It's not that I don't trust my father to keep his word about this being a private get-together, I don't trust Leandra, "The Ice Queen," not to leak it to a reporter or two. Or ten. So far, though, no sign of anyone suspicious lurking around outside the Italian restaurant. I give my father a ten-minute head start before I get out of my car, taking one last look around for any rogue reporters.

When I get inside, I approach the hostess, a way-too-put-together model type who reminds me of Tessa Morgan. I'm suddenly regretting my decision to wear a simple skirt and tights.

"Good evening, I'm Katherine Brenner…"

"Of course. Welcome, Miss Brenner, we've been expecting you." She smiles. "The senator is already waiting for you. I'm Patricia, please, come with me."

I follow her through the restaurant, head down, eyes casting left and right. But all looks quiet in here, too, as she leads me to a set of french doors in the back, lined with scarlet drapes for privacy.

"May I get you something from the bar, Ms. Brenner?" she asks, holding the door open for me.

"Yes, a glass of riesling, please," I say, mentally thanking Drew for introducing me to an adult beverage. It's hard to be taken seriously when you're sucking down a Shirley Temple.

Patty Perfect nods, smiles, and closes the doors behind me. My father pulls the napkin from his lap, gets to his feet, and walks toward me with outstretched arms. I stand perfectly still and allow him to embrace me while I pat his arm, gently. When he lets go, he pushes me back slightly to get a good look at me. I take the opportunity to do the same.

He hasn't aged a day. Maybe there are a few more threads of silver visible in his thick, jet-black hair, but, for the most part, my father looks the same way he's looked my entire life. Tall, lean, and dark, he was always the perfect complement to my mother's petite, fair beauty. Tonight he's looking especially dapper in what must be a four-figure custom-cut navy suit. Only the finest for Tucker Brenner, senator from Virginia.

"Katherine," he says in a soft, choked voice, "I can't believe how much you look like your mother."

Hearing this makes me smile. It's a rare *real* moment for us. Maybe I've been worried about nothing. Maybe this dinner won't be so bad after all.

"I've always thought I looked more like you," I offer, a little shyly.

"Oh, well, you have my dark hair, but it's her coloring and her eyes that I'm looking at right now. And the fine features. Oh yes, you remind me so much of Elaine, it's remarkable."

I feel the blush rising to my cheeks, but I can tell by the wonderment in his eyes that he means it.

"So," I begin awkwardly, "should we sit?"

"Yes, of course," he says, jumping to pull out my chair for me. I allow him to push me to the table.

"How have you been, Daddy?" I ask over the hurricane candle and breadbasket once we're both seated again.

"Very well, thank you. And you? I know you'll be graduating in a couple of months. Is there much for you to do between now and then? Final exams, that sort of thing?"

I'm not surprised he knows that I'm about to graduate, but I am surprised that he cares enough to ask.

"Oh, uh, well, there's a lot, actually. Just about a month of classwork, then I'll conduct a big concert and then it's my oral exams. I'll face a panel of three professors and answer questions taken from pretty much every class I've ever had."

"Sounds like you've got your work cut out for you." He grins. "But then, you've always risen to the toughest challenges. I really do appreciate you taking the time to see me, Katherine."

"You're welcome. I was surprised to hear from Leandra," I admit, plucking a piece of semolina bread from the basket and slathering it in butter.

"You mean *The Ice Queen*?" he asks with a smirk. "You do still call her that, don't you?"

"Maybe…" I hedge with a sheepish smile.

"Well, she and I were both disappointed you weren't able to attend the town hall on campus. That was one of the reasons I agreed to do it—because it was being held here at Shepherd. I was hoping to give you a shout-out from the stage."

Somehow, the phrase "shout-out" just sounds wrong coming out of my father's mouth. I'm guessing The Ice Queen told him it would play well with the millennials.

"Yeah, I figured. To be honest with you, that's why I didn't go."

"What? You can't tell me you're shy. Not when you

conduct in front of *hundreds* of people."

He's teasing, but I'm still stuck in serious mode.

"It's not that I didn't want to hear you speak, Daddy. It's just that I'm a very private person. I'd rather not advertise my identity to the few people in town who don't know who I am."

His brow furrows but he holds his thought when a server returns with my glass of wine. "I see. Are you ashamed of being my daughter then?"

"What? No, of course not. I love you, Daddy. I'm just trying to say that it's one thing for people to know I'm a student somewhere on campus. It's another thing for them to recognize me in the parking lot or in the dining hall. You're—you're not very well-liked, Daddy, and sometimes people can say some nasty things. I'm sure you can understand why I'd prefer to keep a low profile."

"I do understand that, Kate. And I can respect that. But I'm a little confused, surely, you must have so many friends that everyone knows who you are, regardless. I mean, you always did have a huge social circle. How could people *not* know who you are?"

"Daddy, I don't really have any friends."

"Oh, please, Katherine. You're the most outgoing, friendly young woman there could be. You've been like that since you were a little girl."

"Yes, but I'm not a little girl anymore, Daddy," I remind him with a little too much edge in my tone. "In fact, it's not just that I don't have friends. I'm *actively* disliked by most of my classmates."

He considers me for a long beat.

"I'm sorry that's turned out to be the case, Katherine. But now you can appreciate the kind of resistance I get from *my* colleagues."

I swallow the snort that threatens to rise out of my chest. I have the inexplicable desire to hurt him, to make him see and hear and feel all the challenges I've had to overcome simply for being his daughter.

"Yes, well, I'm not a politician. I didn't ask for this kind of scrutiny."

"Of course not," he says with a hint of irritation.

"And I'm sure you can understand how the whole defunding the arts thing—that doesn't go over well with the other music students. Or faculty. And since I refuse to comment on you or your politics, well, let's just say it doesn't make me the most popular girl on campus."

He takes a deep breath and seems to consider this. I'm amazed—and a little disappointed—to see the irritation melt from his expression.

"Yes, I can see how that might cause some tension. Does that mean you've disavowed all knowledge of me?" he says with raised eyebrows and a grin.

His playful teasing is so unexpected that my resolve to injure evaporates.

"What are you, a spy now?" I laugh. "No, of course not! You're my father. I couldn't do that. I *wouldn't* do that."

"I know that, Katherine," he says softly, sincerely. "And I am very grateful that you've managed to keep our business out of the press. I'm aware you get your share of reporters nosing around."

"It's not that bad," I say, sipping my wine. "That jerk from the *D.C. Courier*'s a real piece of work though," I mutter.

"Kevin Kilpatrick," he scoffs. "Yes. You'd be wise to keep your distance from that one."

I don't bother to tell him it's a bit late for that.

"Well, you may have heard I'm considering a run for the White House," my father says, changing the subject.

I nod that I do, in fact, know this little tidbit. He reaches across the table to take my hand.

"Katherine, I'd very much like for you to be a part of

that."

"A part of what?"

"Of all of it! Come out on the campaign trail with me! You'll graduate soon, so you'll have plenty of free time. It'll be you and me on the road… You can give speeches, you can talk to young people about voting— "

"Whoa! Slow down, please," I say, pulling my hand from his and holding it up in a "stop" gesture. "Daddy, this is our first conversation in years. I hardly think we're ready to discuss me coming on the campaign trail with you. I hardly know you…"

"How can you say that?" he counters. "Katherine, please. Don't you think it's time we put this ridiculousness behind us and move on with our lives?"

I can't see the wave of crimson that's crawling up my neck, headed for my cheeks, but I can feel its heat. Suddenly I'm back on the shoot-to-kill train again.

"Daddy, you were the one who started this '*ridiculousness*.' Remember?"

"Oh, now, Katherine, don't be so dramatic," he says with a dismissive wave of his hand.

"'*Dramatic'?* You make it sound as if it was some mutual conclusion that we came to. But we both know that I didn't have any choice in the matter. You threw me out of the house, Daddy. You told me not to come home. Or call. Or write. That was all you, Daddy. All. You."

"I seem to recall you making that choice after I offered you the perfectly acceptable option of studying any one of several fields *not* connected with the arts."

I'm staring at him in disbelief when our server returns with salads. Neither of us speaks other than to thank him.

"Katherine— " my father restarts once we're alone again.

"Daddy," I interrupt him with a sigh of resignation. "Let me save you the speech. I'm doing fine on my own. And no, I'm not angry with you. I was disappointed in you for a long time. Now—well, now I don't know what I feel for you. This is the first time we've spoken directly in more than five years. I mean, what did you expect would happen here tonight? That the past would magically disappear and we'd be the picture of a devoted father and daughter again?"

"I expected to see some semblance of the manners that I know your mother and I instilled in you. That's what I expected to see." He huffs, the charming facade cracking under the weight of his irritation.

I feel my own tide of anger as it rises from my gut.

"She never would have allowed you to treat me the way you have."

"I wouldn't be too sure about that."

"I am. I am *quite* sure about that," I grit, getting to my feet. "You know what? I'm done. I need to go home. I've got to work early tomorrow morning."

"What? Cleaning up like some common maid?" He sneers.

I glare at him.

"Keeping tabs on me, are you?"

He sits back with an officious smile.

"I always keep tabs on my investments."

I suck in a breath and try not to let my rage ratchet up any further.

"Yeah. You take care of yourself, *Daddy*," I say as I turn to leave.

"Please sit down." He sighs. "Let's have dinner."

I shake my head.

"No sir. Thank you, I've lost my appetite. I just want to go home."

"To your ramshackle little apartment in the seedy part of town, right?"

"Oh God! Well, I'm sorry to disappoint you, but I like my apartment. Not to mention, it's what I can afford."

He leans forward across the table, folding his hands in front of him. His negotiating stance, as I recall from my teenage days.

"Perhaps we can do something about that, Katherine. For instance, I might be willing to purchase a little condo for you in exchange for you accompanying me on a few campaign trips in the coming months. We might even be able to work out a stipend for your living expenses."

All at once, I find my anger has been replaced by exhaustion. And resignation. I sink down into the chair next to him.

"Just tell me."

He looks perplexed.

"Tell you what, Katherine?"

"Please, just tell me what it is that you want. That's what you're here for, isn't it? Because you want something?"

He holds my gaze for a long instant before he speaks.

"I'm going to run for president."

"So you've said."

"Ah, yes, well. It's all about optics, how things look. Being a widower doesn't look as good as being married. But it does look better than being single. Especially if I happen to have a daughter by my side, supporting me, on the road with me."

I'm surprised to find myself surprised. Just when I thought I'd heard it all.

"That's why you wanted to see me?"

"Well, yes. Why, what did you think I wanted?"

I want to suppress the laugh that bubbles up from deep inside of my chest, but I just can't seem to manage it. It comes out sounding a little like a cackle and my father does not look amused.

"Oh, I don't know, I guess I thought… No, I guess I'd *hoped* that you wanted to tell me that you love me. That you've missed me. Maybe even that you're sorry. But I could have even given you a pass on that last one if I thought the first two were true. But I see now that they're not."

"I'm not here to apologize for anything, Katherine," he informs me. "Quite the opposite, actually. I think it's *you* who owes *me* an apology. Your antics made me look weak and foolish in front of my colleagues—in front of my opponents."

On impulse, I reach across the table and take his hand in mine. It's big, warm, and soft, just the way I remember from when I was a little girl and he'd hold my hand.

"I'm so tired, Daddy," I say in my sincerest tone. "I work really hard and I'm very proud of what I've accomplished. And maybe you had something to do with that. Maybe you pushing me out like that is what gave me the courage to fight for what I want. And maybe it's what kept me from becoming an entitled, obnoxious socialite. But what you're asking for? I'm sorry, I just can't. I won't *pretend* to be your daughter. Not in exchange for your money. And certainly not in exchange for your love."

Before he can say anything else, I get up again, lean down to kiss his cheek, and walk out of the private dining room. I barely notice the cameras flashing around me as I exit the restaurant.

• • •

FRIDAY APRIL 7TH 9:39 P.M.

D: ***Hey. How you doing?***

K: ***Don't ask.***

D: ***That bad?***

K: ***Worse.***

D: ***I'm sorry.***

K: ***Thanks.***

D: ***Want some company?***

K: ***You're sweet but I'm already in my jammies.***

D: ***You know that's not a problem for me (insert lecherous chortle here)***

K: ***LOL I do know! But I'm wiped. Just can't drag my butt out again.***

D: ***Well, if the butt won't come to Muhammad, then Muhammad must go to the butt…***

K: ***Dude, that's just wrong.***

D: ***No, actually, it's absolutely right. I'm standing outside of your building.***

K: ***Stop teasing!***

D: ***Not teasing. And it's freezing out here! How about buzzing me up?***

K: ***What? No! You can't just show up!***

D: ***Why not? You did it to me, didn't you?***

D: ***K? You there?***

D: ***What are you doing?***

K: ***Sorry, had to get my dirty clothes off the floor.***

D: ***Stop cleaning and let me in already!***

K: ***Fine. I'm up on the third floor, number 304. Watch out for Clinton.***

D: ***Clinton?***

K: ***You'll see.***

Chapter Thirty-Three

Drew

It's so cold that I'm hopping from foot to foot, when she finally buzzes me in. The vestibule is dark, with one of those dim, flickering fluorescent light fixtures that makes that maddening hum. The linoleum floor is yellowed and a little too sticky for my taste. And there's a smell that I think I can place, but would rather not.

I'm just about to start my climb to the third floor when I notice one of the apartment doors open a crack. An elderly gentleman peers out at me suspiciously.

"Good evening, sir," I say with a nod in his direction.

"You got business here?"

"Uh, yes sir. I'm visiting someone on the third floor," I confirm.

Suddenly his door swings open and he's waving a very big, very solid, wood baseball bat at me. "You'd better be! I find out you been making trouble up there and you're goin' to wish you'd worn a football helmet out tonight, you sombitch!"

Ah. Clinton, I presume.

"Yes sir. I understand. I swear I won't be making any trouble."

He gives me the hairy eyeball and slams the door shut so hard I can feel the vibrations on the stairs. I start moving before he has a chance to reconsider.

With my arms full and no elevator, it takes a few minutes for me to actually get to her front door, which opens just as I raise my hand to knock. Katherine is standing there in an oversize plaid nightshirt that hangs down to her thighs. It reminds me of the way she looked in my shirt not so long ago. Damn this girl's got legs. For. Days. I wrest my eyes from them and when I do, my lust turns cold with concern.

There are dark circles under her eyes—which are rimmed in red, as if she's been crying. She offers me an unenthusiastic smile as she holds the door open for me. I'm immediately struck by the size of the apartment. There isn't any. The room, probably in the neighborhood of twenty-five by twenty-five, contains the very barest of essential elements.

In one corner is a tiny kitchenette with a pint-size refrigerator, a two-burner stove, small sink, and microwave. Just in front of it sits a two-top bistro table and a pair of chairs. Bookcases line two of the four walls. They're crammed with books and scores, and one shelf holds a micro sound system and small flat-screen television. A third wall is taken up by a full wall of floor-to-ceiling windows, and the other with the front door as well as two other doors, which I imagine lead to a bathroom and perhaps a closet. In the middle of the room is an open sleeper sofa, the covers pulled back as if I've gotten her out of bed. A narrow coffee table sits in front of it, littered with pages of manuscript paper, pencils, and scores for symphonies and concertos.

I leave my shopping bag on the floor next to the front door while I drop the take-out bags on the two feet of counter space between her stovetop and sink.

"Sorry, if I'd known you were coming I'd have straightened the place up a bit," she says, looking around the room.

I nod toward the huge windows. "I'll bet *that's* what sold you on this place." I watch as her expression lightens considerably. "The view must be spectacular in the daytime."

Katherine nods enthusiastically. "I know it's a crappy apartment, but that view…it's like being closer to heaven, Drew. It's more stunning than you can imagine," she says wistfully.

I walk up to her and put my arms around her waist. "I'd say I'm sorry to show up without calling first, but that would be a lie. I was afraid if I called, you'd tell me not to come. I didn't want to hear that."

"You're right. I would have told you not to come," she confirms with a sigh. "It's been a long, hard day, capped off by a long, depressing night."

"Well, the night's not over yet," I inform her, taking her by the hand and escorting her to the small dining table. I pull a chair out for her and she sinks into it. "I thought you might need a little moral support after seeing your father. I also had a feeling that you might not have made it through your meal, so I picked up some dinner for us."

She looks at the grease-stained paper bags and then back to me. "God, you're sweet," she murmurs appreciatively. "And you're right. It was awful, Drew. He didn't come because he wanted to see me. He came because he wants me to pose as the devoted daughter on the campaign trail. He even offered to buy me a condo."

"Oh, well, if he offered you a condo…" I tease with a grin, slipping into the other chair. She swats me playfully.

"I don't know what I was expecting. Something different, I suppose. But he doesn't change. It's all about appearances. And, now that he might be trying for the presidency, he's afraid someone will come snooping around and find out that I live in squalor and servitude."

"Please, tell me he did *not* say that to you."

I get a rueful grin from her. "He might as well have. He commented on my 'ramshackle' little apartment and my job as a 'common maid.' And you know, it's not like he didn't work his way up. My father wasn't born wealthy, so he knows what it's like to be starting out."

"Yeah, but 'starting out' as a nobody and 'starting out' as the daughter of a prominent politician are two totally different things, Katherine. It's like you told me the other night. It's not the truth that matters, it's what people perceive to be the truth."

"Well, in this particular case, I'm pretty sure they're the same thing," she mutters. "He doesn't want people to realize that I'm out on my own with no support from him. It won't look good, considering the amount of money he has."

"Maybe he should have thought of how it would look before he cut you off," I scoff.

Katherine sighs and shrugs at the same time. "So, what've you got over there?" she asks with a chin nod toward the counter. "'Cause it smells really good."

She wants to get off the subject, and I can't say as I blame her. I'm only too happy to find other things to distract her attention.

"For you, Katherine, it's only the best that Mr. Lu's has to offer. I've got wonton soup, pepper steak, sweet and sour chicken, and fried rice."

"Oh, yum!" she murmurs appreciatively, getting to her feet again. "Let me get us some plates." She stops short when she catches sight of the shopping bag I've parked next to her front door. The one with the big, silver-wrapped present sticking out of it.

"What's with *that*?"

"What does it look like? It's a present."

"For who?"

"For you. Who else would it be for?" I laugh. She doesn't.

"I can't," she says firmly, shaking her head. "I'm sorry, I can't accept it."

"Why not?" I ask, getting to my feet again.

"You know why," she says softly. "You're my professor. I'm your student."

"How can you turn it down before you even know what it is?"

She shakes her head again. "No. I'm sorry, I can't."

"You can," I insist, pulling the unwieldy box from the bag then setting it on the bistro table.

"No."

I roll my eyes at her. "Why do you have to make everything so difficult?"

"I don't *make* anything difficult. Things just *are* difficult. Ironically enough, once I embraced that truth, things got a little *less* difficult."

"Well that's a bit jaded, isn't it?" I accuse.

"I prefer to see it as being a realist."

"Katherine, please open the box."

"Drew…"

"When was the last time anyone gave you a present?"

She doesn't respond.

"Katherine?"

She shrugs. "I don't know. It's been awhile."

"How long?" I press.

"Years," is all she'll admit.

"You're kidding me," I say in disbelief. "No birthday presents?"

She shakes her head silently.

"Nothing when you graduated with your bachelor's?"

This time she just looks down at the floor.

"Christmas? Katherine, tell me he at least sent you a Christmas card."

But, clearly, she can't tell me that. "Drew, you don't understand. It's just the way it is. This," she says, gesturing to her modest surroundings, "this is my life. I've gotten used to being on my own and I like it."

I feel my features softening. Hers, however, are going in the opposite direction.

"Stop it!" she says so harshly that I start.

"What? What did I do?" I hold up my hands defensively, trying to figure how I could have possibly pissed her off by bringing her dinner and a gift. But, as it turns out, that's not what she's pissed about. It's the meaning *behind* the dinner and the gift. And the meaning behind my expression.

"Stop looking at me like you feel sorry for me!" she snaps. "I'm happy. I'm independent. I don't need *anyone* feeling sorry for me. Christ, Drew, up until last month, you could barely hide your repulsion when you looked at me. Sometimes I think I preferred that, actually." She mutters the last bit so softly that I'm not sure I was meant to hear it. But I did.

I stand up and close the distance between us in a single heartbeat, putting my hands on her shoulders so she has to look up into my face. My very serious face.

"I don't pity you, I'm in *awe* of you," I say slowly, softly. "Don't you *ever* forget that. And you didn't repulse me, Katherine, you attracted me. I just—I just didn't know how to face it. My real feelings scared the hell out of me."

"Don't say that."

"Open the present. Please."

I can already tell I've won this particular battle. She rolls her eyes at me. "Fine. If I do, can we be done with this conversation?"

"Sure, I'll agree to that," I say, delivering a kiss to the top of her head.

She examines the shiny package suspiciously.

"It's not a bomb." I snicker, but she ignores me, taking her time.

At last, she leans over the big box, pulling gently at the huge blue bow. After that, she starts to separate the wrapping paper from the tape so she can pull it off without ripping it.

"What are you doing?" I laugh.

"I'm doing what you asked. I'm opening the present."

"That's not how you open a present. You've got to get in there and rrrrip it off!" I make a move to yank on a seam but she swats my hand away.

"Hey! *My* present, right? I can open it with my teeth if I want!"

A smirk crosses my face. "Now *that* I'd like to see."

She blushes at my implication and starts to say something, but thinks better of it and returns to opening the gift. Once the paper is off, she grabs it from either side and gently lifts the box, shaking slightly so that the bottom will fall away from the lid. After a couple of seconds, it obliges her by dropping onto the tabletop with a puff of tissue paper.

She glances up at me and I nod for her to continue. Slowly, she peels the gauzy layers apart and gazes down at the material. It's darker than baby blue, but lighter than navy and softer than cobalt. Cornflower blue, that's what the saleslady at the fancy store in Charlotte told me.

"Oh my God." She gasps softly, pulling the parka all the way out and holding it up so that it hangs its entire length.

"You like it?"

She looks up at me like I've just asked her if she'd like a million dollars.

"Like it? I love it! Drew, it's perfect! Look at the length! It's just long enough to cover my butt and thighs," she informs me as she smooths the length of the coat. Then she turns it sideways and slips her hands into the pockets. "And I love that the pockets are deep enough for me to stuff my hands into…"

"No."

"No, what?"

"No, you're not going to put your hands in the pockets."

She's looking at me like I have three heads. "What are you talking about? How else am I supposed to keep my hands warm?"

"Look in the box," I suggest.

She moves the tissue paper around to reveal a pair of matching gloves. And hat. And a scarf with big blue and white snowflakes.

Katherine's face tightens with growing alarm.

"Hey," I say, my voice full of soft concern. "What's wrong? Don't you like it? I can return it."

"What?" she asks, looking confused for a second. "Oh, no, I love it. It's just that I—it's so nice, is all. And I know this store." She gestures toward the logo on the lid of the glossy black box. "It's expensive. I can't really afford to pay you back or anything," she mumbles, looking down at the floor as she speaks.

"It's a *gift*," I remind her. "A gift. That's it. No strings attached. Honestly, it's just that I hate that goddamn hoodie you keep wearing," I chuckle, standing up and taking the coat from her. I hold it up and open for her.

"Here, try it on."

Reluctantly, she turns around and slips her arms into each sleeve as I hold them up for her. Her eyes are drawn downward as I squat and fasten the zipper at the bottom, following all the way upward as I pull the zipper closed, until our eyes lock. I reach around behind her and pull the faux-fur trimmed hood up, then I stand back so I can survey her with a critical eye.

"Well?" she asks with the most naively sexy smile I've ever seen.

"Well, I think you should only ever wear this color," I say, my voice suddenly husky.

When my lips find hers, they are soft and tentative. When she doesn't push me away, they become more confident. I'm taller than her by a good six inches and she tips her face up, causing the blue hood to slip back off her head. And then my hands are in her hair and holding the sides of her face, pulling her into me. She doesn't resist.

My lips are still connected to hers when I reach between us to unzip the coat, pushing it off her shoulders so that it hits the floor with a soft puff.

I'm walking her back toward her bed, but she doesn't seem to notice as her hands tug at my shirt, trying to free it from the waistband of my pants. When she succeeds, I hold my arms up and help her to pull the garment over my head. It joins the coat on the floor. My pants follow close behind.

"Wait," she says, pulling back for a second.

"What? What's wrong?" I ask between ragged breaths.

She gives me a mischievous smile before clapping her hands twice. As soon as she does, the lights go out, leaving us with only the glow of the moon to see one another by. I chuckle and shake my head, pulling her in close again.

"Oh Christ, I want you, Katherine," I murmur against her neck as I kiss the hollow of her shoulder.

"Then what are you waiting for?" she rasps.

Nothing. Absolutely nothing. I have no intention of waiting a single second longer to be with this woman.

Chapter Thirty-Four

Kate

We're lying on our sides, facing one another when he puts his palm to my face. It's on my cheek, his thumb rubbing back and forth against the bone that runs below my eye. I am riveted, unable to tear my gaze from his face as he touches mine. Then it comes. The moment when I can't wait a single second longer. I reach down with both hands and pull my nightshirt over my head and then immediately press forward. I want desperately to know what his chest feels like against my nipples. I gasp loudly, arching my back with the sensation, unable to keep from rubbing my breasts against him.

Drew groans as he leans forward and claims my mouth with his own. His lips are soft. So much softer than I could have ever imagined. But as our urgency begins to take hold, they become strong and unyielding. His right hand supports the back of my head and holds me tight against him while his left continues mapping the geography of my body. My face. My shoulders. My neck. My back.

Then, he pulls his mouth from mine to deliver a series of tiny kisses across my face. My eyelids, the tip of my nose, my cheeks. I'm giggling until he gets to the spot behind my ear and then I'm moaning. This has, in the blink of an eye, become something different. It's not about sex or no sex. It's about chemistry or no chemistry. And I'll be damned if we don't have amazing, blazing, off-the-charts chemistry.

Even though we're well on our way, I can see that he's reluctant to be the one who takes it past the point of no return. No problem. I'll be the one. I'll be whatever I have to be to feel him touching my body. With his mouth still attached to my shoulder, I take both of his hands into both of mine and place them on my breasts.

"Oh. Oh God, Katherine," he murmurs appreciatively as his thumbs begin to circle my nipples.

Somehow, his lips are on mine again. I whimper as I open my mouth to him hungrily. Yes, it's as if we are starving for this. For each other. I'm not sure exactly how he ends up on top of me, but once I'm flat on my back, he settles himself between my thighs. His warm hands on my hips, my rib cage and back to my breasts again. I can feel his hardness resting against my belly.

"Drew?" I whisper into the darkness. "Do you have…?"

In a flash he's off of me, hanging over the edge of the mattress. It sounds as if he's scrambling for his jeans. I know when he's found what he's looking for, because I can hear the sound of ripping foil. It doesn't take long for the boxers to come off and for it to go on.

I gasp, when he returns to his prior position, my head straining backward against the bed pillow. He takes advantage of the position to start kissing down the column of my throat.

"Jesus," he murmurs. "You are so beautiful."

I freeze, sucking in my breath.

Drew senses the sudden tension in me and he stops all

movement.

"What?" he asks. "What is it? Do you want to stop? Did I do something wrong?"

I shake my head slowly.

"No, no, no. It's just that no one's ever…"

I can't even get the sentence out before he's propped up on his elbows, looking down at me. Even in the moonlight I can see perfectly the mixture of concern and horror on his face. What the hell did I do to make him look at me like *that*?

"Katherine," he says in a voice that's both soft and… what? Frightened. "You're not…you're not a *virgin*, are you?" he asks in a whisper. "I mean, I don't think I can… I'm not sure that…"

I burst into a fit of laughter.

"What? Why are you laughing? This isn't funny," he insists, his dark eyes flashing. But his confusion and subsequent irritation just make me laugh harder.

"It is," I howl, overtaken by a spell of silliness. "It *is* funny!"

But Drew does not look amused, so I try to get myself under control, taking a few deep breaths, wiping the tears of laughter from my cheeks, and meeting his gaze squarely.

"No," I say, putting a hand to his cheek. "No, I'm not a virgin."

"Then what? What is it?"

I give him a bittersweet smile as I reach up and stroke the hair from his forehead. "It's just that no one's ever said that to me before. That I'm beautiful, I mean. I've never thought I was and then, to hear it from you, of all people…"

And then his mouth is so close to mine that I can practically taste his sweet breath.

"Then everyone else is blind, Katherine, because you are stunning," he says, putting his forehead against mine. "I've always thought so. Since the first time I laid eyes on you."

My turn to be shocked. I open my mouth to say something about this confession, but his lips are back on mine and all thought flies out the window. His hands are roaming more assuredly now, his palms running up and down the length of my body from my shoulders down to my hips.

I'm both surprised and excited when he reaches down, his thumbs hooking into the waistband of my panties. I arch slightly so he can pull them down my thighs, past my knees, and over my calves until there is nothing between his hands and my skin.

I didn't lie about not being a virgin, though, I might as well be. I'm afraid that if I tell him that the sum of my experience is a few sticky, unsatisfactory fumblings in the back of my high school boyfriend's SUV, he might put the brakes on, and fast. I don't say a word. Because the last thing I want him to do as he's kissing his way down my body is to stop.

"Oh. Oh my God," I murmur on an exhalation when his mouth finds my right breast. His tongue swirls gently around my nipple until, without warning, he takes it into this mouth and suckles. "Ohhh, Drew," I moan.

My breath is coming fast and shallow now as his right hand snakes in between our two bodies. I know where he's headed and the mere thought of it sends a surge of wetness between my thighs. His mouth has moved from my breast, back up to the crook of my neck at the same time I feel his fingers tracing a slow, tantalizing line along the outside of my sex. It's maddening. I shift a little, trying to entice him further, but he just snickers softly into my neck.

"Uh-uh-uhhh, Miss Brenner. Not so fast," he whispers, his tongue finding the shell of my ear.

And still, the maddening movements around and outside and along the edge until…

"Oh! Oh, Jesus!" I gasp loudly as his finger dips unexpectedly into my folds. I arch upward involuntarily, but his hard chest presses me back down into the mattress at the same instant he finds my clit.

I lose all sense of myself. His soft, slow ministrations become the center of my universe. Slow. Slow. Maddeningly slow. He rubs and swirls until I can hear my own wetness. I'm whimpering and he's nibbling on my neck. My hands are clutching his shoulders with a white-knuckled grip that will most certainly leave bruises. Just when I think I'm going to lose my mind, his clever fingers take on a faster, firmer motion that makes me cry out and arch once again. His mouth covers mine, swallowing my cries as he rubs me harder.

And then, it's as if the entire world explodes around me. A pressure from deep within my core rises and releases in a single flash so intense that my vision actually darkens for a second.

Now I understand.

Chapter Thirty-Five

Drew

She is the most responsive woman I have ever been in bed with. Her body reacts to my every breath and my every touch, and it's so sexy I can hardly control myself. And yet, somehow, I know she hasn't had much experience. Or, at the very least, not much satisfying experience. And when I feel her spasm against the touch of my hand, the intensity of her body, the surprised cry, and her expression of dazed amazement all tell me this was her first orgasm.

Well, I'm going to make damn sure it's not her last. She's barely come back to earth when I pull myself up between her thighs, align myself with her entrance, and push myself in with a single thrust. She's unbelievably tight, but she seems to yield to my presence inch by glorious inch.

She gasps and wraps her legs around my waist, drawing me farther into her than I thought possible.

"Katherine, you feel so amazing," I murmur as I begin to rock slowly, back and forth, back and forth.

Her clear, dark-blue eyes are wide and fixed on mine, her beautiful, soft pink mouth slightly slack.

"Drew," she whispers, "I had no idea anything could feel this good."

A garbled cry interrupts her words as I pick up the pace and thrust more assuredly. It's like I was born to be connected to this woman. I can't even speak. I can only gaze down and watch as her forehead wrinkles and her eyes close, as if she's in deep concentration.

Things are happening fast and I can already tell I don't have much time here. I reach down between our bodies, finding her slickness and rubbing her swollen clit with my thumb. She gasps so loudly I think maybe I've hurt her for a second, but then she's murmuring my name over and over, her head thrashing from side to side on the pillow. When I feel her nails rake down my back, I thrust harder still. Suddenly Katherine's eyes fly open and she screams as she comes.

The feel of her tightening, fluttering, spasming around me is more than I can bear.

I explode and it's like nothing I've ever experienced before. The intensity leaves me panting as I collapse atop her, brushing her face with my lips and feeling my heart beat against her chest.

Chapter Thirty-Six

Kate

I'm lying, head nestled into the crook of his arm, my left leg slung over his, my hand resting lightly on his chest. We've been quiet for a while now, lapsing in and out of light slumber, each of us processing what's happened in our own way. Finally, he's the one to break the silence.

"Regrets?"

"None," I say, not needing a single second to consider my answer. "You?"

"None," he echoes. And then he chuckles, filling my ears with the rich sound as it reverberates through his chest wall. "But, you know…"

"Yeah, I know."

"What?" he asks sitting up a little to get a better look at my face. "What do you think I was about to say, Miss Smartypants?"

"Okay, well, first of all, I don't seem to be wearing any pants, smart or otherwise." I giggle for just a second but then make myself sober up so he knows that I get what he's saying. "You're going to tell me that this can't happen again."

His brows arch in surprise. "Exactly. But not forever. I mean, not unless you don't want to…"

"Oh, I want to," I inform him with an enthusiastic nod.

"Good." He smiles down at me. "That's really good."

Before I can stop myself, I'm blurting out the question that's niggling at the back of my mind.

"Did you mean it? When you said I'm beautiful?" I feel a little needy and a lot embarrassed for asking. "Or was that just—you know—one of those 'heat of the moment' things that guys say?"

He shifts his head so that he's looking up and out through the window, where the outline of mountains is just visible against the clear night sky.

"Always," he says after a long beat. "I've always thought you were beautiful. Since the first time I laid eyes on you."

His words are soft and thoughtful. And I promptly ruin them by snorting. Loudly.

"Oh, *please*. You did nothing but scowl at me that first day of freshman theory."

"That wasn't the first time I saw you." He grins down at me.

I sit up on the bed so I can get a better look at his face.

"No? Then when?"

"It was the night *before* that. I was working late in the office, preparing for *my* first day of classes at Shepherd. It was after eleven and, as I was leaving the building, I heard this music. I followed the sound to the practice rooms and found you holed up in one, playing the piano. Your eyes were closed. There wasn't any music on the stand. You were just playing. And you were stunning."

"Huh," I say thoughtfully. Too thoughtfully.

Drew looks down at me. "What are you huh-ing about?"

I shrug. "I don't know, I guess I just never pictured you as the stalkery type," I say with a big, cheesy grin. "Did you snap a picture with your phone, too?"

Before I can finish my teasing, he grabs me by the waist and flips me on my back, reversing our positions in a flash.

"Hey, I thought we just agreed no more hanky-panky," I protest, laughing.

"We did. After today," he says, leaning down to kiss the spot behind my left ear. "I mean, as far as abstinence goes, we've already blown this day."

"Well, I can't argue with that logic," I say with a giggle that quickly morphs into a gasp as he shifts and nibbles his way down to my belly. "But it hasn't been that long. Are you telling me you're already good to go…again?"

Not that I know a ton about these things, but I do seem to recall there being a shelf life on my last lover's erections.

"Oh, I don't need to be ready for what I'm about to do to you," he says, looking up at me with a wicked grin that sends a delicious jolt right to my core. I don't mention that this will be yet another first as he kisses around my belly button and moves southward.

When he gets to his destination, he pulls my thighs apart gently, nudging his shoulders under the bend in my knees. I feel his warm breath on my thighs as he kisses first one side, then the other. I'm coiled tight in anticipation of what's to come, feeling thrilled and embarrassed at the same time. But my insecurities are gone with a single stroke of his tongue against my center.

Oh my dear good God.

All at once I gasp, ball the sheets in my hands, curl my toes, throw my head back, and stiffen from my hips up. And that's just the first lick. By the time he's taken me in his mouth, alternating sucking with tonguing, I'm certain I'm going to go out of my mind with the overwhelming sensation.

He is so good. It's like he knows instinctively where, when, how hard, and how fast. I am writhing underneath him when I feel a long, strong finger breach me, curling inward to hit a spot inside that makes me—

"Drew!" I yell, arching my back and thrusting my fingers into his thick hair. "Oh, Jesus, Drew…I can't…I think…"

He pulls his mouth from my body just long enough to utter his demands in a harsh whisper.

"Come for me, Katherine. Let me feel you come. Let me hear you come."

His commanding tone is so incredibly hot. And his words, in combination with his tongue and fingers, are more than enough to push me right over that invisible edge.

When the world splinters, shatters, and rains down around me, I know with absolute certainty that I will only ever be his.

• • •

SUNDAY APRIL 9TH 11:30 P.M.

D: ***I wish you were here. With me. In my bed.***

K: ***Me, too.***

D: ***God, I don't know how I'm going to get through class tomorrow without kissing you senseless.***

K: ***Don't you dare, Dr. D! You know the rules. No special treatment. Senseless kissing definitely falls into the category.***

D: ***What if I kissed Evan first? Then it wouldn't be 'special' treatment.***

K: ***Evan the bassoonist? I thought you didn't like the scruffy goatee thing.***

D: ***I don't. But I'd make an exception if it meant I could taste your mouth again…***

K: ***TASTE MY MOUTH? That sounds really gross!***

D: ***Oh, but I assure you, it's not gross at all. Maybe we should get together so I can show you…***

K:***Nice try, Romeo. Keep your ass off my balcony, please.***

• • •

TUESDAY APRIL 11TH 12:42 P.M.

K: ***SOS! May Day! Hellllllp! I'm trapped in Tessa Morgan's office!***

Chapter Thirty-Seven

Drew

I'm juggling Italian subs, chips, and drinks when I get to Tessa's office. But I've done this dance a time or two and I've got a system in place that involves nudging the door open with my elbow, catching it with my foot, and squeezing through before it can slam in my face.

"Ugh. You would not believe the morning I've had…" I'm saying when I come across the threshold. But when the door swings all the way open, I stop dead in my tracks. Katherine is sitting in the chair across from Tessa. She looks up at me helplessly.

"Oh, I'm sorry to interrupt…" I mutter and start to back out the way I came in.

"Drew? Wait, come back here," Tessa calls out.

I step back inside, plastering a pleasant expression on my face.

"Can you come in and sit down for a second?" She gestures toward the chair next to Katherine.

"Oh, well, you know, I really should go and…"

She raises a single eyebrow, daring me to finish that sentence. She knows full well I have no place to be but here, having lunch with her. The bag from SubPort is proof of that.

"Fine. Of course," I say gruffly, dropping lunch on the side table and taking the empty seat. Tessa smiles brightly at us from across her desk. I hate that smile. It's smug and condescending, and it's a clue that she's up to something.

Shit, shit, shit! It isn't possible that she knows about us, is it?

"Drew—rather, *Dr. Markham*," she corrects herself. "Kate stopped by to turn in her graduation paperwork. She's just informed me that she won't be needing any tickets to commencement."

"Oh, that's too bad," I say noncommittally, not sure where the hell Tessa's going with this. All I know is that Katherine looks as if she's praying for a sinkhole to open and swallow her whole.

"Yes, well, I was just saying that she really should speak with her father about attending. I'm sure we could arrange for extra tickets if he needs to travel with security, or an entourage…or even other politicians he might like to bring along."

Now I see what she's getting at. Tessa wants to take one last stab at getting into Katherine's business. I didn't much care before, but I do now. I clear my throat.

"Miss Brenner, I imagine you've already spoken with your father on this topic. And I would also imagine he's a very busy man…"

"He is, Dr. Markham," Kate agrees a little too enthusiastically. "He's a very busy man."

"But too busy to come to his only daughter's graduation? Surely he can find the time for something so momentous, Kate."

Tessa may be speaking to Katherine, but she's looking at me. She obviously wants me to try and intervene somehow.

Holy shit!

I bite my tongue to keep from snorting. This is hilarious. I feel like I'm in a Mozart opera.

"Well," I begin slowly, pretending to give the situation careful consideration. "I think you're right, Professor Morgan, in that we should offer Senator Brenner any accommodations that might make things easier and more secure if he were to attend commencement ceremonies. But, if I'm not mistaken, isn't that the week he's set to bring his big bill to the floor?"

I'm totally pulling this out of my ass. I have no idea when the jackass is going to try and convince his colleagues to pull funding from the arts, but mid-May sounds about as good a time as any. Katherine jumps onto my bald-faced lie as if it's a life raft at the scene of the *Titanic*.

"Oh yes, it is, Dr. Markham," she says, her expression morphing from agony to relief. "Professor Morgan, you are so incredibly thoughtful and I am going to make sure that my father knows how concerned you've been about this. I'm sure he'll be as grateful as I am."

Hah! That's my girl. In a matter of fifteen seconds she's extricated herself from this situation and made Tessa feel appreciated.

Fucking. Brilliant.

Tessa is beaming as Kate gets to her feet. "Please excuse me, I have a lesson to prepare for. But really, I'm very grateful, Professor Morgan." She turns in my direction and gives me a quick nod. "Dr. Markham," she says, her voice a little less friendly.

"Well, I'm here for you anytime, Kate," Tessa gushes. I'm about to breathe a sigh of relief when she speaks again. "Kate, I love that scarf with the snowflakes. Where on earth did you ever get that?"

Oh shit. Shit, shit, shit.

I didn't tell Katherine that Tessa recommended the store. If she tells her where it came from, Tessa's bound to put two and two together. And that's never a good thing. For anyone.

"Oh, thanks, Professor Morgan," Kate says, forcing a smile to her face. "I, uh—I got it from my father. Along with a beautiful coat. He noticed I didn't have one when he was on campus last week. Next thing I know, this one shows up. He's very thoughtful like that," she says, and I'm amazed she can keep a straight face.

"Of course he is. Please send him my warmest regards," Tessa croons.

"I will," Katherine assures her, turning to leave again. And, while Tessa can only see the back of her head at this point, I can see her face quite clearly.

"Oh. My. God!" Katherine mouths with huge eyes.

My sentiments, exactly.

• • •

The phone is ringing when I return to my office after lunch.

"Hello, Drew Markham's office," I say, slipping behind my desk and waking my computer from its nap.

"*Drew Markham's office*," the voice on the other end of the line mimics.

"*Who is this?*" I demand. After an hour of Tessa's nonsense, I am so not in the mood for a freshman prankster.

"Jesus Christ, Drew, what the fuck happened to *you*? Dude, it sounds like you've got a stick up your ass!"

Wait a minute… I know that voice.

"Danny?"

"Who else?" He chuckles.

"Oh my God! How are you, man? It's been too long! How's Vivica?"

"She's amazing, Drew. Marrying her was the best thing I've ever done. Nothing like the love of a good woman to keep you on the straight and narrow, you know?"

I do know.

"Oh, *fuck*." He groans from somewhere in New York City. "Goddammit! I am such an asshole. Drew, I'm so sorry. That was the most insensitive thing I could have said. Please forgive me, man…"

"No, no, no," I assure him, shaking my head as if he can see me through the phone line. "Nah, it's okay. I'm just happy that you two are doing so well. I was sorry not to see you over the holidays."

"Yeah, well, the Vienna Symphony New Year's Eve concert doesn't open up every day, you know."

"I know. I saw the broadcast on TV and you were amazing, Danny. Dude, you'll be replacing that has-been at the New York Symphony any day now." I grin.

"From your mouth to God's ears, my friend. But hey, enough about me. Let's talk about *me*."

"Oh yeah, cause that's something new…" I tease.

"Seriously, Vivica and I are actually in Charlotte visiting my folks."

"What?" I sit up straighter in my chair. "Why didn't you tell me you were coming?"

"I'm sorry, it was a last-minute thing. But hey, I was thinking maybe you could come down for a visit while we're here."

I'm about to tell him that there's no way I can get away, not right now. But then a thought occurs to me.

"Hey, Danny…"

"Uh-oh. I *know* that tone, Drew. What do you want to tell me?"

I take a deep breath, close my eyes, and leap—headlong—into the most terrifying disclosure I've ever made in my life.

"Danny, I've met someone…"

• • •

WEDNESDAY APRIL 26TH 4:04 P.M.

D: ***How you holding up?***

K: ***Meh***

D: ***You nervous?***

K: ***What do you think?***

D: ****SNORT* I think you're probably climbing the walls and I wish I could come and hold you.***

K: ***Me, too. Will you be there? In the auditorium?***

D: ***Would it make you feel better or worse do you think?***

K: ***Better. I think. Maybe. Possibly…***

D: ***If you want me to leave, why don't you give me a sign.***

K: ***Like what?***

D: ***Like…scratching your nose with your left hand.***

K: ***While hopping up and down, naked under a full moon?***

D: ***Oh, well, now, that I'd NEVER miss!***

K: ***I'll be fine.***

D: ***I know.***

K: ***I'm just a little bit terrified. First rehearsal with the "big boy" orchestra.***

D: ***Tonight it's a "big girl" orchestra! It's YOUR orchestra!***

K: ***Hmmmmmm***

K: ***Oh, hey, I almost forgot! Thanks for the care package! Very sweet but you didn't have to!***

D: ***What care package?***

K: ***Don't play coy with me, Dr. D!***

D: ***Seriously, K. I didn't send you a care package. What was in it?***

K: ***Really? You didn't? Then who the hell sent it?***

D: ***WHAT. WAS. IN. IT?***

K: ***It had ramen noodles, jars of peanut butter, instant coffee (blech!), and my fave candy combo, sour gummy peaches and choco-covered almonds.***

D: ***Ugh. That last one was a "blech" for me. No, I swear I didn't send it.***

K: ***Well who then? That's a little creepy.***

D: ***OH.***

K: ***Oh, what? Do you know?***

D: ***Yeah I think so.***

K: ***Christ, D, spit it out already!***

D: ***Your dad.***

K: ***What? Are you out of your mind?***

D: ***Who else knows about your crazy candy combo?***

D: ***K? You still there?***

K: ***Yeah, I'm here.***

D: ***You okay?***

K: ***I don't know. I think hell might've just frozen over.***

Chapter Thirty-Eight

Kate

"I can't do this," I say, pacing Russell's office.

"Hey, what happened to all that self-confidence I saw in your lesson?"

"It's dead, Russ. Flattened, stomped out. Didn't you read that article in the local paper?"

He scratches his snowy-white, scruffy stubble and considers me.

"I did."

Of course he did. Everyone did. The bastards insinuated I'm in total support of my father's politics because I met him for a "clandestine rendezvous" at the restaurant. They went on to call me a coward and accused me of not attending the town hall because I was afraid of facing my classmates and professors. One guy's blog actually *dared* me to stop hiding and make a public statement. To make matters worse, there are pictures of me coming out of the restaurant, head down guiltily. I look like a felon taking the perp walk.

"Hey, Kate! Stop daydreaming and focus," Russell orders loudly, snapping his fingers in front of my face. "You can't let this bullshit get to you or you'll *never* be a conductor."

"Yeah, well maybe that's not looking like such a bad idea right now," I mutter.

"Uh-uh, not on my watch. Put on your big girl panties and shake it off," he growls, grabbing my shoulders and giving me a hard shake. "You haven't done anything wrong. Not a damn thing. So cut the crap and let's get going before you're late to your first rehearsal."

My eyes latch onto his.

"Russ, what do I do if they won't play for me?"

"They'll play for you, Kate."

"But how do you know?"

"Because I know you."

I'm about to tell him how lame that answer is, but he holds up a finger for me to let him finish.

"Kate," he continues, "do you know what made me such a successful conductor?"

I shake my head no.

"Some conductors are hard-asses. They go in, expecting the orchestra to bow down before them, following every direction to the letter, never questioning his judgment. There are other conductors who come in all buddy-buddy, trying to be friends with the musicians. This almost always backfires because they have no respect for him when he does that.

"The orchestra wants a leader. Someone to look at the roadmap and guide them on their journey. You know, like one of those stupid ESP things."

It takes me a second to figure out what he's talking about.

"Do you mean a GPS?" I chuckle.

"Whatever. But here's the thing, they also want a human being. They want to know the reasoning behind your thinking and how it applies to them. These aren't children—even though they may act like it sometimes. You could easily be working with some of the most brilliant musical minds of the last century. It's all about mutual respect."

"Exactly. How can I expect them to respect me as a conductor, when they don't respect me as person?" I whine.

"Have faith, Kate. They'll come around. But you have got to get that balance right. I've had success because I've mastered the ratio of leadership to respect. You will, too."

I sigh and nod, not quite sure how I'm supposed to magically master this in the next five minutes.

"Hey, what about your guy?" he asks.

I freeze.

"What?"

"Oh, come on, Kate. I can tell you're still seeing someone. Is he coming to watch you conduct? Having him in the audience pulling for you might be just what you need."

Truthfully, I don't know if Drew will be there.

"Nah, he didn't want to make me nervous," I say at last.

"Yeah, well, that ship has sailed, wouldn't you say?"

"Hah! Are you kidding? It's halfway across the Atlantic by now!" I snort.

Russell picks up my score from his desk and hands it to me. He knows I don't need it since I've already memorized it. It's more of a safety net than anything else.

"Enough with the self-pity, my dear. It's time to do some conducting."

He opens the door for me and we slip out into the hallway. Every other time, Russell's office feels as if it's a mile away from the main building. Not tonight, though. It feels as if I'm walking into the concert hall in the blink of an eye.

"I'm going to watch from back here," he says, close to my ear. "I'll be here if you get into any trouble. Which you won't."

"Right," I say, sounding unconvinced.

The orchestra is already out on stage, noodling on their

instruments and chattering away. When the stage manager sees me, she signals the concertmistress who, in turn, signals the principal oboe to play an A so they can tune.

Russ takes a quick look around. When he's sure no one is paying attention, he leans down and gives me a quick peck on the cheek.

"Don't want to start any rumors about the two of us," he kids, trying to ease the tension a little. "That's the last thing you need right now."

Oh God. If he only knew.

Chapter Thirty-Nine

Drew

It's clear that she's in trouble from the second she sets foot on stage. There's no hiding anything under the harsh lights overhead and she looks so damn pale. Also, she's shaking. Shaking so hard that I can see her from where I'm standing in the wings on the other side of the stage. This is *not* good. Katherine steps up onto the podium, puts the score on the stand, and starts to riffle through the pages. She seems flustered as she flips from section to section, looking up nervously every once in a while.

"Uh, good evening, everyone," she says quietly.

No one replies. Not one person in the whole goddamned orchestra.

"I'm really happy to have the chance to conduct you," she starts to say after a long, awkward silence.

"Well that makes one of us!" someone calls out from the percussion section.

She glances in their direction, but chooses not to comment.

"Could we please start at the second movement? The Largo?"

Nobody moves.

Little shits!

It had been my intention to just sneak in here, watch her conduct a little, and then sneak out. I didn't want to let her know I'd be here because I didn't want her to be nervous. I'm rethinking that plan now as I pull out my phone and start to text.

You can do this. I'm right here in the wings watching you. And I am in AWE of you.

She jumps slightly, startled by the vibration of the phone in her pocket. She pulls it out and reads it, then puts the phone next to her score on the stand. She looks down, shifting nervously.

"What's the matter, Kate? Can't do anything without the TV cameras and reporters around to see you?"

That little catcall has come from a trumpeter. I recognize him from my junior Music Theory class.

Note to self: *Fail his ass.*

A month ago, I would have told you that I hate Katherine Brenner. But that's not how I feel today as I watch her onstage, the confidence leaching out of her with every passing second. I have a split second to make a decision here. She doesn't know I've done it. If I tell her, it might make things worse. Or, it might turn this thing around. Before I can talk myself out of it, I pick up my phone again and start to type quickly.

Danny Gillies is here. He came to see* you. *SHOW HIM, Katherine.

She leans over the stand to read the message when it appears on her screen. I watch as she stares at it for a few seconds, her eyes growing as big as saucers. She looks up slowly, scanning from stage left to stage right until her eyes finally land on me. Her brows go up in a question.

Are you serious? they're asking me.

I smile and nod my confirmation.

The transformation is instant. And it's breathtaking. Suddenly, Katherine Brenner is a little taller, her head a little higher. She's not shaking anymore and a peaceful expression passes across her face as she looks out over the musicians. *Her* musicians.

She leans over unexpectedly, loosens the laces on her shoes and kicks them to the stage floor. Her socks go right after them and she's barefoot on the conductor's podium. Some of the musicians are snickering at her, but she doesn't seem to notice them anymore. She simply takes a deep breath and flips the score closed.

"Let's start again, okay?" she suggests to them with a smile. Before they can answer, she does exactly that. "Good evening, everyone," she says in a steady, confident voice.

At least a few of them mumble return greetings this time around.

"Great. Okay, let's get started with the slow movement of the Dvořák, please."

I hold my breath for a split second, thinking they might not listen to her. But the orchestra players shuffle pages and find their spots. When they appear to be ready to play, Katherine raises her right hand and looks out over the group expectantly. I watch as she gives a quick nod and then her hand drifts into the slow downbeat that starts the ethereal opening chords of the symphony. A few bars in, she cues the English horn for its big solo, only to bring the rehearsal to a screeching halt a short time later.

"I'm sorry to stop you, Mike," she says to the soloist. She leans over the podium as if the extra six inches will put her right in front of him instead of a good fifteen feet away. She swallows hard and knits her brows together, looking like she's trying to figure out how to phrase something. When she speaks again, it's as if she's having a casual conversation with a friend.

"This solo is a lament and a victory at the same time. You know it's based on the spiritual 'Goin' Home,' right? Well, just imagine yourself the voice of someone singing that melody. You're preparing to depart this world, fully expecting something glorious to come. It's bittersweet. Sad to leave, but also *so* excited to arrive."

I can't help but notice that the whole ensemble has shifted slightly forward, drawn in by her words as she drapes herself casually over the podium.

"Mike," she continues, "I want you to make that horn sing. *Sing*, okay? We'll follow you, buddy. You just take it where you think it needs to go and we'll be there with you. Can you do that?"

I can see him nodding slowly, processing what she's just told him. She gives a quick nod, straightens up, and repeats the entrance. This time when the solo comes in, it's a little tentative for a moment. But only for a moment. As the English horn player gains his footing—and his confidence—the simple, haunting melody blossoms. I watch the corners of Katherine's mouth pull up in pleasure as her hand marks the beats for the rest of the orchestra. Mike stretches and pulls and wraps his fingers around the melody. When it's over, Katherine stops the orchestra. She looks at Mike, a huge smile spreading across her face.

"Ladies and gentleman, Michael Prate!" she says, holding her hand out toward him. The rest of the ensemble starts to applaud along with her. The musicians seated closest to him slap him on the back. When they've finished, they look back at her.

"You guys are *so* going to rock this." She grins. "We don't have a lot of time today, so let's table this movement for now and move on to the last movement. Allegro con fuoco. You all know what that means right? Fast—with *fire.* This thing is the big finale and it's got to be white-hot. So give it everything you have."

They can barely turn to the right page on their music stands before she's got her arms up, waiting for all eyes to train on her. As soon as she's got them where she wants them, she drops into the downbeat like a starter dropping the green flag in a race. And they're off!

This movement is intense from the first note, with the strings playing a melody reminiscent of the theme from *Jaws*. But then they collide with a wall of brass. Trumpets, trombones, French horns, and tuba are in lockstep as they thunder with a fanfare.

But the strings come back with a dizzying flurry underneath them. Each section is a piece of the puzzle—the strings have part of the melody, but it's not complete until it's accented by the horns. And on and on it goes, each piece snapping into place to create the big picture of sound. The winds and strings chase one another throughout, periodically punctuated by a hint of the fanfare, echoing the past and foreshadowing the future.

Through all of this, I cannot take my eyes off Katherine. As she conducts, she leans back so far that I find myself holding my breath, certain she's going to fall backward. But she doesn't. Somehow, she defies gravity. And her arms, the very definition of fluidity, don't seem to be privy to the same physical constraints as the rest of us. It's like a left brain/right brain thing in reverse. The right hand providing the structure, the direction for the musicians to follow while the left pulls the emotion from them.

Under her direction, fluttering winds and swirling strings

compete for attention until the fanfare comes back again. This time, it's bright, but solid. Chunky and drawn out against first the timpani rolls, and then a hard, accelerating beat by the rest of the orchestra. At some point every instrument, no matter what family it belongs to, is part of the percussion section.

Watching her conduct with her eyes closed, I realize now what a gift it must be for a conductor to have a—what did she call it? An *eidetic* memory. She throws cues to individual players and sections across the entire orchestra without even looking at them. But they're watching her. In fact, the entire orchestra is riveted, barely looking at the music on their stands as they play a piece they hadn't even realized they'd memorized.

The raucous fanfare is back now and Katherine's gestures are bigger and bolder. Her right hand moves in a broad, sweeping gesture that the musicians mirror in their playing. With her left hand, she shakes her fist in time with the timpani as it pounds and pounds and pounds. It is the heart of the orchestra. The heart of Dvořák's symphony.

Out of nowhere, everything slows and darkens into a twisted variation on the English horn's earlier solo, "Goin' Home." A phantom horn rises as the strings swirl up and up and up. And then, it's the fanfare in slow motion. The timpani rolls. And then it pounds. *Bang. Bang. Bang. Bang.* Like hammer blows that give way to a single, perfect ethereal chord that ends it all. Katherine does not drop her arms, nor do the musicians lower their instruments until the only thing left of the last note is its shadow.

When her arms finally relax, a slow, broad smile spreads across her sweaty, ecstatic face. Her eyes are still closed, so she doesn't see the orchestra musicians jump up in unison to applaud. The briefest hint of confusion passes as she processes what she's hearing. She opens her eyes, which immediately grow wide with shock. The orchestra is hooting and hollering.

The obnoxious trumpeter is whistling now and I decide to pardon his earlier infraction.

I'm so caught up in her—in her success and her beauty—in everything she does, that I can't keep my eyes off her. Nor can I control my crazy-stupid, lopsided grin as I applaud from backstage.

When I finally do tear my eyes away from Katherine, I happen to glance across the stage, to the wings on the other side. Russell Atherton is watching me intently. I slip back into my normal, impassive expression, as quickly as possible and nod a greeting at him. He doesn't return it. Probably because he's too busy trying to work out what he's just seen unfold between his prized pupil and his sworn enemy.

• • •

"Danny! I thought that was you!" Russell's voice booms above the noise of noodling instruments and chattering musicians.

Kate is going over a few notes with the concertmistress when he finds me out in the rows of seats talking with my old college roommate.

"Russ!" Danny exclaims, throwing his arms around the ghostly man and patting his back enthusiastically. "Where have you been hiding yourself? I thought you said you'd be at the conducting conference last fall."

"I didn't realize you two were in touch," I interject and am met with a withering glare from Russ.

"Do you think you're the only one who knows Danny?" he asks me coolly.

I ignore the comment.

"Russell, stop being an old coot," Danny teases, poking Russell in the ribs. "I was visiting my folks in Charlotte and Drew asked me to take a drive up here to…"

I catch his eye and shoot him a warning glare. Luckily, he

gets the idea before Russell notices.

"...to surprise you and Maureen," he concludes and I breathe a sigh of relief. If Russell thinks I brought Danny here to see Kate conduct, he'll know something's up between us.

Russ eyes me skeptically but decides to believe our guest. "Well, I'm glad to see you no matter what the reason," he says.

"Hey, Russ," Danny says softly, conspiratorially, "I see your fingerprints all over that girl." He's nodding with his chin toward Kate, who's still up on the stage. "She's something else, my friend."

Russell grins proudly. "She is, isn't she? Can you believe she was a piano major?"

"I know," Danny says, before he can stop himself.

Shit.

"You do?" Russell asks, suddenly confused. "How?"

"Drew told me." Danny sees his mistake immediately, but doesn't miss a beat. "I was just asking him about her. I was wondering why I knew her name but hadn't seen her come through the conservatory."

"Ah, well, she got in as a freshman pianist but it didn't work out. You know who she is?"

Danny nods. "I guessed, yeah. Why didn't she audition for me this year?"

Russell looks uncomfortable all of a sudden. "Well, it's not really my place—"

"He doesn't want to embarrass me by telling you that I didn't have the money for the application fee," comes Katherine's voice from behind us. All eyes swing to her. But she doesn't look embarrassed at all. In fact, she looks radiantly happy.

"He offered to lend it to me, but I wouldn't accept. I decided I'd come and conduct for you later this year after I've graduated from here and had some time to squirrel away a little cash. I was hoping to try for early admission," she explains.

"And you would be Kate," Danny says, taking one of her hands in both of his. "What a pleasure to meet you. Your conducting is"—he pauses, seeming to search for the right word—"a revelation."

She blushes from below her neckline all the way up to her forehead.

"Uh, well, thank you," she murmurs, suddenly bashful "It was quite an honor—and a surprise—to conduct for you."

"Miss Brenner," I say, turning on my coolest tone, "Dr. Gillies and I went to school together. He was visiting the area and asked to sit in on a rehearsal. I think you've made quite an impression on him."

Katherine looks at me and back at Danny before putting an arm on Russell's shoulder.

"I didn't realize you and Dr. Markham knew one another, but you should know that Russell has mentioned you many, many times."

Russ looks pleased to be back in the loop again.

"Well, Kate, I was very impressed by what I saw this evening. Both in your handling of a difficult situation and in your conducting. You can be sure I won't be forgetting your name once I get back home to New York and back to work at the conservatory. Now, if you'll excuse us, my old roommate here owes me a dinner before I head back down the mountain."

"I wish you'd just stay at my house," I mutter.

"Sorry, Drew. My mother's pancakes wait for no man. If I'm not there in the morning, I forfeit my stack. Russ, please give me a call when you're headed up to New York again, okay?"

"I will," Russell assures him with a smile. "It was good to see you, Danny. Drew," he acknowledges me with a curt nod. "Come, Kate. Let's go back to my office so I can give you some notes."

Katherine gives me a quick glance back over her shoulder as she follows him out of the concert hall, leaving me alone with my friend.

"Oh, Drew," Danny groans softly, shaking his head. "You are *so* fucked, man."

"I know, I told you. I just can't stay away from her. And my God, the way she conducts..."

Danny's shaking his head. "Not her, man. *Him*. Russell."

"Oh, he's just being a dick, as usual. He's like that all the time since Casey."

"Christ, Drew, get your head out of your ass! Russell was almost your *father-in-law.* You know him better than that. Dude, he knows *you* better than that."

My heart skips a beat. He's right. I can feel the horror etched on my face. It's reflected in the piteous way my old friend is looking at me.

"Drew, man, you do *not* have the luxury of thinking Russell Atherton is stupid. Or blind. He knows about you and Katherine Brenner. It's just a matter of time before he *realizes* that he knows."

And just like that, I hear the ticking of the time bomb as it starts its countdown toward inevitable destruction.

• • •

WEDNESDAY APRIL 26TH 9:22 P.M.

K: ***OMGOMGOMG! That was SO amazing! I can't believe you invited Danny Gillies to come and see me conduct! You sneaky bastard, you! I hope you boys are having some fun tonight. Please thank him again for me. I have to go back to Russell's office now so we can go over the video he took of me conducting and give me some notes before the next rehearsal. MY rehearsal! SQUEE!!!!! In less than a month I'm going to conduct in front of my biggest audience ever! You'd better be planning on coming, Dr. D! May 10th—the Wed before orals. Xoxo K.***

Chapter Forty

Kate

It's ten thirty by the time I get home from my post-rehearsal postmortem with Russell, and all the spots close to the apartment building are gone. But I don't mind. Between the conducting, Danny Gillies, and my toasty new blue parka, I'm lost in my own swirly, dreamy, happy place. I look up at the stars in the black sky and smile. I'm happy. And that's something I haven't been for a very long time.

I'm so caught up in my reverie, that I don't notice the shadowy figure ahead of me until I've walked right into him. Before I can recoil, he's locked his hands onto my upper arms, squeezing tightly. I can just make out the blue-green color of his eyes, though they don't look as bright in the dark.

"Kate, Kate, Katie Kate," Stalkerazzi Kevin sings cheerfully. "So nice to see you again! It's been awhile since our last date."

"Let go of me!" I spit at him, but he just sneers down at me.

"Oh, don't be like that, Kate. C'mon! I just thought I'd pay you a visit. Why don't you invite me up to your apartment? I was going to surprise you there, but for some reason my key doesn't work anymore. Did we change the locks, Katie?"

I force myself past the initial jolt of fear and try to pull away from him. But he's bigger and stronger and he just tightens his grip.

"Help!" I yell.

He pulls me close to him in an airtight embrace, putting his mouth to my ear when he speaks.

"Now, Kate, you don't want to cause a scene, do you? What would the papers say about a fleet of police cruisers in your parking lot? Come on, why don't we go on up to your apartment and have a chat? I'd just love to hear some of your personal thoughts on your father and his political views."

He lets go of me without warning and I'm so off-balance that I fall to the ground with a thud. I'm not hurt, just stunned. And really, really pissed.

"Did you just put your hands on me and—and *push* me?" I growl up at him incredulously.

"Nah, I think you're just clumsy." He grins. "But hey, look at you with a new winter coat. I'm sure it softened your landing. What happened? Did Daddy feel guilty when he saw you shivering outside of the restaurant last week?"

"I thought we agreed you weren't going to follow me anymore, you son of a bitch!"

"No, no, no, Katie! After our little encounter, I was even more intrigued by you. You're a tough cookie. I like tough, Kate. I like it very much," he says with a self-satisfied grin.

Son of a bitch. Time to wipe it right off his face. I lunge forward toward his shins and he falls backward, substantially harder than I did. I crawl out of his reach and scramble to my feet, already fishing for my cell phone. But it's not in my pocket.

"Looking for this?" he asks, producing the phone from *his* pocket.

Damn! He must have grabbed it when he was holding onto me just now.

"You're insane! You think you can just show up outside my building and threaten me? And for what? A sound bite?"

He sits up slowly, wincing with the effort. "Fuck! I think you fractured a vertebra!" he whines as he lumbers back up onto his feet.

"That's not all I'm going to fracture if you don't give me my phone back and get the hell out of here!"

"Yeah, right, Katie…"

Before he can finish his obnoxious thought, I move to kick him in the ribs. My mistake. He's totally expecting that. When he grabs my sneaker and pulls, I go down again, this time flat on my back. I hit the frozen ground with a grunt, even as he's getting up again. We've switched positions now, which might have been a bad thing, except for the fact that I can see what's behind him…and he can't.

"I reckon you might wanna rethink that," Clinton says, baseball bat leaning against his shoulder.

Kevin spins to the side and I see several expressions pass over his face. First, his mouth forms a surprised *O*. After that, his brows draw into an angry *V*. Finally, his mouth twists into a perfect *U* as he smiles at the old man standing there. I'm wondering what other letters he might be able to imitate when he swings around to face Clinton, who doesn't move so much as an inch. That is, until Stalkerazzi pulls back his arm to punch him. Apparently Clinton doesn't like that idea too much, because the bat shoots straight out like a bayonet, nailing Kevin in the chest. Hard. He doubles over and drops to his knees on the icy asphalt, the phone flying out of his hands.

"Katie, your phone fell over there on the sidewalk,"

Clinton says with a nod. "I'll keep an eye on this sombitch, you call the police."

Stunned by everything that's just transpired, I scramble up onto my feet again and retrieve my phone so I can dial nine-one-one on this creep. Again. Once that's done, I make the other call. The one I'm afraid to make because I know if I do, he'll freak. The one I'm afraid not to make, because I know if I don't, *I'll* freak.

Chapter Forty-One

Drew

She's waiting for me just inside the front door of her building when I pull up. She comes out and hops into the cab of my truck with a small gym bag over her shoulder. I pull the truck into an empty space, throw it into park, and pull her across the bench seat into my arms.

"Are you okay?"

She nods into my chest without looking up at me.

"Did he hurt you?"

I struggle to keep my voice even as I ask that question. She shakes her head no and snakes her arms around my waist to pull me closer. I rest my chin on top of her head.

"It's okay, Katherine. It's going to be okay."

When she finally looks up, her eyes are glittering with the tears she's fighting back.

"He ripped my new coat," she says in a miserable whisper. "I'm so sorry."

I smile and kiss her forehead.

"Not to worry. We'll get you another one. And we'll add Destruction of Property to the charges against the asshole."

This makes her smile, too.

"I see you packed a bag this time. Does that mean you don't want to sleep in my shirt?"

A hint of pink colors her cheeks.

"Funny," she says, "I seem to have forgotten to pack my pajamas…"

• • •

The fire is warm, the pillow is soft, and the music of Bach is filling my dreams. But somewhere from deep inside my slumber is the nagging sense in the back of my mind that I need to get up and check on Katherine. My eyes flutter open and I'm peering into the familiar glow of my fireplace. I'm wide awake now, I'm certain of it. And yet, somehow, the Bach from my dreams has spilled over into my reality.

Because I'm *not* dreaming it, I realize suddenly. I get off the couch where I seem to recall being with Katherine before we both passed out from exhaustion. When I turn around, I see her. But she doesn't seem to notice me as I move slowly in Bach's direction until I'm standing behind Katherine as she plays the piano. I don't let on that I'm there, I just stand in silence, in the shadows, where I can see her hands on the keyboard.

There's a famous scene in the old movie, *The Miracle Worker* in which teacher Anne Sullivan tries, with unrelenting persistence, to reach into the dark, silent world of Helen Keller. In one iconic scene, Anne spells the word "water," with her fingers, into Helen's hand. As she does this, she puts Helen's hand under the water, trying to get her to make the connection between it and the word being spelled into her hand over and over again. Those five letters cause an epiphany, an instant of understanding so explosive that it blows a hole through the previously-impenetrable wall of darkness and silence, bringing color to Helen's blind eyes and music to Helen's deaf ears.

As I stand here my mind recalls this image so clearly, with such potency, that it nearly knocks me off my feet. And I watch. Katherine is seated on the bench, eyes closed and head tilted back rapturously. The fingers of her left hand walk the easy distance between the bass notes while, on the right, they actually *spell* out a trill, a line, a slowly unraveling melody. Her wrists arch slightly, delicately as she lifts and relocates them again and again. The gentle motion across the octaves belies the strength and commitment of her fingers as they spell out the Aria from Bach's Goldberg Variations from memory.

In a single, earth-shattering beat, it's as if my world explodes, suddenly filled with the richest of sounds and the most vibrant of colors. Katherine Brenner has broken through a wall I hadn't even realized I'd erected. When her hands come to rest at the end of the Aria, she stops. As if sensing my gaze upon her, she opens her eyes to find me shocked and dazzled all at once.

I see the puzzlement in her eyes and she opens her mouth to speak, but I am sitting beside her on the bench before the words can slip free. Before I can stop myself from putting her face in my hands and drawing her lips to mine. She doesn't fight me. Instead, her arms wrap under my arms and up my back to my shoulders, pulling my chest so close to hers that I can feel her heart beating underneath the white cotton shirt that she's wearing. My shirt.

She tastes soft and sweet, her mouth opening hungrily to mine. I hear a soft whimper from her and I pull back just enough to get a good look at her face. Her eyes are half closed, her lips cherry red and glistening from our contact.

"Do you…do you want me to stop?" I ask in a whisper.

She shakes her head. "No. Please, don't," she says, leaning forward to find my lips again. I don't make her lean too far, pressing myself down to her while I reach behind and pull her closer.

Before I know what I'm doing, I'm on my feet and taking her with me. We're stuck together in a tangled, stumbling embrace as we somehow move from one end of the large room to the other. I grunt when my hip hits the sharp edge of an end table, and her wayward elbow knocks over a book that's balancing on the edge of a shelf.

"Oh, to hell with this," I mutter, suddenly bending down and scooping her up in my arms, the same way that I did when I carried her in from her car. But this time she's not fighting me. This time, she throws her head back and kicks her feet in joy.

• • •

"This is SO not how I imagined this night would turn out," I grumble while I search the closet for the comforter. I find it on the top shelf, all tucked away in its zip-up bag, where my mother put it on their visit last year.

"Hey, I love to be swept off my feet and carried up to bed as much as the next girl, but we've got to stick to the plan. See, not so much work," she adds, as we each take a side of the blue-and-white striped cover and snap it up into the air so it wafts down into place on the bed.

"I know it wasn't much work. I was just saying it would have been a lot less work if you'd sleep in my bed instead of in here," I reply grumpily.

Katherine stops and puts her hands on her incredibly sexy hips.

"Hey," she clucks at me. "What did I just say? You know the rules, Dr. Markham. No more hanky-panky till I've got that diploma in my hot little hand."

"I can think of a few other things I'd like to put in your hot little hand," I mutter and am rewarded with the *thwap!* of a pillow to the head. I give her a sheepish grin. "Can't blame a guy for trying."

I'm relieved to see her like this, decompressing instead of deconstructing. I was afraid her run-in with that creep journalist—not that he even deserves that title—would leave her a mess. And maybe she is a little shaken, but she seems to feel safe here with me. And I like that. A lot.

She sits down on the edge of the bed and surveys her surroundings.

"This is a really nice room."

"Thanks. It doesn't get used very often."

"I was surprised Danny Gillies wouldn't be using it tonight. Didn't you invite him to stay when you asked him to come and watch me conduct?" she asks pointedly.

Oh. So, I guess we're doing this now.

"I did offer. But you heard him, he has breakfast plans in the morning."

"Why did you ask him to come, Drew?"

The question isn't an accusation, so much as a curiosity and I'm relieved by that. I've been afraid she'd be angry that I took the liberty of asking my friend to come without consulting her first.

"You know why," I say quietly, holding her icy-blue gaze with my own. When she doesn't reply, I sit next to her on the mattress.

"He's a nice guy," she says at last.

"He is. And he was very taken with you."

"You mean because we're…together," she deduces. Incorrectly.

"No. Not because 'we're together.' Not because *we're* anything. You blew him away with your conducting. Hell,

Katherine, you blew me away with your conducting."

She looks at me out of the corner of her eye.

"Really? You swear?"

I wrap an arm around her and pull her to me, resting my chin atop her silky dark hair. It smells like lilacs today.

"I swear it. And I'm sorry, I should have asked you first. Honestly, I wasn't even going to tell you he was there. But you were struggling. I wasn't sure if knowing he was there would make things better or worse, but I rolled the dice. And it seems to have paid off."

She nods underneath my head and then, with absolutely no warning, Katherine hurls herself at me, knocking me flat on my back on the bed.

"Hey, what's up with that?" I laugh.

She climbs on top of my waist and straddles me, looking down with those enormous blue eyes and perfect porcelain skin. Her lashes must be more than an inch long.

She reaches down and puts a hand to my cheek.

"Thank you for tonight—for Danny. And thank you for coming to get me, Drew. I was really scared."

"I know. And you don't have to thank me. I'm just so relieved that the bastard didn't hurt you."

I feel my heart rate quicken with the thought of him touching her.

"I think he might have, if he'd had the chance," she admits quietly and I see now how scared she was.

"Katherine, why didn't you report him the first time, when he locked you in his car?"

Her turn to shrug.

"Because usually the threat of police is enough to scare them off. But this guy, he's more aggressive than most. The less-reputable guys often are, and they can get a little pushy. Physically, I mean. But I've never had any of them actually assault me physically like that before."

"Thank God for your neighbor."

"Yeah, thank God for crotchety old Clinton. And his baseball bat," she says, sounding suddenly exhausted and it occurs to me just how much she's been through today, good *and* bad.

I flip her over so she's underneath me, then place a chaste kiss on her forehead. "All right, Miss Brenner. To bed with you," I say, getting to my feet and crossing the room to the closet for an extra blanket. "It can get a little chilly up here on the north side of the house," I explain. "So keep this nearby, just in case…"

When I turn back, Katherine's eyes are closed and her chest is already rising and falling in a deep, steady rhythm. I put the blanket over her gently and press one more kiss to her cheek.

"Sweet dreams, Katherine," I whisper and leave the room silently, keeping the door open just an inch. Just in case.

• • •

MONDAY MAY 1ST 11:32 A.M.

K: ***OMG! Just heard from police. The attorney general is indicting Kevin K for assault. It's actually going to go to court!***

D: ***That's great!***

K: ***No, it's not.***

D: ***What? Why not?***

K: ***Because it's the last thing my father needs right now. As soon as my name is brought up they'll be all over him.***

D: ***What are you supposed to do? Just let him get away with it?***

K: ***No. But you don't understand…***

D: ***I do. This is about YOU not your father.***

K: ***Same difference. When I was in high school, I got***

busted with a fake ID at a bar.

D: ***What?! YOU! Miss Goody Two-Shoes??? Drinking underage? I'm shocked!***

K: ***Yeah, well that was back when I had friends. Someone recognized me and took a pic. Was in the paper the next morning. His popularity took a 5% nosedive when they accused me of being a spoiled "wild child" and him of being an absentee father.***

D: ***And what's all this got to do with now?***

K: ***He doesn't need another dip in the polls. Not if he's going to run for POTUS.***

D: ***You care too much, K.***

K: ***Yeah, it's a bad habit of mine.***

Chapter Forty-Two

Kate

"No, no, no!" Russell yells so loud that I jump, dropping my arms mid-Dvořák. I turn to face him.

"What? What did I do?" I ask, palms facing skyward. This is the third time he's stopped me in twenty minutes. I've seen him in a bad mood before, but this is the first time he's ever taken it out on me.

"That transition. You're missing it by at least half a beat, Kate," he calls out to me on the stage from where he's sitting out in the house seats. His arms are crossed and his snowy-white brows are drawn down in irritation.

I'm not missing anything. He knows it, and I know it. Time to figure out what the hell is going on once and for all. Still barefoot, I sit on the edge of the stage and slip off to the main floor three feet below. He doesn't move as I approach the middle row where he's seated. When I'm next to him, I sit down.

"What's up?" I ask quietly.

won't teach me anymore unless I break it off with you."

"Son of a bitch!" I hiss under my breath, pulling Katherine back to me.

I rub her back gently and am reminded of that first night. The night she was so sick.

"It's okay, Katherine. I'll talk to him."

She looks up, horror-stricken.

"What? No, Drew, he hates you! He was talking crazy, accusing you of driving his daughter to suicide."

"Oh, that again?" I say with a chuckle as I tuck a strand of hair behind her ear. "He's been saying that since the day she… well, since she's been gone. He needs to blame someone and he can't bring himself to blame Casey. So, I'm the next logical choice."

"But…"

"No, 'buts.' Come on, let's go upstairs. You don't have to work in the morning, do you?"

She shakes her head and I get to my feet, extending a hand to her. She accepts it and I hoist her up.

"Good. I'm off in the morning, too. We'll get you into a nice, hot bath and you can get some sleep. I promise I'll square this with him, okay?"

She nods but doesn't look at all convinced. Come to think of it, I'm not convinced, either.

• • •

If Russ is surprised when I throw open the door to his studio without knocking, he doesn't say.

"What the *fuck*, Russell?" I spit at him once I've closed the door behind me. "What's wrong with you?"

He gets up from his desk, standing just a few feet in front of me.

"This isn't about what's wrong with *me*. It's about what's wrong with you!"

"No, actually, this isn't about either of us, it's about Katherine. You really think it's fair to just drop her because she and I…because we…"

I don't know how to finish this sentence and I'm kicking myself for not thinking this through a little more before storming in here.

"Seems to me, Drew, that there's a provision in the handbook prohibiting relationships between students and professors. And, knowing my ex-wife the way I do, I suspect Maureen would have your goddamn head on a silver platter if she knew what was going on."

"But you're not going to tell her," I inform him.

He gives me a disbelieving grin.

"And why the hell wouldn't I, Drew? I could finally get you out of my life once and for all. No tenure. In fact, no job for poor Dr. Markham! And a big, black *X* on your record for indecent behavior with a student."

I take a step closer and poke his chest with my finger.

"You won't tell anyone about this because it will destroy Katherine," I say flatly.

He sucks in his scrawny chest, eyes blazing.

"Keep your goddamn hands off me, Drew. You know I'll kick your ass from here into next Tuesday," he hisses.

The truth is that he probably could. Russell's much stronger than he looks. I know this because we've tussled before, over Casey. But this time I stand my ground, folding my arms across my chest and raising a questioning eyebrow.

After a very long, very heated minute, his face relaxes a fraction and I sigh with relief in my head.

"What are you doing with her?" he asks in a low, gravelly voice. "Are you just using her to get to me? To torture me again?"

Unbelievable.

I sigh again, out loud this time, and take a step back from the man who was almost my father-in-law.

"I was wrong, Russ. This isn't about you or me *or* Katherine. It's about Casey."

He doesn't disagree, so I continue.

"No. I swear to you, on her grave, that I am not doing this to get back at you. Or to torture you. I think I love her, Russ," I mumble just loud enough so no one who might be lurking in the hallway might overhear us. "I didn't think I could. I mean, not after Casey. And, Christ! I tried not to. And I was almost home free. Almost. But now…I just want to be with her. We've only got to keep it under wraps until she graduates."

I can't tell what the hell is going through Russell's head. He might be plotting my death. Or, he might be planning our engagement party. You never know what *The Ghost* is going to do.

"All right."

"All right?"

"All right," he repeats.

"All right, *what*, Russ?"

"All right, I won't say anything about you two."

Oh, thank Christ…

"And Katherine?"

He looks down at the floor, clearly ashamed of his earlier behavior with her.

"I'll apologize," he says softly. And then, his head comes up and he meets my gaze squarely again. "Because I love her, too. Teaching Kate is what kept me sane after…after Casey."

I consider debating the meaning of the word "sane" as it pertains to him, but decide to keep my mouth shut.

"Russell, I've said this before but I want you to hear me this time. If I'd had *any* idea what Casey was thinking… She was the love of my life, Russell."

His translucent blue-white eyes bore into mine and I think, for a split second, that he just might spit on me. But he doesn't. Instead, this gruff, nasty, grumpy man starts to cry.

I'm more at a loss than I was when Katherine started to cry that first night at my house.

"Russ," I begin, and before I can stop myself, I've wrapped my arms around him. He doesn't fight me. Instead, he leans into my embrace, his hands balling the back of my shirt as he sobs inconsolably.

"I just—I just miss her so goddamned much."

I feel my own eyes start to water.

"I know," I whisper. "Me, too. If you only knew how many times I've gone over it in my head. I should have known. I should have seen something."

I push him away from me slightly so he can get a good look at my face when I say this.

"There was nothing, Russell. I swear. *Nothing*. She was too smart for all of us. She knew she couldn't give any of us a single clue because we were all watching her too closely."

He nods.

"I know that, Drew. I just—I wouldn't listen. Maureen warned me so many times and I didn't listen. Maybe if I'd listened..."

I shake my head.

"Man, there was nothing that could have stopped Casey when she set her mind to something. Not you, or me, or Maureen, or all of us combined. Maybe if we hadn't lost the baby. *Maybe*. But I'm not even sure about that Russell. Christ, I've never said this to anyone else, but I sometimes wonder if that wouldn't have made things worse. Postpartum depression and all that. Or maybe it would have saved her? I just don't know."

The tears are flowing freely down my face now, too. This time, he's the one to pull me into an embrace. And, for the first time in nearly six years, grief trumps blame.

• • •

WEDNESDAY MAY 3RD 5:16 P.M.

D: ***Come over.***

K: ***No.***

D: ***Why not?***

K: ***You know why not.***

D: ***What, you don't think I can be trusted to keep my hands to myself?***

K: ****SNORT****

D: ***I've a steak on the grill and two potatoes in the oven. There's a bottle of riesling chilling and I've even got an apple pie for later. With coffee. Real coffee. Not that instant shit your Secret Senator sent you.***

K: ***LMAO! All right, all right. But I'm not staying over.***

D: ***Bring your toothbrush and clothes for tomorrow anyway. Just in case.***

K: ***Just in case what? Another rogue blizzard comes our way?***

D: ***Stranger things have happened.***

K: ***Fine. Fine. But I've got to work in the morning so it can't be a late night. AND you know the rules about the other stuff.***

D: ***I do.***

K: ***And you plan to abide by them?***

K: ***D? You there?***

D: ***Just thinking.***

K: ***About what?***

D: ***Loopholes. For every rule there's always a loophole…***

K: ***Not this time, buddy :)***

D: ***Are you leaving now?***

K: ***No.***

D: ***Come on, don't back out!***

K: ***I'm not. I got in my car the second you mentioned steak. I'll be there in ten minutes and I expect to be greeted with a kiss at the front door.***

D: ***Just try and stop me!***

Chapter Forty-Four

Kate

When the clock strikes midnight on the worst day of your life, no one is there to warn you. It's not something you circle on your calendar. You don't get a heads-up or a reminder phone call or a *Save the Date!* postcard in the mail. And it sure as hell isn't as if you just wake up *knowing*.

I'm sure some people would say that's a good thing—that they'd rather not see it coming. I am not one of those people. I'd rather know. Because, the way I see it, the only thing worse than being blindsided, is looking up at the second of impact to see that someone you know is driving the car that's about to flatten your ass. Then, instead of all those happy memories and faces of loved ones that should be passing before your eyes, the only thing you can think is *'Dude! What the fuck?'*

"Have a good day," Drew mumbles from somewhere under the covers of the bed.

I bend over and kiss the back of his head.

"I'm sorry, I didn't mean to wake you," I whisper.

He rolls over and gives me a sleepy smile.

"Nah, I have to get up soon anyway. I have a meeting with Maureen this morning. She's going to have a look at my final presentation for the tenure committee."

"Oh! So, there might be something special to celebrate tonight," I say with a coy smile.

He reaches out and grabs me by the waist, dragging me back into bed with him.

"Drew!" I squeal as he manages to flip me over on my back and cage me in with his body.

"Ha! I've got you!" he proclaims triumphantly. "And I'm going to keep you here, with me, in this bed. All. Day. Long," he says, delivering a kiss between each of the last three words for emphasis.

"Oh no!" I say with false dismay. "Whatever will you do with me all day, you wicked, wicked man?"

"Wouldn't you just love to know," he murmurs, now kissing the spot behind my ear that makes my eyes roll back in my head.

"Jesus, Drew, that feels amazing…" I murmur and then pull away slightly to get a good look at him, all sleepy, sexy, and tussled. "Are you sure this is okay? I mean, I'm still a week away from orals and my conducting final. I'm not officially graduated yet, Dr. Drew…"

"I was thinking we could do a practice test."

"What? Ahhhhhh…" I can't even finish my thought when his mouth reaches where my neck meets my shoulder. Another "point of interest" along the map of my body that he's been drawing in his head. This guy doesn't miss an inch when it comes to my erogenous zones, tugging at the collar of my shirt so he can kiss my bare shoulder.

"Oh, please…" I murmur.

It's a plea for him to stop before it goes too far. At the same time, I want him to go so far that he *can't* stop. I'm clearly unclear on which outcome I want right now. Actually, that's not true. I know what outcome I *want.* I just don't think it's an outcome I can have and still get to work on time. But, when his warm hands find their way up and under the bottom of my blouse, I know that all hope is lost.

"Drew, you're going to make me late," I half whine, half groan when he pushes up the soft cups of my bra so he can get his hands on my breasts.

"You want me to stop?" he asks just as his tongue finds my belly button.

"Ugh, no. Please, don't stop..." I moan, getting his comment about an oral practice test.

He looks up at me just long enough to flash his self-satisfied grin, and then he's traveling to points southward, unzipping my jeans then easing them, along with my panties, down to just below my hips. I start to lift my backside so he can pull them all the way off, but he stops me.

"Uh-uh," he says, stopping the downward pull of my clothes when they're mid-thigh.

"But I can't really—you know—I can't..."

"Spread your legs?"

He seems to relish finishing the sentence for me. But before I can comment, I feel his hot, soft tongue dipping into my hot, soft folds.

An unintelligible gurgle comes out of my mouth, and I arch my back. I try to separate my thighs, but it's no use, they're held tight in their denim bindings. In the meantime, one of his hands is back on one of my breasts, reaching up to gently roll my nipple between his thumb and index finger.

He's doing a damn fine job of swirling, licking, and tracing every spot except for the one I'm silently begging him to touch. I'm on the very edge of my sanity as he comes close and pulls back again and again. The bastard knew exactly what he was doing when he pulled my pants only partially down my legs.

I can writhe under him as much as I want, but I have almost no room to maneuver myself. I cry out in frustration and hear him chuckling between my thighs.

"Please, Drew," I whimper from above him. "Please…"

My eyes fly open and I arch off the bed again when he sucks my most sensitive flesh into his mouth. He moves his other hand to my stomach, holding me down so I can't fight against the intense pleasure that's mounting faster than I can process it.

"Oh, Jesus, Drew!"

I'm practically wailing when he finally decides to put me out of my misery with tiny nibbles, making the world explode around me.

You wouldn't *think* this is how the worst day of your life would begin.

• • •

I may be late for work, but I'm happy when I get there. I grab an apron from the back and throw my hair up under my cap. I've got a smile for everyone I encounter. But it's still early yet. Things don't pick up until I've been there an hour or so. That's when I notice the strange looks I'm getting. I pop into the bathroom to make sure Drew didn't leave a huge hickey somewhere visible. Nope. Nothing out of the ordinary, so I must be imagining things.

When I get back out onto the floor, I spot them at their usual table. At least, it was their usual table until the whole coffee incident. Joanie, Ken, and company have been ducking me since then. Not today, though. Today, all four of them are sitting on the same side of the table, no one sitting across from them. It's bizarre, really.

She's snickering. He's sneering. They're all leering and pointing. And here I thought we were past all this. Well, no matter what, I'm not going to let them ruin this day that has started so spectacularly well. I walk right up to them with a broad smile.

"Good morning," I greet them cheerily. "Can I get you guys some fresh coffee?" I offer as a goodwill gesture.

That's when I notice the newspapers. Four people. Four papers. With some secret signal they've prearranged, they pick them up in unison and open them so that the front page is facing me. Or, rather, the front pages. All four identical front pages. I'm still smiling as I glance down at them, but the smile doesn't stay there for long.

• • •

THURSDAY MAY 4TH 7:12 A.M.

K: ***Drew! There's an article in the paper about us. That SOB Kevin Kilpatrick. How did he find out? Was he following us? Shit!! PLEASE call me NOW.***

• • •

THURSDAY MAY 4TH 7:22 A.M.

K: ***Where ARE you? I've been trying to call you…***

K: ***I'm on my way to your office. I'll go in the back entrance***

Chapter Forty-Five

Drew

The familiar *ping* of a text sounds and I'm about to dig my cell out of my bag when Maureen sticks her head into my office.

"Drew, may I have a word?" she asks.

"Oh, good morning, Maureen. I was just putting the finishing touches on the opening comments for my tenure presentation."

She looks over her shoulder before coming in and closing the door. I offer her a seat but she shakes her head.

"Drew, the tenure meeting's been canceled."

The phone *ping* turns into a phone ring. I grab it, glance at the screen and mute it. Katherine's going to have to wait a few minutes while I get this sorted and get Maureen out of my office so I can return her call in private.

"When has it been moved to?" I ask, starting to flip through the calendar on my desk. "Is it still this month?"

She closes her eyes and rubs the bridge of her nose between her index finger and thumb. After a long pause, she looks up at me again.

"I'm going to ask you a question and I need for you to be completely honest with me. All right?"

Uh-oh. I do *not* like the sound of this, or the fact that she just dodged my question.

"Uh, sure. What is it, Maureen?"

She takes a long pause, draws a deep breath, and finally asks.

"Drew, are you having a sexual relationship with Kate Brenner?"

I don't even realize I'm holding my breath until it comes out of me in one big, blustering puff.

"I—uh—why are you asking me that question, Maureen?"

"Is it true, or not?"

In the split second I have to consider my answer, I weigh the pros and cons of lying versus coming clean. Turns out the latter weighs more than the former, at least in this instance.

"Yes," I say in a whisper.

She's looking at me as if she'd like to wrap her hands around my throat.

"What. Were. You. *Thinking*?" she hisses, chewing off each word individually. "Do you have *any* idea what kind of a liability you've exposed us to? She could sue us for sexual harassment. And, considering your contentious relationship over the years, she'd win. Easily."

Is that all she's worried about? I shake my head confidently.

"She wouldn't do that. She'd never do that."

Maureen cocks an eyebrow. "What makes you so sure?"

"I just am," I say.

"Really, Drew? Then how do you explain this?" she asks unfolding the newspaper and holding it up for me to see.

It takes me a second to process what I'm looking at. It's a picture of Kate. And me. We're kissing out in front of my house. Oh my God. But it's not until I read the headline that

I feel all the blood drain from my head.

Senator's daughter makes the grade in professor's arms.

"Maureen..."

"No."

"Maureen, please..."

"I said no, Drew. There is no room for interpretation in the university's policy here. Sexual relationships between students and professors are strictly forbidden. This, Drew, looks like a relationship."

"Maureen, you're right. It is a relationship. And I know how hard that must be for you to hear, after Casey."

"That's where you're wrong, Drew," she says, her voice dropping in volume but rising in intensity. "There's nothing more I want to hear from you than that you're in love. That you're happy. That you're having a life after my daughter. But this was just beyond foolish. Did you really think no one would find out?"

I really did think that. But it doesn't matter now, because I can't un-ring that bell. What I find more disconcerting here is the question of *how* they found out. We were so careful. And this picture, it's at my house. I could maybe understand it if we'd been careless about our behavior in public. But someone would have had to tip off this reporter in order to get him to my house at that time.

"Do you know who did this?" I ask her.

"Are you seriously asking me that question?"

"I am. Do you know who tipped off the press?"

She's shaking her head as if she can't believe what she's hearing.

"Drew, you did this to yourself. And, I have to say, I'm shocked. You, of all people."

I take a long, slow breath and try to slow my racing heart.

"Will this take me out of the running for tenure?"

Maureen looks incredulous.

"Tenure? Drew, we'll be lucky if I can keep the president from firing you! Senator Brenner was on the phone to him at five o'clock this morning demanding your job!"

This can't be happening. Not to me. I realize, in that instant, that it's not just happening to me.

"I—I'm sorry to do this to you," I say, my quavering voice barely above a whisper. "I'm sorry to put you in this position."

"You damn well should be," she spits. "Maybe if I'd known, I could've helped you figure out a way to make it work. But now..." She's shaking her head. "It's not like this is an internal thing that can be swept under the rug. This is printed in black and white. And believe me, it may just be the local paper today, but it'll be national news by tonight."

I can scarcely wrap my head around this. In the span of ten minutes, my career has ended. Over. Period. Done. My world is suddenly spinning out of control and I don't have the faintest clue how to make it stop.

She sighs. "Go home, Drew. Figure out what you want your official response to be. I'd recommend resigning before you can be terminated, but that's your call."

"I can't go," I mutter. "I have final review sessions this afternoon."

"No, actually, you don't. You've been given a week's suspension while Human Resources sorts through this mess. You prepare your oral exam questions, though. I expect you'll be back to work in time for those. The last thing we want is for other students to claim unfair treatment because you didn't deliver the exam after teaching them all those semesters."

I get to my feet, overtaken by a feeling of numbness.

"I really am sorry, Maureen."

"I know you are, Drew," she says quietly and leaves my office.

I'm still reeling as I pack up my bag, turn out the lights in my office, and shut the door behind me. I need to get to Katherine before she comes over here to the music department. God only knows what the idiots here will have to say to her.

• • •

I'm not sure how long Kevin Kilpatrick's been trying to get my attention when I finally hear him calling my name out in the parking lot. I stop to see him sitting in a white car, driver's door open, one leg in and one leg out. He's parked right next to me. He's waiting for me.

Son. Of. A. Bitch.

"You fucking douchebag!" I yell before I can help myself. I fly across the ten feet that separate us. He's holding up his hands as I drag him out of his BMW and push him hard against the front quarter panel. So hard that it dents under his weight.

"Dude! The car!"

"The *car*? You better pray to every god you know that I don't put your fucking face through the windshield of this car!"

He's laughing. The motherfucker is actually laughing. "Okay, okay! Calm down, Doc, chill!" he says, holding his hands up in gesture of mock surrender.

"When did you know? How? Have you been following me this whole time?" I demand, my fists wrapping hard around the lapels of his jacket.

"What? No! Doc, I *didn't* know," he protests. "Not until yesterday."

"Yesterday?"

"Yesterday. She told me where the two of you would be. Where I could find you for a photograph."

"*She* told you?"

"Aw, I'm sorry, Doc. You didn't see that one coming, huh? I told you, Kate Brenner isn't the innocent little ray of sunshine she pretends to be."

"She told you about us?"

He shrugs. "Who else would tell me? I mean, who else knew where you'd be? Who else knew who'd you be *with*?"

I feel as if someone has punched me in my gut. I let the slimy creep go and step back, raking a hand through my hair and trying to process what he's telling me. That she's betrayed me. That *is* what he's telling me, isn't it?

"But, why?" I mutter, more to myself than to him.

"Revenge, Doc. Pure. And. Simple."

I spin on him again and this time he's smart enough to move just out of my reach.

"What the fuck are you talking about?" I spit.

He shrugs. "Kate Brenner hates her father. He kicked her out when she was a teenager and cut her off. She wanted to ruin him. Nothing like a good old-fashioned scandal to ruin a politician."

"But she and I…we were…I…" the words just won't form in my mind or in my mouth.

All of a sudden Kevin Kilpatrick looks sympathetic. "In love? Right? Is that it? Maybe you were, Doc. But her? Well, from what I hear, you gave her plenty of reasons to *not* love you over the years. Honestly, I can't totally blame her. Apparently you treated her like shit because she reminded you of your ex. Is that a lie?"

I can only stare at him. The only way he could know that is if she'd told him herself. Jesus Christ. She did this to me. Kilpatrick takes my silence as assent.

"You embarrassed her. You threatened her. I mean, it was pretty fucking brilliant, actually. She gets you to fall for her. Maybe even call in a few favors to help her get into that swanky music school up north? Then she lowers the boom. Kills two birds with one stone. Destroys your career *and* your heart. It's not her father's fault, but it certainly opens up a can of worms about their relationship and makes him look like a real shit heel in the process. In fact, if little Katie Brenner spins this just right, she comes out looking like the girl who was abandoned by her father and forced into a relationship with a professor who took advantage of her."

"Drew?"

I jump at the sound of my own name and a soft touch on my shoulder. I grab the hand and yank. Tessa comes stumbling into my field of vision.

"Drew! Hey, stop it! What's wrong with you?" she shrieks at me.

"Oh God, Tess, I'm sorry, I thought you were…" I can't even say her name.

"Hey, aren't you that reporter?" she says, suddenly turning her sharp tone and narrowed eyes on Kilpatrick.

"At your service," he says with a crooked grin and a mock bow.

"What did you do?" she hisses at him. "I saw that article, you son of a bitch!"

"Ah, well, I think that's my cue to go. The good Doc over here will fill you in, I'm sure."

Tessa has extricated her hand from my grip and put it on my forearm possessively. My friend. She's my only friend on the face of this fucking earth. Kilpatrick gets back in his car and starts to pull away, pausing briefly and rolling down his window.

"Hey, tell Katie Kate I said thanks, okay?" He's chuckling as I watch him pull out of the parking lot.

"Drew? Are you okay, Drew?" Tessa is asking me, her voice growing more alarmed.

"No, Tess," I murmur. "I'm never going to be okay again."

"So, it's true then? You and Katherine Brenner?"

Her eyes are so full of concern that it breaks my heart. Here is yet another victim of my selfishness.

"It is, Tessa. I mean, it wasn't before, but, it's a long story. I just don't understand how she could do this to me. To us."

She gives my arm a gentle squeeze.

"Drew, are you saying that *she* did this? That Kate set you up?"

"She must have. No one else knew. We were so careful," I mumble, shaking my head and staring at my feet as if the answer to this clusterfuck might be written across the top of my shoes.

Tessa moves her other hand to my back and pats me gently. When she speaks again her voice is considerably softer, as if she's trying to calm a spooked horse. "Oh, Drew. I'm so sorry. I wish I'd known. Maybe I could have done something. Maybe I would have seen something. But you're right. You were careful. I mean, you must have been because you were even able to keep it from me."

I'm only half listening to her as my mind desperately searches for any straw to clutch at. *Anything* that would make this be something other than what it looks like. But there's nothing. Kevin Kilpatrick is a sneaky fuck, but there's no way he just happened to stumble upon our relationship. He was tipped off. He knew when we'd be together.

Only someone who knew could have told him.

Only someone who hated me would have told him.

• • •

THURSDAY MAY 4TH 7:35 A.M.

K: ***Where are you? I'm just pulling into the lot now. Going to your office.***

• • •

THURSDAY MAY 4TH 7:38 A.M.

K: ***Drew, you're really starting to scare me. You're not in your office or the classroom. You should see the looks I'm getting... Holy fucking shit. Please call me! Going to check with Dr. Morgan.***

Chapter Forty-Six

KATE

His office is dark when I get there at seven thirty, but Tessa Morgan's isn't. And I don't know what else to do.

"Uh, Professor Morgan?" I ask quietly from the door.

When she looks up, I know she knows. Her jaw is set, her face is stone.

"Kate."

"I was just wondering if you'd seen—Dr. Markham?" I make a concerted effort not to call him Drew. She notices and her lip curls up with the hint of a snarl.

"Why yes, Kate. This morning. Right after Maureen told him he was no long under consideration for tenure and that he would very likely be fired for sleeping with a student."

Oh my God. This is so much worse than I thought.

"I—uh—wonder if you know where he is?"

She leans forward across her desk and narrows her pretty green eyes. The snarl isn't a hint anymore, it's a full-blown, living, breathing part of her face now.

"I don't believe that's any of your concern, Kate. And, even if it were, I can tell you that Dr. Markham has no interest in seeing you."

"But why?" I ask before I can help myself. "I didn't do anything!"

"Didn't you, Kate?" She sneers. "He has money, he has connections, he has a lot of things that a girl like you could use to her advantage. And then, when you're done with him, how convenient he is to throw in your father's face. Well played, Kate! Well. Played."

As she says this last part, she actually starts to applaud.

Horrified, I turn around and run. And run. And Run.

• • •

THURSDAY MAY 4TH 7:45 A.M.

K: ***You know I'd NEVER do anything to hurt you, right?***

• • •

THURSDAY MAY 4TH 7:47 A.M.

K: ***Okay, enough of this shit. I'm on my way to your house. Why won't you answer my calls or texts? You KNOW I could never do this to you, Drew! Don't you?***

• • •

I can't get to him fast enough. Every second that ticks by with him believing I've betrayed him is a second of suffering I can't bear for him to have. I run to my car and drive to his house as quickly as I can. When I get there, I ring the bell until he finally comes to the door. But I see immediately that this isn't right. He isn't right. His face is hard, his eyes are chillingly vacant.

"Drew…" I begin breathlessly.

"Go home, Miss Brenner," he says flatly. "I don't want

you here."

"Please, just listen to me. This isn't my fault…"

"You're right, it's not your fault. It's mine. I should've known better than to trust you in the first place. What were you going to do after you graduated, huh? Once you'd gotten what you wanted from me. Were you just going to disappear? Or did you think you'd just hang around to use me for a while longer, maybe see if you could get a few bucks out of me while you were at it?"

"You can't possibly believe that I would do that to you," I whisper.

"Oh, but I do, Miss Brenner."

"Please stop calling me that. Please. I'm Katherine."

"What did you think I could do for you, *Katherine*?"

"Drew…"

I reach out my hand to touch him but he pulls his arm away as if I'm a poisonous snake about to bite him.

"Don't touch me. Don't you ever touch me again," he spits with such acridity that I take half a step back.

"What? What did I do? Just tell me and I'll make it right!" I say, fighting against the inevitable spiral that I see coming.

"Oh, please. You played me. I know it, you know it, and soon everyone else will know it, too."

"I have no idea what you're talking about!"

He just smirks and shakes his head.

"I'm such a fool," he says, his voice filled with self-loathing. "You are *so* good. You had me convinced that you cared for me. And, my God! The act you put on! Tell me, did you somehow make yourself sick on purpose? Or was it just a happy coincidence that I was forced to take care of you? Tell me, Katherine. Tell me all of it. And then tell me what you stood to gain from it. Really. I want to know—what's worth ruining someone's life over?"

"I love you!" The words feel like a roar in my mind but

they come out sounding more like a squeak. "I would *never* hurt you. I swear to God, Drew, you've got to believe me!"

He looks up at the ceiling, stroking his chin and pretending to consider. "Hmm, now let's see," he begins, his voice dripping with sarcasm. "You somehow convinced me to sleep with you; to trust you. Then you used me to get to my connections at the New York Conservatory. Then you showed me just how much you care by tipping off a reporter about the *consensual* relationship that is about to end my career. Oh yes, Miss Brenner. I believe you."

I start to fight him, but suddenly, I can't fight anymore. The hatred in his eyes is so much worse than the disdain that used to be there. This man will never believe I haven't done something to sabotage his life and his career. And I will never forgive myself for allowing him to get close enough to hurt me.

"You're going to think about this," I say in a voice barely above a whisper, "and you're going to realize the mistake you've made."

"Oh, believe me, *Miss Brenner*, I am well aware of the mistake I've made," he returns in a tone as cold as ice. It robs the breath from my lungs.

I'm not sure how long the tears have been streaming down my face, but I can taste them in my mouth. They accentuate the morning chill as they run down my neck and under my collar, reminding me that I'm not wearing a coat. Again.

"Please," I repeat in a voice that I can barely hear, "I'm Katherine."

"No. What you are is a callous, immature little girl who used me to get what she wanted at the expense of my career. Of my life. Were you laughing at me, *Katherine*?" he asked with a cruel emphasis on my name. "Were you making fun of my grief for my fiancée, *Katherine*? Were you telling all your little friends how you were screwing around with me,

Katherine?"

I shake my head.

"Please!" I beg.

"Go home, *Katherine*. And then go to hell," he hisses and slams the door in my face.

I stand, staring at the spot where he just was, shaking with the sobs that are rising from my chest. I ring the bell again and again until it finally just stops ringing. He must have found a way to disconnect it so he wouldn't have to hear it. I start pounding on the heavy oak door with my fists.

He's got to hear me. He's got to listen to me. I bang and bang until blood runs from my knuckles. I don't know how long has passed when I finally slip to my knees on his doormat, the word "welcome" screaming up at me in its irony. I weep openly, sobbing his name and begging him to open the door.

There's another temperamental mountain storm set to roll through the area and even as the early sun gives way to clouds, I sit there. I can feel the plummeting temperature around me, but I sit there. I'm still sitting on the floor of his porch when the police cruiser pulls up in the driveway and a middle-aged woman in uniform gets out. She walks up to where I am, shaking with grief and cold.

"Hey there, sweetie," she says gently as she squats down to my tear-blurred eye level. "It's freezing out here. Where's your coat?"

The question makes me sob even harder. The woman's eyes are filled with compassion, as if she understands exactly what she is looking at: a broken heart.

"Katherine? Is that your name?" she asks. He must have told the dispatcher who I was when he called in the complaint to the police.

I nod dumbly, crying until the hiccups rise from my chest.

"Katherine, you need to go home now, sweetie. You can't stay here any longer."

I cry harder and the officer looks down at the ground, as if the answer is written there in front of her. Finally, she meets my eyes and takes a deep breath.

"Katherine, I'm so sorry, but if you don't go on your own, I'm going to have to bring you into the station and book you on trespassing charges. He wants me to do that, but I think maybe you just need to go home. Do you think you can drive?"

Drew wants to have me arrested? There it is. He really and truly believes that I could do something like this to him. No. There is no coming back from this. Not for him. Not for me. And with that realization, I can finally stand up on my shaky legs. I wipe my tear-stained face and nod my assent to the officer.

"You know what? I'm going to follow you home, okay, honey? I know you're going—I just want to make sure you get there safely. Okay?"

I nod again and allow her to take my elbow and lead me gently back to the Corolla. In a few minutes I'm headed back down the hill for the last time, my tears falling on the steering wheel just as they did the day he found me in front of his house.

• • •

THURSDAY MAY 11TH 8:45 P.M.

D: ***I'm glad you've finally stopped texting and calling. I was about to have my number changed. This is not an invitation to contact me, it's just a suggestion that we keep things professional tomorrow when you come in for your exam. Making a scene by crying or complaining is only going to make it harder for you. I'm getting on with my life and I suggest you do the same. After tomorrow we'll never have to see one another again. Please DO NOT respond to this message.***

Chapter Forty-Seven

Drew

The rage has been steadily building in me all week, and now that I'm finally allowed to go back to work, I'm ready to let it loose. I stomp into the kitchen and start pulling bottles down from the cabinets. I need a drink and wine is not going to cut it tonight. Brandy? Scotch? Vodka. Yes, that bottle I have stashed in the subzero will do quite nicely. I pour myself a shot and knock it back. Another one. Then another, and I feel my body start to uncoil just a little.

In my absence, Maureen has arranged for a teaching assistant to conduct the review sessions for my classes and that suits me just fine. I have no desire to be the butt of jokes in my own classroom. By not being there, I've missed the smirks and snickers of my students and colleagues. I can't even bring myself to take Tessa's calls right now. What I cannot get out of, however, are the orals.

First thing tomorrow the Graduate Oral Examinations panel meets in the small conference room. Barry Green will handle the Music History questions. I'll take Orchestration and Theory. Maureen is in charge of all general music topics including Research and Music Education. One by one, my grad students will come before us and answer questions culled from every class they've taken. Among them will be Miss Katherine Brenner.

At first, the thought made me uneasy. I wasn't sure how I'd react to being so close to her. Seeing her at my door had been hard enough. But then again, I hadn't really been prepared for that. I was still confused and uncertain about her role in all of this. But now I know. I've had enough time to work it all through and there's no doubt in my mind that she did this. And, when she stands before the committee tomorrow, I plan to be ready. More than ready, in fact.

I pour myself one more shot and take it with me to the kitchen table, where I've spread out my old exams and set up my laptop. I've been poring over all my notes going back four semesters, digging out the most obscure questions I can find. Policies stipulate that all students receive test questions from the same semesters. They do not, however, stipulate that each student receive the exact *same* questions. So special little Katherine Brenner will have an entirely new special little oral exam I've created just for her.

Maybe I can't fail her, but she sure as hell can fail herself.

• • •

I'm in an excellent mood as I take my seat at the conference table with Barry and Maureen. There's a fresh carafe of coffee and a tray of pastries. The students are much too nervous to even look in my direction, let alone snicker or sneer about what they've read in the papers.

I don't ask to see the roster because I want to be surprised when she walks in the door. The anticipation builds so much throughout the morning that I barely touch the sandwiches they've brought in for our lunch break.

"What's the matter, Drew, chewing up all those students spoiled your appetite?" Barry jokes with a snort.

"Something like that," I mumble as I pick at some potato salad.

Maureen has been careful to stick to business with me today. She hasn't said a word about my *situation*, and I'm thankful for that. For today, at least, I can pretend that everything is back to normal. Now, she's skimming her clipboard of names.

"Well, so far not one fail in the bunch this year. That's very impressive, gentlemen. A testament to how well you've taught these students," she says with a smile.

"Day's not done yet, Maureen," I mumble.

"That's true, Drew, but we've pretty much hit all of your students. Anyone who fails this afternoon is on Barry's watch," she says, teasing my colleague.

Wait. She's forgotten something. Or, rather, *someone*.

"All except for Katherine Brenner," I correct her. "I have her questions ready to go."

Maureen turns to me with a confused frown.

"What? No, her orals have been postponed," she says.

I feel myself grow warm with anger. So, she's found a way to wiggle out of it? I should have seen this coming. She's probably trying to find a way to get around having me on her panel because she knows I'm going to make it a living hell for her.

"And how exactly did *that* happen?" I ask with an irritated huff.

Maureen is staring at me, uncomprehending.

"Drew, don't you know what happened?" she asks.

"What? Did Daddy manage to get her excused or something? Or does getting one of your teachers fired get you a pass on your orals?" I snort derisively and catch a flash of irritation cross her face. She's about to comment when Barry pipes up from across the table.

"Kate's in the hospital," he says through a mouthful of pastrami.

I feel the breath leave my chest, unbidden. This has to stop. I have to stop caring about whatever it is she's involved in now.

"Well that's a little convenient, isn't it?" I ask, snark dripping from my words.

Maureen stares at me, clearly surprised by the outburst. And why wouldn't she be? I've done a total one-eighty since the last time we spoke. When I was a drooling, sniveling, lovesick cuckold.

"Drew, I hardly think she's faking a broken wrist," Maureen says dryly.

I scoff. "It's an oral exam, Maureen. The state of her wrist is irrelevant. What did she do? Slip on the ice in those ridiculous sneakers she's always wearing?"

Now my boss's gaze hardens. Her eyes squint a little as her brows draw together. She's pissed. Something's not right here.

"Drew, Kate was attacked Tuesday night. Some overzealous reporter from DC. She had him arrested on assault charges and he lost his job. When he got out on bail, he decided to come back for a little revenge."

My mouth is now grazing the linoleum floor. "What?" I gasp. "Is—is she all right?"

"Well, yes. And no. She managed to give the guy a good swift kick where it hurts, if you know what I mean. He was still balled up on the ground, crying and shoving snow down his pants when the police arrived. But when Kate went to the hospital to have the cast put on, the doctor noticed she was having trouble breathing. The poor thing's got double pneumonia on top of everything else. When they couldn't get an acceptable oxygen level on her, she was admitted. I understand it's gotten quite serious. I'm sorry, I assumed you were…in touch with her."

She says this last part pointedly.

Suddenly, all I can see is Katherine sitting on my front porch with her back against the door, sobbing my name over and over again. No coat. No hat. Not even a fucking pair of gloves.

"Where?" I whisper, my voice filled with concern I didn't know I still felt.

"He followed her to—"

"No," I cut in. "Where is she *now*?"

Maureen stares at me curiously.

"All Saints." She pauses, considering me carefully before she continues. "Barry, would you please excuse us for a few minutes?" she asks, her eyes never leaving mine.

"Huh? Oh yeah, sure," Barry mutters as he gets up, taking his lunch with him.

When he's gone, Maureen takes off her glasses and rubs the bridge of her nose.

"What the hell, Drew? Just last week you were telling me how much you care for Kate. Now, all of a sudden, you seem to hate her again. What on earth is going on with you?"

"I did care about her. But she played me, Maureen. It was her. She told the reporter. She used me to get back at her father. She took advantage of my grief for Casey and she—"

I stop short because I don't see what I was expecting in Maureen's face. It's not sympathy for what I've gone through. It's not relief that I finally understand what I've done. It's rage. Pure, unadulterated fury.

"Are you out of your goddamned mind?" she yells at me.

I'm so stunned that I can't say anything. I have never seen Maureen this angry. Or heard her this loud.

"Good lord, Drew! And here I thought you couldn't

muck this up any worse."

"W-what?" I finally venture.

"Could you *be* a bigger idiot?"

I think it's a rhetorical question, but she seems to be waiting for an answer. My mouth opens to say something, but there isn't anything, so I close it again.

Maureen closes her eyes and takes a deep breath, clearly willing herself not to come across the table and stab me with her plastic fork. When she starts again, her voice is a little softer, but it's still laced with anger.

"And what, exactly, is it that you think she was using you for?"

"My money—"

Maureen jumps all over the two words.

"So, she asked you for cash?"

"Well, no. But I bought her an expensive coat—"

"Did she ask you to buy it for her?"

"No."

"Did she know you were going to buy it for her?" she presses.

"No, but—"

"But what? Did she ask you to pay her rent?"

"No…"

"So it *wasn't* money," Maureen says, dismissing that theory. "What else, Drew? What else do you think she used you for?"

This isn't a question, it's an accusation and I don't like it one bit.

"My connections," I say confidently.

"What connections are those?"

"My connections at the New York Conservatory. She wants to go into their conducting program and she found out Danny Gillies and I are friends."

"Oh!" Maureen says, looking suddenly disappointed. "So it was her idea for him to come here and see her conduct."

"I—uh—well, no, not exactly…"

"What do you mean?" she asks suspiciously.

"I didn't tell her he would be there. It was a surprise," I admit, feeling foolish suddenly.

And just like that, she's on the warpath again.

"So how did she use you for your connections then?"

"She knew I went there. She asked me all kinds of questions about the program and the faculty. She wanted to know what Danny was like," I inform her.

"You mean, like any student who was interested in attending your alma mater?"

I shake my head. "It wasn't like that, Maureen. I showed her pictures of me and Casey at Danny's wedding…"

Shit! This isn't sounding as convincing as it did when I was working it all out over vodka.

"What are you going to tell me, next, Drew? That you have some magical penis and she used you for sex?"

Before I can react to that—not that I have any clue how to react to that—she continues.

"Drew Markham, you're a goddamned fool if you think that woman was anything but in love with you. I know her better than you think, and she doesn't have it in her to be ruthless. But, apparently you do. And that, I did *not* know," she says, shaking her head at me in clear disgust.

It hits me then, like a piano falling from the sky. I have screwed this up beyond comprehension. Before I can think about it, I put my head in my hands, nearly jumping out of my skin when I feel a warm touch on my shoulder.

"It looks to me like you might just love her," she says quietly.

I nod without raising my head.

"Then go to her. She's sick, she's alone, she's scared, and I'm going to guess she's heartbroken, based on what you've told me. Go, Drew. Go show her she doesn't need to be any of those things anymore."

Chapter Forty-Eight

Kate

He's there, holding my tiny hand in his big one. Stroking my thumb with his. He tells me he loves me, and that I'm his. That I'll always be his and that he's so sorry he let me down. My heart swells with love for him. Just like it did when I was a small child.

"Katie?"

I don't recognize the voice.

"Katie, come on, honey, time to wake up," the voice coaxes me.

I mumble something unintelligible, even to me.

"Katie…"

"Stop calling me that…" I whisper hoarsely.

"There you are! Open your eyes, hon. Come on."

I want her to shut up so I can get back to my dream, but somehow, I know she won't let me until I give her what she wants. Slowly, painfully, I open my eyes against the light of the hospital room.

"Hello, darlin'!" the tall black woman says as she leans over me. Her smile is bright and her eyes are soft.

"I don't know you," I murmur.

"No, you don't. But I know you! My name is Beverly. You can call me Bev. I know you're Katherine but it don't seem like you like to be called Katie."

I shake my head no and let my lids droop closed again.

"Uh-uh! Wake up, Katherine!"

I open to her again and am rewarded with that brilliant smile.

"Please let me sleep. I was dreaming about my daddy."

"Oh, darlin', he just stepped out to get a cup of coffee. I promised him I'd try and get you to eat something."

Wait. What?

I force myself to focus.

"My father is *here*?"

"Yes'm. He's been here for a couple days now, but you've been too out of it to realize it."

"Why is he here?"

Something about this question strikes Beverly as funny.

"Oh, you're just a silly one, aren't you? He's here cause he's your *daddy*."

I shake my head.

"No, you don't understand," I explain. "He doesn't care that I'm in the hospital—"

"Of course I do."

I'm wondering how it is that my father's voice is coming out of this woman's mouth. But it's not, is it? Because her mouth never moved. God, I'm so confused.

Beverly steps away and is replaced by the tall, lean, handsome figure of Senator Tucker Brenner.

"Of course I care," he repeats, taking the seat next to my bed.

I feel my eyes grow wide and my breathing gets even

shallower.

"Are you real?" I ask with a slight tremor. I'm afraid of what the answer might be.

He smiles at me and chuckles, the way he did when I was a kid.

"Yes, Katherine, I'm real," he says, reaching over to pull the rolling table across my bedside. He picks up a bowl and spoon that are sitting there. "The doctor says you need to eat, sweetheart. I need you to have a little broth for me. Can you do that, do you think?"

I nod and watch as he fills a spoonful and carefully brings it to my lips. I open my mouth and swallow the warm, salty liquid.

"Good girl," he says happily, already filling another spoonful. We repeat this process until the broth is gone and he sets the empty bowl and spoon back on the table. Beverly quietly pulls it out of the way and adjusts my pillows under my head.

"You came," I say to my father, still not completely certain he isn't a figment of my imagination.

He nods.

"Why?" I ask.

He reaches out with his big, soft hand and brushes the hair from my forehead.

"Because you needed me. And, for the first time in your life, Katherine, I realized *that* was more important than anything else on the face of this earth."

I try to respond, but I'm just too tired. My eyes slip closed and I feel a smile on my lips as his hand strokes my cheek.

"More than anything else, Katherine," he repeats as I fall back to sleep.

Chapter Forty-Nine

Drew

When I arrive outside her hospital room I take a minute to catch my breath before I push open the door. But I needn't have worried about alarming her because she's out cold.

"Can I help you?" comes a voice behind me. I turn to see a tall, slender black woman, probably in her sixties. She's wearing a nurse's uniform and a name tag that identifies her as Beverly Keen, RN.

"Uh, yes, I'm here to see Miss Brenner. I'm her…uh… friend."

She cocks a suspicious eyebrow at me. "You don't sound so sure about that."

I consider concocting some fake story, but that never works, so I settle on the truth.

"Truth is, I'm not sure. I screwed up. Big time. And now she's here and all I want is to beg for her forgiveness. Please. If she wants me to go, I'll go, but I just have to see her," I plead as her eyes soften.

"You can stay for a little while, but she's not going to accept any apologies tonight. That girl is sick. Very, very sick and right now she's resting so deep that she probably wouldn't hear a bomb explode in the room next door."

"I understand," I say, in a rush to accept her offer before she changes her mind. "I'll just sit here next to her for a while. I just want to be close to her."

She gives me a harrumph and leaves us alone. I pull one of the recliners as close to her bed as I can and sit, leaning forward to take her hand. It's chilly and I'm reminded of that night that I had to climb into bed to warm her.

In the glow of the room's soothing, amber lighting, I can see how pale and wan she is. Her hair hangs in thin strings around her face, which looks gaunt now. Has she been eating? It seems like she's lost a good chunk of weight.

I look at the IV pole behind her. That's likely where her nutrients are coming from right now. Not to mention some serious antibiotics. A clear plastic hose snakes its way out of a panel in the wall behind her bed, becoming a cannula across her face, delivering oxygen through her nose. I want nothing more than to climb into the bed and scoop her into my arms. I want to tell her how sorry I am and that I want to make it better. That I love her. Because I do. But the most I can do for now is kiss the back of her delicate little hand and stroke it with my thumb.

"Please forgive me," I whisper so softly that she wouldn't have heard me, even if she were awake. At least, I think that's how softly I say it.

"I wouldn't count on forgiveness coming anytime soon."

I jump, startled by the sound of a man's voice in the room just a few feet behind me. When I turn around, I see him. Even though his face is half obscured by the dark shadows of the room, there is no mistaking who he is.

"Senator Brenner."

The look on his face is sheer disdain. I recognize it because it is an expression that I, myself, have perfected. It occurs to me that the young woman sleeping besides us has been the unfortunate recipient of that glare from both of us. God, it's a wonder she trusts anyone.

"Dr. Markham," he replies flatly.

How does he know who I am?

"Of course I know who you are," he says and I wonder for a split second if I've asked the question out loud.

"Do you really think I wouldn't vet anyone who is involved with my daughter?"

I take a deep breath and match his expression, despite the unsettling feeling that he can read my thoughts.

"I wasn't aware you had any interest in anything involving your daughter," I reply icily.

He gives me a cool smile. "You mean like the fact that you're sleeping with her? And she's one of your students?"

"I'm not. I mean, I was, but…"

"Uh-huh. I know. You're not now, not since you called the police on her. But you were. Isn't that right *Doctor* Markham?" He sneers. Wow. This guy is an even bigger dick than I am. "In fact, the physicians here seem to think it was that little incident that left my daughter with pneumonia."

And that would be my jugular.

"Senator Brenner, considering the fact that you've barely uttered a word to your daughter in years, I don't see how any of this is your business," I swat back at him. He's about to say something when the door flies open, spilling muted light from the hallway across the room. Beverly is back with a big frown.

"What is going on in here?" she hisses.

Neither of us replies.

"All right, gentlemen. I think visiting hours are *over*."

"I'm not leaving her," I insist firmly, quietly.

"How much you wanna bet?" the senator retorts

menacingly.

I jump up so we're only separated by a few feet.

"Anything. Anything on God's green earth. I did this to her, and I'm not going to take so much as a step outside of this room until I know she's all right," I inform him.

Beverly considers me for a beat, and then the senator.

"All right. Katherine needs rest right now, so here's what we'll do. There's a private VIP lounge on the next floor and it's empty right now. You all can wait there, maybe get something to eat. I'll come and get you later on when the doctor makes his afternoon rounds."

I look at Tucker Brenner. He looks at me. We nod, stand, and leave the room, our uneasy truce forged.

"It wasn't Katherine, you know," he tells me matter-of-factly once we're settled in the lounge.

"What?" I ask. But I know what he means. I'm just not sure I believe him.

"You know very well 'what,' Dr. Markham. I'm telling you that Katherine was not responsible for that article."

"Senator, I don't think this is a discussion you and I should be having. I think Katherine and I—"

"No, Dr. Markham. You listen to me and you listen carefully, because I don't want you upsetting my daughter with your nonsense. I don't care what Kevin Kilpatrick or anyone else told you, Katherine is not the one who told him about your relationship. She'd never do that to someone she cared about. Not you. Not even to me."

I shake my head, unable to reconcile my fury with her over my concern for her.

"I'm sorry, Senator, but there was too much. He knew too much. She was the only one. I'm sure you don't want to hear that she would do something like this to make you look bad…"

"I've known about your relationship almost since it

started, Dr. Markham. If I'd wanted to squash the story or spin it or broadcast it to the Associated Press, I'd have done it. I can assure you, you sleeping with my daughter has no impact on my career."

"Well it sure as hell had an impact on mine," I mutter with more anger than I intend to.

"Yes, well, perhaps you should have thought of that before you took her to bed."

He's right. But I don't care. And all I want to do right now is share some of this bone-crushing guilt that's sitting on me.

"What about you, Senator Brenner? You're her father. The only family she has in the world. How could you have abandoned her like that?" I throw at him, careful to twist the knife.

"I didn't," he says, not at all surprised by my attack. "Not really, anyway. She's never been truly alone. I've always had eyes on her."

"I don't think it works like that. She never knew you were there, watching. She always felt alone. I'm pretty sure that means she *was* alone."

He seems to consider this and when he speaks to me again, he sounds resigned. Tired. Regretful.

"As much as I'd like for you to be wrong about that, you're not. Dr. Markham, I know you'll find this hard to believe, all things considered, but I do love Katherine. And I think you'll find she loves me, too."

"Why would she?" I ask in a tone that isn't mean, so much as curious. He seems to get the distinction and explains.

"She understands that I don't hate music or dance or theatre or art. I'm not some Neanderthal who doesn't understand the need for aesthetic beauty in the world," he says, then drops his gaze to the ground. "What I am, is a man who loved a woman more than life itself. *She* filled my world with music. And when she died, it died with her. Every note on the piano was a nail in her coffin to me. It was a reminder of what I had lost. The pain was so intense that I had no recourse but to try and *force* it to stop in the only way I knew how."

"By making the music stop," I say, astonished that I understand what he's saying perfectly, because I've lived through this as well.

He sees this and nods, a sad smile filling his features.

"That's right. And when Katherine wanted to make a life *making* music, well, I just couldn't abide that. I tried reasoning with her, but she wouldn't listen. In the end, it forced my hand in a way I never wanted to see come to fruition. But the pain…I couldn't live with the pain anymore. It was killing me."

Now I am nodding, too. "I—my fiancée…" I begin, but stop, leaving the rest unsaid. Turns out, I don't have to say any more than those few words.

"I know about her. I'm so sorry. I could see what was happening when I investigated this thing further. Clearly you made the music stop, too, but in a different way. You don't compose anymore. You starting teaching, probably thinking it would make it hurt less. And then came Katherine."

"I tried to keep her at a distance."

"But that doesn't work. Not with her. She gets under your skin, that girl," he informs me, shaking his head. Then he turns to the side and takes a good long look at me. "I see you, Drew," he says suddenly and I am startled by his use of my first name. "You built a wall around your heart. Katherine tore it down. It's what she does." Senator Brenner stands up and walks away from me to look out the window, still speaking as he does. "But, whether you know it or not, you have a bigger problem on your hands right now."

"I doubt that," I mutter.

He turns to face me from across the room.

"Dr. Markham, if there's one thing I've learned over

the years, it's the art of motivation. Not your own, but other people's. Before things ever even start to go south, you need to have a good look at the people around you. Then figure out who has the most to gain from you losing everything. *That* will be the person who betrays you in the end—if you're not prepared for it."

"Senator, I have no idea what you're getting at, so please just spit it out already," I say, tired of trading enigmas with this man.

"Fine. Here it is, then. Humor me for just a minute and assume my daughter had nothing to do with that article in the paper. If you take her out of the picture, who else has something to gain from your humiliation?"

"No one," I say stubbornly. "I'm sorry, Senator. I care for Katherine and I want to get to the bottom of this. But, as much as I want there to be someone else who could have done this, there just isn't."

"Is that so?" he challenges with a raised brow. "Who else was in the running for the tenure spot, Dr. Markham?"

"No one. I'm the only one with the qualifications."

"You're the one with the *highest* qualifications," he corrects. "Who would be in line after you?"

"No one. There is no one," I insist. "There's me. The next person is one degree, three years' experience, and several publications away from me."

"Exactly. A huge chasm to overcome if you were interested in the position, isn't it? There's no making up that kind of a breech unless the person ahead of you is no longer eligible."

"Well, sure, if you want to twist it around that way," I admit with more than a little skepticism. "But that's absolutely not the case here. The next one in line would be Tessa Morgan and we're very close friends."

His lips curl up into a sad smile. A knowing smile.

"Very close, hmm? Close enough for her to catch the clues that you were involved with someone? Close enough to be jealous that that someone wasn't her? Close enough to know your schedule and where you could most likely be found by a reporter looking for a salacious photograph? Are you and she *that* close, Dr. Markham?"

I'm confused. And then I'm not. I shake my head. "No. Absolutely not. She'd never do that to me. She cares about me and what happens to me."

"Does she? Does she really? And, if she does, are you sure her motives are *just* friendly?"

I open my mouth to tell him how wrong he's got this, but I find the words are stuck in my throat. I've always known that Tessa has wanted more from our relationship than I was willing to give. I've never been ready for anything—for anyone—after Casey. And when I was, it was Katherine. Sure, if she knew, she might be upset. Pissed off, even. But *only* if she knew.

Holy. Shit.

She knew.

The force with which this realization hits me is enough to knock the breath from my body. I am such a fucking idiot. How could I have not seen it?

"Betrayal is a brutal thing," the senator is saying even as my head is spinning. "There's the impact of the betrayal itself. Then there is the aftermath. The sting of knowing that someone you trusted has intentionally inflicted injury upon you."

No, no, no. No way! Why? How? I can't process the questions that are flitting through my mind.

"We've failed Katherine," he says to me. "And I don't know how either of us can ever make it up to her. I don't know how she could ever forgive either of us. What I do know is that whether or not we can, she will. My daughter's heart is bigger than the both of us, Drew."

"I don't know what to do," I whisper, swiping at the rogue tears that have slipped past my once-steely veneer.

"Oh, I think you do. Get to the bottom of why this Tessa person is trying to hurt you and Katherine. Then you make it right with my daughter. I think you're the only one who can."

I'm on my feet and out the door before we can exchange another word. And all I can think is that I hope to God he's right.

• • •

The door swings open so hard that it slams into the adjacent wall and rattles the windows of Tessa's office. She doesn't jump. She doesn't gasp. She doesn't even look alarmed.

"Why?" I ask, breathlessly.

I can see by the look on her face that I don't need to explain what I'm asking. She already knows.

Tessa shrugs. "Five years is a long time to wait for the next tenure slot to open up, Drew."

"But—but you're my friend!"

Now she smirks at me and her face twists into a sneering mask.

"Friend. Yeah, that's exactly what I've been. Sweet Tessa. Dear Tessa. Good old Tessa. Always there for you to talk to, cry on her shoulder. Tessa who was there to pick up the pieces when that psycho bitch Casey killed herself. I was patient, Drew. Oh, was I patient. I just *knew* there'd be a time when you were ready. And I'd be there, waiting for you with open arms. And you'd see me as more than just your *buddy*."

I shake my head in disbelief. "What the hell are you talking about?"

Now she's shaking her head. "Such an imbecile you are, Drew. So blind. But you know what? I'm not blind, Drew."

"Tessa, you don't know what you're talking about—"

"Don't I?" she spits at me. "Funny, how Kate shows up with a new coat and accessories from one of *my* favorite stores right after you ask my advice on where to get a gift for your *mother*. Didn't think I caught that one, did you? Well I did," she informs me snidely. "And, Christ, Drew, the way you and Russell Atherton were at each other's throats and then…you weren't. The way you'd smile when you thought no one was watching. Suddenly you weren't complaining about Kate Brenner. Suddenly you were telling your old pal Danny what a great conductor she is and getting him all the way here to see her—that girl that you 'hate' so much. Yeah, I was watching, Drew. I saw all of it. And then, I made sure Kevin Kilpatrick saw it, too."

She's crazy. Totally, completely, certifiable. How could I have *not* seen this before now? I'm trying to decide how to respond to her little monologue when she opens the top drawer of her desk and pulls out a thin silver chain with a heart dangling from it. Engraved on the heart are the initials "KB."

"What is that?"

"Why, it's Kate's bracelet! I suppose you didn't notice it? Well I did. On several occasions, in fact. And then, I spotted it in a very interesting place. On the floor mat in your car that day we went out to Ruby's."

"So you took it?"

She shrugs. "I'm not even sure why I grabbed it. I just did. And I put it in my pocket for a rainy day. Well, guess what, Drew? It's raining," she says with a smile that sends a chill down my spine. "Oh, sure, I licked my wounds for a while, but then it struck me. Maybe I couldn't have *you* but I could have your job. Something I wouldn't get as long as you were qualified and eligible. That's when I saw my opportunity."

I know what's coming and, for a moment, I consider

getting up and walking out of this office before Tessa can say another word. But I realize that I can't, because I deserve this. When Tessa was hurt, her first instinct was to destroy me. When I was hurt, my first instinct was to destroy Katherine. Yes, I deserve every putrid thing she's about to tell me because I believed the worst of the person who I loved the most.

"When you refused to give him any information about Kate, Kevin Kilpatrick came sniffing around *my* office," Tessa informs me now. "And, lucky for him, I kept his business card. We struck a deal. I told him everything I knew and where he was most likely to find the two of you together. All he had to do was agree to tell you it was Kate who gave him the information. And how convenient! There I was to help you pick up the pieces of your broken heart. Oh, sweet, gullible Drew. *You* screwing a student is the best thing that's ever happened to *my* career. So, thanks for that, at least." She looks so pleased with herself. I can't decide who I'd rather kill—her or myself. Quite possibly both.

"Tessa," I say slowly, quietly, as if I'm approaching a skittish woodland creature. "I had no idea you felt that seriously about it. About *us*. I—I just didn't want to screw up our friendship."

She leans forward across her desk.

"That's bullshit and you know it. All this time, all these years, you've told me you weren't ready for a relationship. You didn't want a relationship. What you meant is that you didn't want a relationship with *me*. Right?"

She's right. I can't deny it. Maybe if I hadn't been such a coward for so long, we wouldn't be here—in this ugly, fucked-up situation—now. I take a deep breath and a seat, my eyes fixed on hers.

"I am sorry," I apologize in a considerably less agitated tone. "I'm really, really so sorry. You're right. I wasn't honest with you, Tess. I didn't want to hurt you, but that's exactly what I ended up doing."

She sits back in her office chair, arms folded in front of her chest.

"Yes, well, too little, too late. Don't you think?"

"I do, actually."

She seems surprised by this comment and one of her perfectly plucked eyebrows arches with interest.

"Good. I'm glad you realize there's no going back from where we are."

When I don't reply, she seems to soften the least little bit.

"Not that we can't try to go forward. Start again. With time, maybe, we could get back to what we've shared all these years. Maybe even more," she ventures softly.

I consider her carefully. She's beautiful. And smart, and funny. Any man would be lucky to have Tessa Morgan in his life and in his bed. Any man but me, that is. I give her a small, sad smile. She returns it tentatively.

"You're right, Tess," I say, my voice hoarse with emotion. "There is no going back. But there's no going forward for us, either."

"What—what do you mean?" she asks, her well-practiced, hard-ass facade cracking before my very eyes.

"There will never again be anything between us. Not friendship. Certainly not love. At this point, I don't even hate you. I'd have to care about you to hate you. I could have maybe gotten over your betrayal of me. Maybe. But what you've done to Katherine…what you made *me* think of Katherine…I just can't."

I stand up and take Katherine's bracelet from the desk and turn toward the door.

"Wait. Drew, what are you saying?"

I stop, but I don't face her.

"I'm saying that we're done, Tessa. I hope you enjoy your tenure. I hope it keeps you laughing over wine and has dinner with you and goes to movies with you, because I suspect it's going to be the only friend you have for a long time."

She gasps from behind me, but she doesn't utter a single word as I open the door to her office and walk out of it for the last time.

Chapter Fifty

Kate

I am lost, deep within a cloud. I try to move, but this isn't your garden-variety puffy, fluffy cloud. This one is thick as pea soup and it's heavy, like a wet blanket pinning my body flat. My every attempt to move or shift or even open my eyes is met by an oppressive resistance. After a time, I just give up and allow myself to sink back into the white fluffiness, my mind hovering within a kind of limbo…aware but not. Alert…but not. Alive…but not. I have no idea how long I hang like that in the ether. It feels like months.

When I finally break through the cloud shroud, my entire body constricts with my effort to draw a deep breath. The resulting wheeze is loud and ends abruptly in a fit of coughing so violent that I sit bolt upright, opening my eyes to a room I have no recollection of entering.

"Katherine?"

My head swings in the direction of my name and I'm met by stormy brown eyes. Drew looks as if he's been hit by a truck. Repeatedly. His clothing is wrinkled and his hair disheveled. There are deep creases across his face from where it rested against the back of the chair he's been sleeping in.

"What are you doing here?" I croak.

He gets to his feet and puts his hands on my shoulders, gently pushing me back against the pillows behind me.

"I was worried about you," he says, now adjusting the cotton blanket so that it covers my chest.

He's taking care of me. Again. It's that thought that brings it all crashing back to me. The awful fight. The way he left me on his porch. The police. Each memory hits me like a slap to the face, so that when he moves to put his soft palm to my cheek, I flinch away from his touch. An instant of confusion crosses his face, but then I see it all come flooding back to him as well.

He drops his eyes to my hand on the bed next to me, bruised around the site where they put the IV needle. When I follow his eyes, I see it. My bracelet has been returned to its rightful place on my wrist. It takes him a long moment, but he looks up finally and I can see it all in his eyes. His regret, his pain, his loneliness. But I can't let his hurt be my priority. I know better, and look where it got me. I will never be so foolish again so long as I live. Never.

"Katherine," he begins softly, "I don't know what to say. *'I'm sorry'* seems so inadequate. I was wrong. God help me, I was so, so wrong and I'd give anything to do it over again."

I snort, as best I can in my present condition, but it only sends me into another coughing fit. He moves to pat my back but then he pulls away. Smart. The way I'm feeling I might just tear his arm off with my bare teeth. It takes a full minute before I can speak again.

"Yeah, I'd give anything to go back, too, Drew," I rasp weakly, closing my eyes against the throbbing pain behind them. "I'd give anything to be able to turn back time so I could kick my own ass before I let my guard down. Before I let myself believe you could possibly be the one person in my life that I could finally count on."

He reels back, as if a physical punch accompanies my words.

"Katherine, I—"

I hold up a trembling hand and he stops. "Please, Drew. Please just go. We don't need to see one another again. Under the circumstances, I'm sure Dr. Morgan can arrange a substitute on my orals committee."

Something I don't recognize flashes across his features at the mention of Tessa Morgan's name. He shakes his head firmly.

"No. No, no, no. That's not how this ends," he declares stubbornly.

His words make me smile faintly. "Oh, but it is, Dr. Markham," I inform him bitterly.

"No. First of all, it was Tessa. She used you, Katherine. She used you to get the tenure position. She's the one who called Kevin Kilpatrick. She figured it all out and gave that son of a bitch the story."

I sit bolt upright and gasp at the burning sensation that fills my lungs.

"What? Are you *kidding* me?"

He shakes his head solemnly. "She found your bracelet in my car. I'd asked her where I could buy a nice coat for my mom and she suggested that place. That place in Charlotte where I bought your coat."

"Oh, fuck! You didn't!" I moan, pressing my palm to my forehead. Men! Stupid, clueless men! "Of course she recognized the scarf, you idiot!"

"I know, I know," he groans in response, shaking his head with regret. "She started to put all the pieces together. She was jealous of you. Of us. And she thought that this would somehow get her what she wanted. When she realized I was never going to have feelings for her, she decided to settle for going after my tenure slot."

"Holy crap," I mutter more to myself, than to him. "That bitch. She started this mess for a little job security?"

He nods. "That and some unrequited affection she had for me," he says, floating a shy smile. But I'm not biting this time.

I snort again.

"Poor Drew. All the girls want you. Oh, wait…all the girls but *me*, that is."

He winces visibly.

"Please don't say that."

I shrug.

"Whatever. Just go. Go before we're both splashed across the front page of the tabloids again. Go before you end your career. Go before you ruin my life any more than you already have."

The supreme sadness that settles over him is unnerving. When he stands up, I realize he's actually going to do it. He's going to leave because I asked him to. But part of me hopes… what? I shake my head slightly as if it will thrust the ridiculous thoughts from my mind.

But Drew doesn't leave. He inches closer to where I'm lying.

"Move over," he says.

"What?"

He tries to sit next to me, pushing me up against the bedrail.

"Move. Over."

"Go to hell."

And then he's shoehorning himself into the small hospital bed.

"Get out!" I object, wheezing with the effort. "No, I don't want you here!"

But he doesn't listen. He nudges me to the right, situates himself to the left on his back and pulls me against him until my head is nestled in the crook of his arm, my casted arm draped over his chest. I'm enraged and I push at him, trying to force him out, but he is as immoveable as a mountain.

"Drew, I don't want you here!"

"It's okay, Katherine," he says in a soothing tone. But it doesn't soothe. It enrages me.

"Get the fuck out!" I say louder. He just holds me tighter.

"You're going to be okay," he says in that same manner that makes me want to strangle him.

"No!" I shriek, if you can call a loud, hoarse croak a shriek. "I don't want you here, you son of a bitch! You said you loved me and then you threw me away!"

Whoa. Where the hell did *that* come from? Wherever it is, Drew just pulls me tighter to him.

"It's all right," he says in a voice barely above a whisper. "I've got you now. I'm not going to let you go again. Not ever, Katherine."

I open my mouth to spit venom at him, but that's not what happens. Against all fury, against all rage and determination, a strangled, deep-seated wail emerges from some dark place within me. I don't even recognize myself as I gasp in as much oxygen as my pained lungs will allow and release it in a sobbing rush.

Drew puts his free hand, the one that isn't wrapped around my side, on my forehead and strokes my hair back off my face. "It's okay, Katherine," he repeats again and again until I am clinging to him, face buried in the safety of his chest, tears cascading and dampening his shirt underneath where my cheek rests. He shushes me, holding me firmly against him, gently stroking my hair, and catching my falling tears with his thumb.

I don't know how much time has passed when my sobs peter out into their hiccupping, shuddering aftermath. Drew just holds me.

"Never," he whispers. "I will never let you down again. I swear to God, Katherine. I swear it."

Epilogue

Drew

No one is more surprised than Barry Green when the tenure committee awards the new position to him. And with it came a nice bump in salary. So nice, that he asked if he could rent my "cabin." Seemed like the perfect solution to me after I'd made the decision to leave town. Why stay? There's nothing for me there now.

I resigned in order to spare Maureen from having to fire me. Tessa, on the other hand, did not. Big mistake. Convinced she was in the right, she stood firm until the bitter end when she was dismissed for breaking the university's privacy policy, endangering the well-being of a student, and willfully disobeying a directive from her superior.

It got ugly. Very, very ugly.

And, while Maureen was far from pleased with my professional behavior, she generously forgave my personal behavior, supporting me in my decision to leave North Carolina to pursue other opportunities. And to put a little distance between myself and the past.

When I was packing everything up, she and Russ came to the house to help me go through the last of Casey's things that I'd tucked away in the attic. I didn't keep much. I couldn't keep much. Just a few small mementos and our engagement picture. I pulled the back off the frame and slipped the tiny black-and-white sonogram photo inside for safekeeping. It seemed only right to have the two together.

I sold the truck and gave my neighbor Joe my snowblower, along with a very fine selection of spirits from my basement bottle collection. The contents of the house were divided up between Barry, a storage locker, and the moving truck. All the books and my favorite pieces of furniture. My kitchen supplies. And, of course the piano. It's all already waiting for me in my new apartment in New York City.

New city. New apartment. New job. New life.

"Thank you for flying Atlantic Air," the pretty flight attendant says as I file past her and out onto the Jetway.

JFK is busier than I remember. After the slow, comfortable pace of rural North Carolina, I'm not certain how long it'll take me to get used to this faster speed of life. It's loud, and bright, and everywhere around me, people are moving with purpose and determination. In a small way, I envy them—having a tangible place to go and be and do. Even as I pull my rollerbag down the escalator to baggage claim, I have no idea what awaits me outside these walls.

Though, I know exactly what awaits me inside of them.

I don't see her at first, in the mob of people waiting to greet the newly arrived passengers such as myself. Mothers are crying tears of joy, children are jumping up and down excitedly. Boyfriends and husbands and fiancés are holding bouquets of flowers.

She's just standing there, in the middle of all of them. Her hair is tied up in a messy bun atop her head, a few stray strands lying across her face. I can already sense how they'll feel under my fingers when I tuck them behind her ear. She's smiling sweetly, patiently, contentedly, as our eyes meet on my downward crawl from one floor to the next. They are the bluest eyes I've ever seen, with flecks of gold and long, dark lashes.

It feels like an eternity until I'm finally on firm ground again. I walk up to her with more confidence than I've ever had in my life and pull her into my arms, inhaling the peach and lavender scent of her hair. Her arms wrap around my waist and her head tips up toward my face.

"Hi," she says softly.

"Hi." I smile down at her. "I've missed you."

"I've missed you, too. It's been a long six weeks."

"Well, I had to get things wrapped up. And no way you could miss the start of the semester."

Her turn to smile. "I know. I'm just saying that I'm not as comfortable…that I can't…" She stops, closes her eyes for just a second, and tries one more time. "I don't want to be alone anymore."

I put my cheek against hers and press my lips to her ear so that she is the only person in the world who can hear me.

"You will never be alone again, Katherine."

If you're lucky, when the clock strikes midnight on the best day of your life, someone is there to warm you. If you're lucky, it's something you see coming. Something you can circle on your calendar and look forward to for days and weeks and months. If you're lucky, people will remind you it's coming. And, when that lucky day comes, you will wake up just *knowing*.

I know.

Acknowledgments

For me, writing began as an emergency stopgap against a bout of depression. What was supposed to be just a few paragraphs meant to 'get me out of my own head' turned into a novel. And then another…and another. For me, writing was a surprise in the truest sense—it was something I didn't even know I wanted until I got it. And now I cannot imagine spending a day without putting words to paper. *Solo* is very near and dear to me in that it's my first traditionally published book, but it was definitely not a 'solo' endeavor. My greatest thanks to just a few of the people who made this book possible…

Tom—As I write this, you're sitting next to me, exactly two weeks after the event that nearly took your life and changed mine forever. Thank you for living. Thank you for loving me.

Janet and Kwaku—my parents 'in absentia.' I'm so grateful for your constant, unquestioning love and support, as I'm sure my parents would be.

Vanessa—My hero. My cheerleader. My friend. My sister. No, YOU'RE the best!

Karen—For always checking on me. For always worrying

about me. For always encouraging me. For always, somehow, making the obstacles seem smaller.

Kelly—you make being your friend so easy, and so fun. Thank you for always finding time to chat, to write and to read.

Mike and Crucita—Who don't always get it, but are proud of me anyway…and always.

Jennifer Mishler—You're so much more than my editor. When you called me and said, 'Hey, let's do something together!' I had no idea where we'd end up. Thank you for making me a better writer. Now buckle-up, baby, cause it's gonna be one wild ride!

Stacey—You never doubted this day would come, and every chance you got, you made sure that I knew it.

Ernie— You keep me sane. You remind me to be happy. You help me to navigate all the detours that life throws into my journey. This wouldn't have happened without you.

To those who watch over me from beyond this world: Marie, Gregory, Carol, and Mario. Your words are whispers in my ear, your guidance a gentle push in the right direction.

My greatest and most humble gratitude to my Heavenly Father who gives me the inspiration to create, the courage to pursue and the faith to believe.

About the Author

Lauren Rico was going to be principal French horn of the New York Philharmonic. That was her plan, anyway. The New York Philharmonic had no idea of her intentions, and that's probably a good thing, since she wasn't an especially good French horn player!

Lauren was, however, an exceptionally good classical music radio host. She has made a career of demystifying classical music for her audiences by taking it off a dusty old pedestal and putting it into a modern context.

Lauren has recently discovered a passion for writing, which she's managed to combine with her love and knowledge of the classical music world.

Discover more New Adult titles from Entangled Embrace...

Confessions of a Former Puck Bunny

a *Taking Shots* novel by Cindi Madsen

Confession #1: *I used to be a puck bunny.* But after a hockey player broke my heart, I gave up all things hockey. Unfortunately, if I want to graduate college, I'll need the help of Ryder "Ox" Maddox—my sexy, hockey-playing tutor. The closer we get, the harder it is to remember why I need to stay away. If I'm not careful, I'll fall for Ryder, and then I'll be totally pucked.

Trusting Tanner

a *Collins Brothers* novel by Lexi Lawton

Tanner Collins is perfection—tall, dark, sinfully sexy—and completely out of Juliana Shea's league. Knowing she'd never survive a repeat of her last disastrous relationship, she parks Tanner firmly in the friend zone. But man, he's hard to resist. Juliana is exactly what Tanner wants, and he slowly wins her over with kindness and humor... Until with the flick of a "send" button, their hope for a future together is shattered. But Tanner isn't the type to give up on what he wants—and he wants Juliana.

A Star to Steer Her By

a novel by Beth Anne Miller

Ever since her last dive ended in bloodshed, Ari Goodman's been terrified to go back into the water. But the opportunity to spend a semester at sea is too good to pass up. So is Tristan MacDougall. Rugged, strong, and with demons of his own, Tristan heals her with every stolen moment they share. But when a dive excursion goes wrong, their only hope for survival is each other.

The Rule Book

a *Rule Breakers* novel by Jennifer Blackwood

Lainey Taylor's Second-Assistant Survival Guide: 1. Don't call your hot boss the antichrist to his face. 2. Don't stare at hot boss's, um, package or his full sleeve of tattoos. (No. Really. Stop!) 6. Boss's dimples are lust-inducing. Do. Not. Give. In. 9. Whatever you do, don't fall for the boss.